CRIM
IN THE COLLEGE

A fiercely addictive mystery

CATHERINE MOLONEY

Detective Markham Mystery Book 11

Joffe Books, London
www.joffebooks.com

First published in Great Britain in 2021

ISBN: 978-1-78931-698-8

PROLOGUE

There was something about an Oxford winter that got right into your bones. Bill Knowles leaned gingerly against the wall at the bottom of staircase eleven in Sherwin College. The stonework was so clammy with condensation and damp that it was no wonder the students had runny noses whenever he clapped eyes on them.

Not that too many students were left in college on that Saturday, 12 December, most having made tracks as soon as term finished the previous weekend. They had that many bleeding holidays, he thought sourly, it was a wonder they did any work at all.

And now the sodding projects manager had dragged him in at the weekend to investigate dry rot. As if it couldn't have waited till after Christmas. The wife was livid he couldn't take her shopping at the Westgate, so he'd be in the dog-house till god knew when. The only upside was he didn't have to face her gobby mother and sister (aka the Gruesome Twosome) and listen to them moaning on about men being a waste of space. It was a wonder to him that the poor bastards they married hadn't done a runner long ago.

A rheumatic twinge in his back made him wince. At least the Westgate was nice and warm, he thought irritably.

Even in summer Sherwin College always felt arctic, especially the older buildings. The gawping tourists oohed and aahed about its 'charm' and 'character', but as far as he was concerned you could stick all that Olde English bollocks. Give me central heating and decent carpets any day, he thought crossly, instead of all this mouldering heritage malarkey.

He felt even crosser as tantalising smells suggestive of a roast dinner wafted across the quadrangle from the Great Hall. Looked like those coppers down for the police conference were going to have a slap-up feed after a morning banging on about firearms or statistics or whatever the hell it was they were debating today. He could feel his mouth watering at the thought.

As for *him*, well he'd be lucky to get some curled-up sandwiches and cold tea knowing the skinflint head porter. Nothing was too much trouble for the boys in blue, but it'd be slim pickings for anyone else.

A fresh wave of resentment surged over him. He wasn't even sure what he was supposed to do about the dry rot. It wasn't as if they were going to fork out for a new staircase. More like, they'd expect him to do some sort of bodge job on the cheap — shore up any dodgy timbers and make sure it wasn't a death-trap.

He was willing to bet the bursar and fellows didn't even know about this. It was just another bright idea of snot-nosed 'Johnny Clipboard' desperate to impress the principal.

Bill sighed and, watched his breath spiral into the freezing air of the staircase. Trying to put off the evil hour when he would have to chip away at the floor of the exposed crawl space under the staircase to access the wooden supports, he peered out into the quadrangle.

Although it was only early afternoon, the light was already starting to fade and third quad, as it was called, was wreathed in a vaporous mist that made Bill think of ghosts and graveyards. No lights shone from any of the rooms that overlooked the courtyard, since the conference guests were accommodated mainly in second quad and would anyway now be piling into the nearby Great Hall.

There was something unsettling about a day like this. Something about the swirling fog which made him think of childhood stories about shapeshifting creatures that slid along the eaves of ancient buildings before vanishing into the murk.

Altogether it was a mournful prospect and he shivered, suddenly craving the bright lights and hubbub of the Westgate . . . even the maddening inanities of his womenfolk as they bickered over Christmas bargains.

As he stood there, the college librarian appeared on the other side of the quad and began walking towards the Great Hall. Eerily, she looked for all the world like a sleepwalker, otherworldly, swimming in a milky sea as though skimming through his dreams.

Bill felt a sudden wish for snow instead of fog. Proper picture-postcard crunchy snow with the footprints of the college population etched into the white like some pristine code that only the initiated could read.

Yeah, give me snow any day, he thought. *That's* what you want before Christmas, not this nasty cotton wool stuff that gets in your lungs like you're choking . . . or drowning.

He gave himself a shake.

No way did he want to be stuck on this staircase once it was properly dark. Even with all these coppers around, it still felt creepy. Better start digging up that crawl space and work out what was amiss. With any luck, repairs would keep till after the holidays . . .

Twenty minutes later, Bill sank back on his haunches wiping sweat, dust and cobwebs off his face.

He'd transferred most of the rubble to a waiting wheelbarrow, so that he could take a closer look at the wooden struts, sunken at least four feet into the ground, but there remained a stubborn patch of what appeared to be debris mixed with tar and other builders' sludge. *Messy job*, he thought. Evidently the previous builders hadn't thought to mix their concrete properly before re-levelling the floor. First off, he needed to chisel off what he could with a pickaxe.

Chiselling completed, he reached for a spade and set to shovelling.

Suddenly he recoiled.

A bone protruded from the newly chipped rubble.

That's all I need. Some moggy or other poor animal must've gone down into the exposed foundations and ended up with a barrowload of debris dumped on top.

Only . . .

As he turned over another spadeful, Bill's bowels turned to water.

Despite the cold of the staircase, he suddenly felt hot.

There were too many bones for a cat or rodent.

There were lots of delicate bones . . . looked like they belonged to a hand . . . what did they call them, phalanges or metacarpals . . . ?

Easy, fella, he told himself, mindful of his dicky ticker. *Easy.*

With these places — centuries-old in parts — who knew what might turn up. There were probably monks and peasants and whatnot buried hereabouts, just like folk had come across in other colleges.

Deep down, though, Bill failed to convince himself. He knew the staircase was overhauled in 2000 and the builders were bound to have turned up anything like that — any *remains* — then . . . Even though it was twenty years ago, the university apparently had strict rules about that kind of thing. Mister 'clever dick' Projects Manager had impressed it upon him from the outset, like he fancied himself George Clarke or one of them lah-di-dah archaeologist types: 'Anything like that, Bill, everything stops and we notify the relevant authorities *tout de suite.*'

Tout de fucking suite.

That poncy phrase just about summed up why he hated the affected little git.

But there was no getting away from it.

The bones *couldn't* be from medieval types cos they'd have turned them up way back in 2000. And then, like as not, they'd have ended up under glass at the Reynolds Museum.

A fine example of a displaced Tudor burial . . .He didn't watch *Time Team* for nothing.

Bill was starting to feel light-headed.

C'mon, he urged himself. Just dig it up and chuck whatever you find in the wheelbarrow. Leave it to mister clever dick to sort out the rest.

Thunk.

The spade closed on something hard and substantial.

He steeled himself.

It was a skull.

Unmistakeably a human cranium.

* * *

Afterwards, Bill couldn't quite believe he hadn't had a coronary right there on the spot.

The wife had told him to sue the college. 'They left a *body* down there,' she squawked. 'A *body* for you to find . . . And you with your iffy heart and all.'

An iffy heart that he never told them about.

There had been something horrible about the sightless sockets staring back at him.

A memory had come to him as he rocked back on his heels staring at it.

His grandson excitedly yammering away about the princes in the Tower.

'They found the princes' bones in a box, grandad. Under a staircase in the Tower of London!'

But instinctively, he just knew this wasn't any old monk or historical skeleton or fairy-tale nobleman.

This was more recent.

Thank god those coppers had been on site. They could take over now.

Bill had lurched unsteadily to his feet and manoeuvred himself out from under the crawl space.

Standing on the threshold of staircase eleven, he had looked out into the misty quad and taken a deep breath.

The curtain was about to rise on what became known as the Oxford College Murders.

1. JANE DOE

DI Gilbert 'Gil' Markham had always found the restrained Gothic style of the Sherwin College chapel very much to his taste. It had been a place of sanctuary, somewhere to escape to during his undergraduate days and it fulfilled that purpose now as he reflected on the startling developments of the previous day.

It was Sunday morning and he felt a strong inclination to linger, savouring the warmth of a shaft of sunlight streaming through one of the high chapel windows.

He had been looking forward to nothing more exciting than jam roly-poly and custard followed by a soporific address from Oxford's divisional commander when Bill Knowles had burst into the Great Hall with news of the grim discovery beneath staircase eleven.

'Looked like the ole lard bucket were gonna keel over,' DS George Noakes had declared afterwards with all the severity of a fellow chubster who had been put on a strict diet following the previous year's health scare. 'Anyway, it's par for the course with a place like this, innit . . . You're bound to trip over skellies all over the shop with it being medieval an' all that.'

Gil was amused by his wingman's assumed sang-froid, Noakes having clearly made up his mind not to be impressed by the City of Dreaming Spires. 'One more for the museum,' Noakes had continued comfortably, declining to be distracted from his pud. '"Jane Doe from Henry the Eighth's times" or whatever. The punters'll go gaga. *Kerching*!'

But even Noakes was obliged to revise his opinion when informed that these remains were highly unlikely to be ancient, given nothing of the kind had been called in by the builders who renovated that same staircase twenty years previously.

Judging by the reaction of Markham's boss DCI Sidney (or 'Slimy Sid' as he was known to the troops), one might have thought Markham had personally engineered the discovery in order to wriggle out of the 'seminal' session on restorative justice scheduled for that afternoon.

'It's almost as though murder follows you around,' Sidney observed disagreeably on hearing of the find beneath the staircase where Markham had lived as a final year student.

'He made it sound like you fricking well dumped them bones there yourself!' Noakes exclaimed wrathfully. 'Like you were doing a Doctor Crippen or summat . . . when anyone'd know you had your nose in a book all the time.'

He tried to ignore the implication that he was far too *busy* to have murdered anyone. 'Thanks for the vote of confidence, Sergeant.'

Too late, Noakes realised his gaffe. 'Not that I'm saying you were the murdering kind, boss.'

Markham grimaced. 'When in a hole, Noakes—'

'Stop digging,' DC Doyle and DS Kate Burton chorused in unison.

The young detective constable and DS Burton, the earnest fast-track psychology graduate who was the other member of Markham's close-knit 'gang', were visibly delighted to be in Oxford.

Only Noakes resolutely refused to succumb to its picturesque charms.

But then George Noakes was a law unto himself . . .

As he sat there, Markham congratulated himself on having kept Noakes out of the clutches of Sidney's henchmen on the retirement plan committee and the rubber-soled mob at the office for police conduct. No mean feat given Noakes's spectacular talent for alienating his superiors. And, of course, there'd been Noakes's breakdown at the end of the Bluebell murder case. Noakes and Markham had found themselves in the tightest of corners, but somehow it had bound the two men even more closely together.

Markham well knew that he and Noakes were called 'The Odd Couple' by CID's resident wits, but he could not conceive of ever being able to dispense with his point man. If anything, watching his upwardly mobile contemporaries greasing away to Sidney and the top brass at this conference made him all the more appreciative of Noakes's unvarnished authenticity, even if his political incorrectness made life decidedly tricky at times.

'Can't you rein the man in, Markham,' was Sidney's never-ending complaint. 'He gives an appalling impression of service values.'

Noakes didn't give a flying fajita for 'service values', but he never mis-stepped when it came to comforting the anonymous victims of murder or making 'toerags' squirm once they were in his sights.

Moreover, the DS was instinctively simpatico to his legendarily chilly and fastidious boss, somehow taking in Markham's unuttered past as a victim of childhood abuse without anything explicit on the subject having ever passed between them.

Added to all of this — and his lips quirked at the incongruity — Markham's teacher girlfriend Olivia Mullen was a staunch adherent of Noakes, revelling in his subversiveness and touched by his devotion to 'the guvnor'. She was just about the only person able to get away with teasing the old warhorse — certainly the only one able to dispel any grouchiness.

The thing was, for all Noakes's run-to-seed slobbishness — the salt and pepper thatch that never *would* lie down along with the hangdog features, paunchiness and shockingly bad dress sense — he had a romantic, almost poetic, chord in his nature which vibrated to Olivia's lightest touch. Hugely admiring of her willowy ethereal looks and long red hair, he confided once to Markham that she put him in mind of 'them witches in picture books' (a typically mixed compliment, but Markham got the gist) and never objected when she discoursed on books and poetry on the basis that 'her voice was like music or a choir doing one of them oratorio thingies'.

These troubadour-like tendencies did not go down well with Muriel Noakes, the sergeant's snobbish overbearing wife who had a soft spot for Gilbert Markham ('*such* a charmer and *so* reliant on George') but little time for his 'ditzy' partner with the bohemian hair and clothes.

It was a wonder to many back home in Bromgrove how Noakes and his 'missus' had ever ended up together, but Markham knew that, whatever the truth of the matter, his DS was bound to Muriel by ropes of steel. They were regulars on the ballroom dancing circuit — 'poetry in motion' was one surprising description of the stumpy policeman and his Bet Lynch lookalike wife — and Noakes was fiercely protective of Muriel and their daughter, Natalie. When Noakes found out during the Bluebell case that Natalie was almost certainly not his biological daughter but the result of Muriel's teenage indiscretion, he went temporarily off the rails, almost precipitating a crisis in his relationship with Markham. But the two detectives had weathered the storm and come out the other side, though Markham had no idea whether Noakes had made a clean breast of everything to the women in his life. Somehow, he suspected family omertà had won the day, so he was destined never to have an answer to that question.

Initially, Kate Burton and Noakes had been as prickly as a pair of cacti. A psychology graduate, she was earnest, quietly tenacious and according to Noakes 'an all-round smarty pants'. Her parents had opposed a career in the force ('no job for a woman'), but she had won them round to the point where they were inordinately proud of her success.

Earmarked for great things, she had appeared to waver after splitting from her fiancé in the fraud squad and deferred taking her inspector's exams.

It was an open secret in CID that she carried a torch for Markham, but he had been incredulous when Noakes finally took it upon himself to deliver a few home truths, dismissing it as an over-developed sense of respect for her boss.

'Nah guv, you can take it from me, she's got it bad,' the DS replied, before adding graciously, 'but I'll give her this, the lass never made a tit of herself down the pub or owt like that.' Seeing as Burton was virtually teetotal, a sozzled meltdown was unlikely to occur, but this was small comfort to Markham in the circumstances and he vowed to raise the subject of her promotion again once an opportunity presented itself.

At least she and Noakes had now shaken down well together, each valuing the other's loyalty and dedication. Burton no longer flinched at her colleague's breaches of PC good taste while he refrained from excessive eye rolls when she 'went off on one', as in sharing her prodigious knowledge about various branches of psychology ('the world and everything'). Indeed, their shared enthusiasm for true crime documentaries had even resulted in some amicable fact-sharing that had proved useful in recent investigations. Noakes had mellowed to the point that he was almost fatherly towards his eager colleague while *she* had come to appreciate the nonconformist integrity that ran through him like a stick of rock. Markham suspected Burton still occasionally resented the intimacy he shared with Noakes, but these days she was less touchy about being a third wheel.

DC Doyle, for all his youth, was what Markham thought of as a Steady Eddie. Now he had obtained a criminal law degree and passed his sergeant's exams (though he hadn't yet been made up to his new rank), he would doubtless be moving to pastures new in due course. In the meantime, he was a valued member of the unit. Gangling, ginger-haired and personable, he was affectionately irreverent towards Noakes, who was his invariable confidant when it came to matters of the heart (since for some reason the course of true love never did run smooth) and the prospects of their beloved Bromgrove Rovers.

Yes, Markham was highly satisfied with his little band whose loyalty was unquestionable (despite Sidney's best efforts) and regarded it as a stroke of good fortune that they were all at the conference together.

His gaze drifted to the black-and-white chequerboard tiling of the chapel floor. Something about the symmetry of its patterns soothed him and he lingered on, enjoying the sunlight and the peace.

As houses of god went, this little chapel was unpretentious and almost cosy.

At the far end, an oak screen depicted the twelve apostles posing stiffly in choir stalls much like the one in which he was sitting. Was it his imagination, or did Judas Iscariot — carrying the money purse with its thirty pieces of silver — bear more than a passing resemblance to DCI Sidney?

Above the screen an arched stained-glass window depicted a repentant Mary Magdalene, clad in ruby red, raptly contemplating a skull in the depths of a turquoise cavern. Markham had been fond of this image from his student days and knew it was a traditional *memento mori* — as emphasised by the faded flowers and miniature coffin in the background — but the discovery of that skeleton beneath staircase eleven gave it a new and poignant resonance.

Was their victim a woman, he wondered. The Magdalene's eyes seemed to look sorrowfully out of the stained-glass image as though to say 'Yes'.

He recalled the muttered commentary of the pathologist who attended the scene yesterday afternoon. 'Gracile bones . . . circular pelvic inlet . . . most likely female . . . all a bit jumbled.' Markham had shuddered at that.

He missed Doug 'Dimples' Davidson, their usual pathologist back in Bromgrove, the compassionate eyes belying his bluff farmer's appearance. '*Dimples* wouldn't have talked about them bones like they were a bleeding Rubik's cube,' as Noakes put it, not caring at all whether he was overheard.

Beneath the main window were three smaller arches depicting the story of Saint George and the dragon. Something about the earnest gaze of the wimple-clad princess the saint was supposed to have rescued reminded Markham of Kate Burton.

Burton, of course, would be waiting impatiently in the bursar's office behind the porters' lodge, itching to get on with it but reluctant to seem too eager.

He understood that mixture of emotions only too well . . . the adrenalin rush of a murder investigation which was also somehow shameful and vampiric because it derived from the extinction of a fellow human being. As though they were feasting on dead men's bones.

His gaze wandered back to the Magdalene and that sightless skull.

Do not store up treasures on earth, where moth and rust destroy, but rather lay up for yourselves treasures in heaven.

An unwelcome picture of those neglected remains, covered over with cobwebs and runnelled by insect larvae and god knows what else, suddenly rose up before him. But he forced it down. Whoever their victim was, he or most likely she was long past their pain. Nothing could hurt them further.

All that remained was to seek justice.

His mouth twitched at the thought that Noakes and Doyle were probably tucking into a full English in the Great Hall while Kate Burton — keen to get started — was forced to cool her heels in the bursar's office. Personally, he couldn't face a grease-fest with the rest of them, preferring to gather himself in the seclusion of the college chapel.

Sidney, gimlet-eyed, had reluctantly acceded to the principal's suggestion that 'one of their own' take over the investigation. Markham hadn't taken to Sir Paul Mirfleet with his bombast and drinker's complexion, but he jumped at the offer to solve the mystery of staircase eleven. No doubt there would be 'territorial' issues with Thames Valley Police, but they'd cross that bridge when they came to it. Superintendent Ian Charleson from St Aldates was due to see them later on, so hopefully any ruffled feathers could be smoothed down, assuming Noakes didn't trample all over local sensibilities with his size twelves.

The bursar, Philip Greaves, had combined maximum efficiency with minimal warmth towards the DI and his team. Another florid specimen with pinched features, he aped the mannerisms of the principal in a way that Markham found faintly nauseating. But at least he had made over his own rooms behind the porters' lodge for their convenience. 'Prob'ly bugged 'em,' Noakes observed with cheerful insouciance. 'That fella looks like a grade A snoop.' Privately, Markham resolved to do a sweep before installing full incident room facilities.

The minutes ticked by and yet Markham still could not tear himself away from the chapel. His mind travelled back in time to those halcyon student days which had seemed then to stretch out hazily to infinity.

The framed group pictures of students in full fig (sub fusc academic dress) that lined the oak-panelled corridor outside the chapel made him feel sad. So much starry-eyed anticipation. So many hopes and dreams . . . And then the bitter-sweet awakening once the wine of life was drunk, leaving only the dregs.

Nostalgia ain't what it used to be, he told himself wryly looking slowly round the chapel.

The sun had now moved round to the plain-leaded lancet windows that lined both sides of the choir, leaving his stall in shadow.

Markham shivered, as though a chilly finger had touched him, admonishing him for wasting time when there was a murderer to catch.

But was this murder? he asked himself. And if so, whose were the bones interred in the sludge under that staircase . . . such a desolate resting place. Even more horrible when one thought of all the students pounding up and down stairs, blithely unaware of the grave site beneath their feet.

His eyes returned to the enigmatic Magdalene in her strange subterranean lair. The ruby red mantle had somehow lost its lustre, seeming to pool about her feet like an upswell of blood . . . Unconstrained. Unstoppable.

Somehow, he was unable to look away.

Above her in a rose window, God the Father extended his arms wide as though to embrace all lost sheep into the fold.

But there was a wolf in the sheepfold,

And Markham was determined to find him.

* * *

'*Cushty!*'

As far as Noakes was concerned, the bursar's rooms were a distinct improvement on the usual accommodation available for CID investigations.

'He's got one of them George Clooney Nespresso machines an' all . . . *Jammy bastard.*'

Kate Burton was clearly embarrassed by these Del Boy raptures, but Doyle just grinned. 'We're in the wrong job, sarge. Should have worked harder at school, then *we'd* be the ones with the swank office.'

Noakes grunted and continued exploring the bursar's oak-panelled domain, clumping through the Axminster-carpeted rooms — study and tastefully appointed bedroom. Like they were in an episode of *Through the Keyhole*, thought Burton despairingly as she waited for him to complete his inspection.

'Flat screen telly, drinks cabinet an' fridge an' *two* computers . . . Talk about a gravy train!' Noakes plonked himself onto the chesterfield. '*Hey*, d'you think he's got his fingers in the till? Cos this set-up's worth a fortune.'

'They pay vice-chancellors and all the senior people top whack.' Doyle pursed his lips and spoke with all the authority of a new-minted BA Law (2:2). 'Bursar at a place like this . . . He's got to be on a hefty salary.'

'Plus there'll be perks and benefits,' Burton added thoughtfully, looking round at the Old Masters and the vast mahogany desk. 'And they probably do stuff in the private sector.'

Nice work, she mused, *if you can get it.*

'You can tell he's a boozer,' Noakes declared sanctimoniously. 'Ain't seen a nose like that since ole Basher went on the batter at his leaving do.'

Obviously recalling the legendary DCI 'Basher' Briggs, Burton forced a strained smile.

'Mr Greaves has certainly done well for himself judging by this lot,' she said. 'Bursar's a responsible position, though, so he must be up to the job . . . And anyway, there's always a drinking culture in places like this. They're stuck in a time warp: *Brideshead Revisited*.' The censorious sniff with which this last was uttered suggested Burton's views on Oxbridge leaned towards the puritanical.

'*Brideshead Revisited*.' Noakes mulled it over. '*Oh yeah*, I remember now . . . poofters carting teddy bears round the place an' speaking in daft voices.'

Burton looked as though she regretted having ever mentioned the cult classic, but the DI's arrival mercifully prevented further discussion.

Markham smiled at them but his eyes in his lean dark face were sad.

'I've just had a call from the pathologist,' he said.

'Oh yeah, the Jigsaw Man.' Noakes was distinctly unenthusiastic. 'Fitted all the pieces together has he?'

'Indeed he has, Sergeant.' The DI's gaze wandered briefly to an exquisite Madonna and Child which had the chiaroscuro hues of a valuable antique on loan from the college vaults. Then he looked steadily at the team.

'Our victim is a young woman, around twenty years old . . . She was three months pregnant. The bones of the foetus had become displaced from the pelvis, but there's no doubt about it now.'

'Poor lass,' Noakes said gruffly, clearing his throat. '*Pregnant* an' chucked out with the rubbish.'

Burton's throat contracted as she thought of the corpse disappearing beneath cement and slurry, slowly digested to a skeleton.

Doyle looked sick. 'Did the doc say how she died, sir?'

'Strangulation. Apparently there was enough left to identify a hyoid fracture.'

Burton found her voice.

'Is there an ID, boss?'

'We're waiting on official confirmation from dental records, but there's a strong possibility it's a third-year English student who disappeared from Sherwin twenty years ago . . . Catriona Rowlands. She was never traced.'

'How come she jus' *disappeared*, guv.' Noakes got up from the chesterfield and began prowling the deep pile crimson carpet. 'I mean, a girl that age an' a student *here* at Posh Central . . . They musta had some idea.' He kicked a thin-legged side table by way of relieving his feelings. 'An' her in the family way too, jus' don't make any sense . . .'

For all that it was a bright winter morning, the bursar's quarters seemed suddenly drained of light as though the air had somehow turned grey.

The four detectives contemplated each other, pinch-faced.

'Sit down, Noakesy,' the DI said finally. 'It's making me sea-sick watching you wear out that carpet.'

Moodily, the DS complied, taking a savage satisfaction in the fact that muck from his brothel creepers had transferred itself to the sofa's chintz valance.

'The team at the time pulled out all the stops,' Markham continued.

'Not if they didn't check under that bloody staircase they didn't,' Noakes burst out mutinously.

'On the face of it there was no reason to reopen the earthworks,' the DI said levelly. 'The builders working on staircase eleven were adamant no one unauthorised had been there . . . the site foreman was positive about it at the time.'

'"*At the time*"?' Burton had picked up on the ambiguity. 'Does that mean he got it wrong, sir?'

'I've got a hunch that site security wasn't all it was cracked up to be. The firm in question was McMaster & Son who eventually went bankrupt after settling various claims involving breaches of health and safety.'

Noakes's piggy eyes had narrowed suspiciously. 'So they fricking lied.'

'It's a distinct possibility,' the DI agreed. 'But at the time McMaster had a good reputation. There were contracts with several of the colleges and, besides, the last confirmed sighting of Ms Rowlands was in Cornmarket Street. Several students placed her there.'

'What about the family?' Doyle asked. 'Did they have any idea she might be pregnant?'

'Her mother died while she was still at school,' Markham replied. 'Father remarried when she was in the sixth form. I believe there's a stepmother and stepsister.'

Doyle digested this. 'What about the dad, is he still around?'

'He died five years ago,' the DI informed them heavily. 'Ms Rowlands's stepmother and stepsister are out of the country . . . they were planning to spend Christmas in Lech—'

'What's over there then?' Noakes asked belligerently.

'It's an Austrian ski resort,' Markham explained. 'But they'll be travelling home as soon as it can be arranged. And to answer your original question, Constable, according to the case files, the family had no idea why she went missing . . . certainly no notion that she was pregnant.'

It was clear, Burton thought approvingly, that the DI meant to get a jump on the local police.

Then a thought occurred to her.

'Did you ever meet Ms Rowlands, sir. . . I mean you were here twenty years ago, and this is your old college?'

'Yeah, the way Hissing Sid was carrying on yesterday, it sounded like he's got you in the frame for this one, guv,' Noakes observed amiably.

'Very reassuring, Sergeant,' came the dry response. Markham smiled at Burton. 'We were actually in the same year, Kate, but oddly enough I don't have any recollection of how she looked . . . Strange, because the English students were a pretty flamboyant crowd.' His eyes became remote, as though he was looking inwards. He reached into the pocket of his immaculately tailored pinstripe and produced a photograph.

'The bursar was kind enough to give me this,' he said. 'Pass it round.'

The photograph showed a delicate featured, vibrant young woman with big dark eyes and Mediterranean colouring.

'Nice-looking lass,' was Noakes's verdict. His stubby forefinger stroked the picture. 'What a chuffing waste.' Then almost angrily, as was always the case whenever the DS felt he had been betrayed into showing his emotions, 'What about boyfriends? With a stunner like that . . . there had to be some bloke sniffing around.'

Something flared at the back of his eyes causing Markham to wonder if his wingman was remembering Muriel and Natalie, each of them wronged by a man . . .

'Ms Rowlands was apparently recovering from a break-up at the time when she was last seen,' he said.

'*You're kidding me.*' Doyle was incredulous. 'You mean someone knocked her back?'

'She and her boyfriend had split up a month or so before she went missing,' the DI informed them before adding. 'Actually, he's a fellow here.'

'The boyfriend?' This sounded promising to Noakes.

'Dr Jon Warrender . . . Yes, he's a senior research fellow and tutor in Classics.'

'Bully for him,' Noakes grunted. 'Where was he when the lass went missing?'

'A JCR event in the college bar.'

'That's the junior common room,' Burton translated.

'Off his face then.' Noakes never had much time for acronyms.

'Along with most of his peers,' Markham said. 'It was June, so everyone was whooping it up after final exams. An all-nighter.'

Somehow Burton couldn't envisage her elegant boss 'whooping it up'. Dinner for two at an expensive restaurant, she thought wistfully, was more his style.

'If they were partying, he could have snuck off an' done the dirty without anyone clocking him then.' It was obvious Noakes liked Warrender as their prime suspect.

'There was never anything to tie him — or anyone else — to Ms Rowlands's disappearance, Noakes.'

Burton noted the formality of 'Ms Rowlands'. The DI was always mindful of victims' dignity and woe betide any subordinate who so far forgot themselves as to engage in gallows humour.

'There was speculation that maybe she had a breakdown or something traumatic happened . . . maybe an amnesic episode . . . chose to disappear, or possibly she didn't want to be found . . .'

'You mean they thought she might have done a Reggie Perrin . . . faked her own death?' Doyle sounded bemused.

'Well, that was one line of thought. Even so, the case went nowhere.' The DI ran a hand through the curly black hair that had, did he but know it, led to civilian typists back at Bromgrove Station christening him their 'stud muffin of the month'.

'Whass the plan, guv?' Noakes was growing impatient. It was clear that, as far as he was concerned, it was time to feel a few collars, and the sooner the better.

The DI glanced at his watch.

'I've asked the bursar and chaplain to join us,' he said. 'They'll be along any minute.'

'What about the local plod?' Noakes looked as if he relished the idea of a face-off.

'Sidney's squaring it with them. We'll be meeting with Superintendent Charleson tomorrow morning, Noakes. Diplomacy's the order of the day.'

Good luck with that, Burton said to herself, her mind roving over Noakes's hair-raising track record with officialdom.

Catching Markham's eye, she blushed. Something about his expression suggested he knew exactly what she was thinking.

'You and Doyle will be setting up our incident room, Kate.'

'In *here*, sir?' It sounded as if she couldn't believe her luck.

'Well, if we can manage to sweet talk the bursar . . . and convince him we're house-trained.'

Her face fell as she looked at Noakes, but Kate Burton was nothing if not determined.

'I'm on it, sir,' she said firmly.

There was a discreet rap at the door.

The advance party had arrived.

2. INTO FOCUS

Sunday evening found Markham and Olivia in his temporary accommodation at Sherwin College. All was quiet outside save for the occasional hollow echo of footsteps on the flags which bordered Sherwin's immaculate lawn. Now and again the glass of the quaint diamond-paned windows rattled as a gull or curlew swung by, making a diversion on its flight home to Port Meadow for the night. The swirling mist of a typical dank Oxford evening muffled everything, the old-fashioned college lampposts illuminating the murk in little pools of yellow light. As she stood looking down into the courtyard, Olivia experienced something of the same shuddering distaste Bill Knowles had felt the previous evening when poking around the entrails of staircase eleven.

Was it just good old-fashioned jealousy that prevented her from succumbing to Oxford's winter spell, she wondered? Resentment that she'd been denied the 'Oxbridge experience' and consigned instead to an undistinguished red-brick university (her schoolteachers were strong on 'knowing your limitations' and 'not getting above yourself')?

No, that wasn't it, she concluded. More a case of there being something eerie about these old buildings, blotched and stained with damp as though humidity was breaking out on them like a disease. And then there was the nonstop tolling of bells which at this time of year she found more dirge-like than joyful, a sort of sinister sostenuto that she couldn't switch off. So strong was this funereal impression that she found herself remembering the steel girders and plate glass of Bromgrove University with something almost like affection.

'Penny for them, Liv?' her lover enquired behind her.

She shrugged off her morbid fancies.

'Who've they booted out to make room for you, then?'

'One of the junior fellows . . . History tutor . . . She's headed back to the States for Christmas, so,' he gestured expansively, 'here we are!'

'Hmm . . . a kitchenette and your own *en suite* too.' She laughed. 'I presume the others have to share.'

'Oh, Burton and Doyle are up for the authentic student experience — draughty stone staircases, wind whistling round the eaves, wonky floors, vaulted ceilings—'

'Squeaky beds.'

'That too. Needless to say, Noakes was distinctly underwhelmed, particularly with there being no television.'

'He can always catch up with the footie in the Frog and Firkin next door. They've got an obscenely large plasma TV in there.'

'Yes, I believe he and Doyle have already scoped out the local amenities.'

Something in Markham's tone told Olivia that he didn't anticipate there being much opportunity for recreation.

'And then there's the ancient plumbing,' Markham added with an air of resignation. 'That's another gripe. Plus I don't think Noakesy's keen on queueing for the bathroom in his skivvies. Kept grumbling that it was like being back in the section house.'

'Let's hope Muriel packed a bathrobe, otherwise the scouts may wish to avert their eyes!'

They chuckled at the thought of the college servants' likely reaction to Noakes.

'So what does George make of the feudal set-up, scouts tugging their forelock and all that jazz?' she asked. 'I'd have thought it was a bit too *Downton Abbey* for his liking.'

'Oh, he got on like a house on fire with Ernie Braithwaite.' Markham smiled. 'Ernie's a fixture. Part of the furniture. I remember him from my own student days. I believe he's Sherwin's longest-serving college retainer Noakes spoke to him this afternoon as part of the investigation. Turns out he served in the same regiment as Noakes's cousin Jack when he was in the army, so no problems there.'

Olivia hesitated.

'Was Ernie around when this poor girl went missing?'

'Yes. He was Catriona's scout at the time. Seemed badly cut up about her murder.'

'I suppose it *was* murder, Gil?' There was a pleading note in her voice.

'No doubt about it, sweetheart. But look,' he steered her across to one of two comfortable wingback tartan armchairs in front of the cosily glowing electric fire where a tray of coffee and biscuits was waiting. 'Tell me about *your* day first and then I'll bring you up to speed on the case.'

She allowed herself to be ensconced in an armchair.

'Blimey that feels good,' she sighed. 'Bit of a cushy billet this.'

Her expression suggested the accommodation at Rochford College, where she was fortunately attending a residential course, was somewhat lacking by comparison.

Markham poured the coffee. 'What's Rochford like?'

'Oh, I still can't quite believe I wangled this creative writing gig.'

'Always good to have Mat Sullivan on your side,' he observed.

Mathew Sullivan, the deputy head at Hope Academy in Bromgrove where Olivia taught English, was an old friend who had been caught up in a particularly gruesome investigation at the school. It was a case that had strained old loyalties, but their friendship had somehow come through unscathed and they were if anything even closer because of it.

'Well, you know how passionate he is about Bright Young Things,' she said referring to the initiative which linked Oxford colleges with teachers in North-West inner-city schools. 'Really sold it to SLT and the governors.' A reminiscent giggle. 'Laid it on a bit thick actually . . . made me sound like a cross between JK Rowling and Hans Christian Andersen by the time he'd finished.'

'Better watch out, they'll have you doing all the literacy initiatives if you're not careful.'

She nibbled on a chocolate Florentine (god, even the *biscuits* were exclusive).

'It'd almost be worth it if I manage to go on courses like this now and again.'

'Good tutors then?'

'Fantastic. It's a bit embarrassing having to read your own stuff out, but there's a great buzz.'

'Do I get to see any of the *magnum opus*?' Markham asked slyly.

'Not till I'm on the second draft,' was her solemn reply. 'I haven't quite found my groove yet.'

He smothered a smile.

'What's the accommodation like?'

'Standard student set-up, but it's comfortable enough. Certainly not as . . . picturesque as Sherwin.' She hesitated. 'Not quite so *Fall of the House of Usher*.'

He looked surprised. 'You think this place is creepy?'

'You've got to admit there's something foreboding about it at this time of year. The walls are so grey and, well, *damp* . . . Like they're sweating witch-ointment or something.'

'Rochford's pretty historic too,' he countered thinking of the college's gracious mellow buildings in the Queen Anne style.

'Yes, but somehow it feels *benign*, reassuring . . . like a favourite great-aunt. Whereas Sherwin . . .'

Despite himself, he was amused.

'Not everyone's favourite relative then.'

'Not mine.' She looked somewhat shamefaced. 'God, I'm coming over all "arty-farty" aren't I?' She looked thoughtfully towards the windows which, with their heavy damask curtains drawn back, disclosed only the starless inky night. 'It must be that medieval vibe and all the stone . . . Makes me feel like Richard Crookback's lurking behind the ramparts somewhere, waiting to slither out and wreak evil.'

Despite the warmth of the fire, Markham gave a reflexive shiver.

Olivia was instantly stricken with compunction.

'Oh Gil, I'm sorry. The last thing you want is me bringing that up.'

He forced a smile, although her reference to history's most famous Wicked Uncle was an unwelcome reminder of the art gallery murders in which the legend of the Plantagenet king had recurred like a particularly horrible leitmotif. Markham had lost a friend during that case, afterwards declaring to Olivia that it felt as though the entire investigation lay under a curse.

'All behind us, sweetheart,' he said lightly. 'Actually, the workman who found Catriona's remains under staircase eleven felt much the same as you. He was totally freaked out because apparently his grandsons had been learning about the princes in the Tower at school and couldn't stop talking about bones turning up under staircases.'

Now it was *her* turn to shiver.

'How awful,' she said with feeling. 'And pregnant too, the poor, frightened girl.'

'She disappeared in 2000 . . . last sighted on Cornmarket at the end of finals week.'

'The height of summer,' she ruminated. 'Everyone demob happy because the exams were over.'

'*Demob happy* . . . Yes, that's a good way of putting it.' Markham's brows furrowed. 'All punch-drunk with relief and excitement so no one noticed when Catriona slipped out of focus, into the shadows.'

I'm going to refocus the picture somehow, he vowed. *Recall her to life.*

'And then she ended up under the cement . . .' Olivia's eyes wandered to the window.

'It seems her killer took advantage of a restoration project.' There was a marked edge to Markham's tone. 'The contractors were cowboys by the look of things which made it easy to conceal a corpse. The killer just slid it into the exposed pit under the staircase and shovelled asphalt on top.' His mouth twisted. 'Apparently there were wheelbarrows of the stuff and no security to speak of. Perfect for the killer's very own *DIY SOS*.'

'*And that was it?*' Olivia sounded disbelieving. 'She was just written off as a missing person? And nobody thought to check out building sites . . . What were they playing at?'

'There *was* an investigation, Liv,' he sighed. 'Though I grant you, things would be done differently these days . . . It's easy to condemn with the benefit of hindsight, but when Catriona went missing there were works going on all across the city so nobody thought of excavating under college staircases, particularly not when the contractors said everything was kosher.'

She nodded slowly. 'Like the Madeleine McCann investigation, I suppose. The police over there in Portugal chasing their tails and no one bothering to check out construction trenches even though half the holiday resort was being dug up.'

'Correct. Besides, it seems the investigation at the time ruled out foul play — they presumed she chose to disappear.'

'And all the while Catriona's killer must've been watching and *gloating* . . . like one of those sneaky little gargoyles on that parapet outside.' She contemplated the glowing bars of the electric fire. 'D'you think whoever did it is still here, Gil? In college?'

'Possibly. We're proceeding on that basis . . . The killer would have had the worry of knowing that the grave site might one day be uncovered. Plus,' he added sombrely as though the words were dragged out of him, 'I think it's likely they felt somehow possessive of Catriona and wanted to keep her close, keep an eye on her, so to speak.' He thought of Catriona's ex-boyfriend, still in Oxford, a fellow in the very same college.

'God, you make it sound like the Dennis Nilsen spree . . . What did he call it? "Killing for company"?'

More like the Bluebell murders, Markham thought grimly, recalling how that particular investigation had ended.

Aloud he said, 'It's just a hunch, Liv. I've got nothing to go on except gut instinct.'

At this, Olivia narrowed her eyes in suspicion and imitated DCI Sidney's unpleasantly strident honk.

'Be wary of *flair*, Markham. Good solid legwork . . . that's what's needed . . . None of your Flash Harry notions.'

It was an uncannily accurate impersonation and Markham felt his spirits lift.

'You should've seen Sidney's face when the principal said he wanted a "Sherwin man" to run the investigation. His eczema flared up like Erysipelas and he was tugging the goatee so hard I thought it might come off.'

'*Ugh*. I hate the way he always strokes that tufty bumfluff like he thinks it makes him some kind of sex god.'

Markham spluttered.

'*Sidney . . . A sex god*!'

'Well, only in his dreams obvs.' She grinned roguishly. 'Too bad all those mini-skirted students have broken up for the holidays and aren't available to soak up his lethal charm.'

'You forget Sidney's delightful lady wife has spies everywhere,' he replied drily. 'I doubt he'd risk it.'

'Oh yes.' Olivia rolled her eyes at the mention of the DCI's Valkyrie-like spouse. 'Didn't Brunhilde go to St Ursula's?'

'That's right. And firmly part of the Oxford mafia as I understand it.'

'Come to think of it, her name came up when we had drinks with the dean of Rochford College yesterday,' Olivia said.

'How did that go?'

'Oh, he's a nice bloke: Peter Hart. Teaches Classics. His wife, Margaret Payne, is the junior dean.'

'Quite the family affair.'

'That's Oxford for you.' She tried to keep resentment out of her voice. 'The Old Boy Network alive and kicking.'

'I take it they're both Oxbridge.'

'Actually, they were at Sherwin together.'

His antennae twitched.

'Do you know when?'

'I think they did their finals in . . . let me see . . . 2000.'

'Which would make them my contemporaries, and contemporaries of Catriona Rowlands,' he said slowly. 'Yes, I believe I remember those two from OUDS.'

'OUDS?'

'The Oxford University Dramatic Society.' He smiled wryly. 'Like me, they didn't make the final cut . . . good enough for the school play but not dazzling enough for *As You Like It* in the round.'

He laughed at her troubled expression.

'Don't worry, I'm not going to storm Rochford and expose you as a policeman's moll,' he joked. 'At least not just yet. But,' he said carefully, 'it would help to have a word with them, perhaps later in the week.' Markham's voice held a question.

'Fine by me.' Olivia had recovered her equilibrium. 'Anyone who was at Sherwin with Catriona . . . well they've *got* to remember something, right?'

'Well, we were all pretty selfish at that age, obsessed with our own petty concerns . . . oblivious of the bigger picture . . . failing to connect.'

'Perhaps that's what Oscar Wilde or whoever it was meant when they said youth is largely wasted on the young,' she said shakily.

'Well when it comes to Oxford's gilded youth, I've no doubt about it,' Markham agreed wryly. 'When Catriona disappeared there was a flurry of police interest and some excitement in college — reporters hanging around, that kind of thing. I remember being curious about what happened . . . wondering if there wasn't more to it than her just dropping out and walking away from everything or killing herself. But then it was next day's fish-and-chip paper.' His dark eyes were unfathomable pools.

'It's bothered you all these years, hasn't it?' Olivia's voice was full of understanding. 'It's not just about being on the spot or a "Sherwin man". Somehow you feel you owe her. That's why you wanted this case.'

'Yes. Deep down I knew that while I went on with my life, there were people whose lives would never be the same again.'

Including her murderer.

In the silence that followed, the bell in the college clock-tower tolled nine p.m.

The lovers counted each individual stroke.

When the city bells pealed out on the last day of Catriona Rowlands's life, she couldn't have known that for her peers the carillon announced the start of summer festivities — parties, balls and Pimm's — while for her they heralded the approach of eternity. Olivia imagined the young student relaxing after her exams touched by no shadow of what was to come . . .

A thought occurred to her.

'D'you think Catriona died the same day she disappeared, Gil?' Suddenly it felt as though the chocolate Florentine was stuck in her throat. 'Or was she . . . *kept* somewhere, abused or maybe tortured?'

'I think she most probably died soon after she vanished,' he said firmly. 'And I'm willing to bet the kill took place in Sherwin close to staircase eleven. Given the level of decomposition, the pathologist couldn't tell us whether or not she was assaulted or raped.'

'But where do you even start after all this time . . .'

'Those living on staircase eleven and the other staircases in third quad on the date Catriona disappeared,' he said.

'Was there a boyfriend?'

'Yes, though they'd split up. Dr Jon Warrender. He's a fellow here.'

Her expression said it all. *Nepotism, again.*

'I imagine as far as George is concerned it's pretty much all sewn up then.'

Markham gave a mirthless laugh.

'There are a number of contenders for the top spot, Liv. Ernie Braithwaite was very illuminating on the subject.'

'Ernie*?* Oh right, the scout . . . Noakes's new bestie.'

'The very same. He said Catriona was a popular girl and there was at least one other serious boyfriend. Actually, by the sound of it, her boyfriends may have overlapped. If Ernie's to be believed, she and Warrender split up after he found out the other man was on the scene.'

Olivia pulled a droll face. 'Don't tell me . . . the other man works here too.'

'As a matter of fact, yes. Modern Languages don named Drexler.' Markham smiled reminiscently. 'You could see Ernie thought he was an arrogant tosspot.'

She smiled. 'Did *he* say that or are you quoting George?'

'Let's just say Noakesy was at hand to translate.'

'So, two ex-boyfriends are in the frame and now a "Sherwin man" is going to head up the investigation. The whole thing's positively incestuous,' she declared, sinking back into her armchair.

'It gets better.'

Deliberately, he poured them some more coffee enjoying her reaction.

'*Come on,* Gil, the suspense is killing me.'

'Well, the bursar was an undergraduate here too.'

'At the same time as Catriona?'

'Correct.'

'Wow.' She sipped her coffee mulling over the revelation. 'I think I saw him in the porters' lodge when I was signing in earlier, tall and rather snooty . . . barking orders.'

'Yes, that sounds like Philip Greaves.'

'He's not all that bad looking,' she went on thoughtfully, 'if it wasn't for the sneery expression and the nose.'

Markham grinned. 'You're a stern judge, Liv. What's wrong with his nose?'

'Oh, it's one of those beaky purplish types straight out of Dickens . . . The ones that always seem to have a drop of moisture at the end.'

'Delightful. Well you said it yourself, Liv. It must be the cold and damp.'

'Too much claret more like.' Her prejudices were hard to shift.

'Hmm Sherwin has a fine cellar, I believe. Perk of the job.'

'Did George's chum have any dirt for you on the bursar?'

'We call it intelligence gathering,' he said in mock reproof.

'*Whatever*.' She waited implacably.

'Apparently Catriona beat him to various college prizes. Actually, I remember that. He was a dead cert and then this girl came from behind. She also sent him up in the *Sherwin Confidential*.'

'Sent him up?'

'As in, poked fun at him in a sketch. It was nothing malicious according to Ernie, she just had a naughty way with words. "A bit of fun" was how he described it.'

'Did you ever see a copy?'

'Must've passed me by. I never had much time for college politics. But I've put Doyle on it.'

'Greaves looked like a slimy cold fish,' she mused. 'But *murder* . . . That's a stretch.'

'Not when you've got jealousy in the mix.' As Markham knew all too well.

'But he's done well for himself, surely . . . I mean, bursar in an Oxford college.'

'No academic glory though, Liv.' Markham stretched out his long legs, enjoying the warmth of the fire. 'I mean, Greaves was one of my intake and a scholar to boot, but he rose without a trace. I was aware of him,' he shrugged, 'but apart from that he didn't make much of an impact. You've got to go back twenty years when Catriona outshone him. According to Ernie, their tutor was convinced *she* was the one with great potential . . . destined to wind up as the kind of talking head who publishes a string of books and is "never off the telly".'

'Lashings of charisma.'

'Undoubtedly . . . whereas it looks like Greaves never truly fulfilled his potential.'

'So he hated her then,' she said flatly.

'Well if so, he wasn't the only one.'

There was a flush on Olivia's cheek as she leaned in eagerly. No wonder Noakes described her as a sorceress, Markham thought, with those glittering grey-green eyes and the piled up red hair.

'Go on, Gil. I'm all ears.'

'There was a scout who ended up being dismissed for pestering female undergrads. A man called Ray Cunliffe. Catriona was one of those who complained.'

'A sex pest . . .'

'It happens from time to time, 'over-familiarity' they call it.'

'They bloody would.'

'There was also some sort of issue with the Reverend Dr Royston De'Ath. That's the chaplain emeritus—'

'The *what*?'

'Posh speak for a former chaplain — they get to be honorary fellows after retirement from the pastoral side.'

'God, don't tell me *he* was perving as well.'

'There were *rumour*s he was somewhat over-interested in particular students.'

Her tone was grim. 'As in laying on of hands.'

‘Nothing concrete and no official complaints. We’re talking about gossip on the scouts’ network . . . If anyone *did* report him, it was hushed up.’

‘What a beaut.’ Olivia sounded disgusted. ‘You don’t mean to say he’s still here enjoying the “perks”.’

‘Oh, he’s very much in evidence. Still has a high-profile role at Sherwin, heavily involved with liturgy and the like . . . mentors the college organist Andrew Skeffington . . .’

‘Where does Skeffington fit in — is he another one who had the hots for Catriona?’

‘Nothing like that . . . ultra-respectable and a don into the bargain. Did his BA at Courtenay Hall, thought about becoming a Catholic priest but changed his mind. Later, he had a plum job as Director of Music at Southwark Cathedral before Sherwin poached him.’

‘All very illustrious. But if he’s Doctor Death’s sidekick, there’s got to be something hinky.’

‘I’m keeping an open mind, Liv,’ he said mildly. ‘I haven’t met any of them yet except the bursar. The chaplain, a Mr Gardiner, was down in London with Dr De’Ath, so that’s a pleasure deferred.’

She regretted her sarcastic tone. ‘Sorry, Gil, I’m being obnoxious. Sounds like there are a few people who might’ve had problems with Catriona.’

‘She was the kind of girl others were drawn to,’ he said quietly. ‘Like moths to a flame . . . But in the end, *she* was the one who got burned.’

‘What about another woman?’ Olivia caught herself up. ‘But no . . . a woman *couldn’t h*ave managed that, surely.’ The pleading note was back.

‘Catriona was a slight girl . . . doll-like. The pathologist says a woman could easily have done it if she was taken by surprise. She could have transported the body to staircase eleven in a wheelie suitcase or travel trolley, perhaps . . . With all the college revels going on that night, the quads and stairwells were deserted—’

‘But it was still a massive risk.’

'Well, it could have been passed off as some sort of prank . . . especially if someone helped her.'

She stared at him.

'You mean an accomplice.'

'It's possible, Liv. Maybe they didn't even need a wheelie bag. Remember, students were letting off steam that night, maybe all anyone saw was a girl slung over some bloke's shoulder in a fireman's lift . . . playing caveman . . . horsing around, that kind of thing.'

'Everyone slaughtered cos it was the end of exams . . . Yes,' she said meditatively, 'I can visualise something like that.' She held out finely tapered almost translucent hands towards the fire. 'Could be the bloke didn't even twig that Catriona was *dead* . . . thought she was drunk and just dumped her on that staircase so her "friend" could take care of her. *God* . . .' Her eyes were wide with horror. Then, as though to comfort herself, she murmured, 'But you haven't got any women in the frame yet . . .'

'There's an events organiser at *Gaysoc* we need to interview,' he said reluctantly. 'A woman called Alice Matheson.'

'How come?'

'Apparently she "had a thing" for Catriona when they were undergrads.'

'And Catriona wasn't interested?'

'It's not clear what happened, but the friendship soured.' Markham rubbed his eyes vigorously. 'Ernie got a bit queasy round the subject of same-sex liaisons.'

She laughed. 'Ah, just like George then.'

'Oh yes, definitely singing from the same hymn sheet.' He sighed. 'But I just had the feeling there might be more to come on that score. And then there's the family . . .' He attempted to smother a yawn.

'You're tired,' she said. 'And I should be getting back to Rochford.' A mischievous smile made her eyes dance. 'I suppose in the old days when this place was all-male, you'd have had to smuggle me over the wall once the gates were locked.'

'I'll get you a taxi, Liv. *No,*' he declared firmly at the look on her face, 'no way am I letting you walk back by yourself with a killer on the prowl.'

'It's only up the road, Gil . . . Just off the High. And besides, Catriona's killer isn't interested in me, it was twenty years ago . . .'

'Who can say what a madman will do,' Markham muttered darkly. And then, 'You may as well give in graciously, Liv. Come on, I'll walk you over to the lodge.'

Outside, the vaporous mist coiled about their feet like some pestilential exhalation breathed out by the stone flags.

Suddenly Olivia was glad Markham was with her.

A rustle from the adjoining staircase made her jump.

She wheeled round, nervy as a whippet. 'What was that?'

'Just some loose ivy flapping about,' he laughed. 'Look, there's no one there, Liv.'

But for a moment she was almost sure there *had* been . . . someone with glittering eyes shining out of the gloom.

Eyes full of hate.

'Lay off the Edgar Allan Poe tonight, Liv.'

'I'll try *Inspector Morse* instead.'

He gave a mock-theatrical groan.

'Text me when you're safely home.'

'Will do.' She reached up to kiss his cheek, conscious of the night porter watching them from the glass kiosk that fronted the lodge. 'What're you up to tomorrow?'

'A meeting with the local police first thing.'

'Oh dear . . . territorial wrangles?'

'Most likely, yes.'

'Better unleash George, your master diplomatist.'

'It doesn't bear thinking about.' Then his tone brightened. 'At least Kate will have the incident room up and running, so we can hopefully start the interviews.'

There was the sound of an officious cough from the other side of the glass.

Markham signalled to the porter to admit Olivia and reached for his mobile.

'You wait in there, Liv, until the taxi arrives, do you hear me?'

'Fat chance of making a break for it with Fulton Mackay's beady eye on me,' she riposted before sweeping into the lodge with a radiantly insincere smile.

Markham retraced his steps. All he wanted now was a whisky and bed. Thank heaven he had thought to pack the Glenlivet.

Soon all was silent in first quad and the college slept.

3. THE LINE-UP

Monday 14 December dawned cold and bright with a glittering frost.

In the event, Markham's meeting with Superintendent Charleson went on the backburner.

He had just looked in at the porters' lodge only to be accosted by the head porter wearing a troubled expression.

'What is it, Mr Stevenson?' the DI said, instantly alert.

'On staircase eleven, Mr Markham . . . vandals or something.'

'Show me.'

Their footsteps seemed unnaturally loud as they passed through the archway in first quad and up the steps, with the Great Hall on one side of a narrow wooden corridor and the college kitchens on the other.

Then down another flight of steps and on through second quad where a further archway led to third quad and staircase eleven, which was over in the far left-hand corner.

The head porter held back, gesturing Markham to go ahead.

The word, spray-painted in red on the stone wall to the right of the cavernous gap at the bottom of the staircase, had the force of a blow.

WHORE

There was no sign that the yellow police tape had been disturbed, but he glimpsed a flash of colour in the murky depths of the excavation pit.

Markham moved closer and peered in.

Scattered in the tarry sludge, where plastic pegs marked Catriona Rowlands's final resting place, were petals from a red rose. The flower itself looked to have been savagely hacked about . . . like some travesty of a mourning posy.

In light of the unusual circumstances — a twenty-year-old crime scene in a venerable Oxford institution currently hosting a police conference — it had been decided not to seal off the premises on the assumption that there was no immediate threat to life or property.

'Our killer will be lying low,' was DCI Sidney's verdict. 'Won't want to draw attention to himself.'

But whoever murdered Catriona Rowlands had answered some ungovernable compulsion to revisit the gravesite and desecrate it.

Markham turned to the head porter.

'What time did you lock up last night, Mr Stevenson?'

'The wicket gate is locked at midnight, sir. I open it again at 6 a.m. sharp.' The man looked uncomfortable, as though fearful of being caught out in some dereliction of duty.

'And outside those hours?'

'Electronic card or fob . . . same as what you've got while you're here for the conference. Visitors hand them back when they sign out.'

'Presumably students and staff have them too?'

'That's right, sir. In terms of security, it's generally open access these days. Different from olden times when the proctors patrolled to see folk weren't doing anything they oughtn't.'

Something about Stevenson's expression suggested he thought things were managed better back then.

'No need to leap over walls,' Markham said remembering Olivia's joke of the previous night.

The head porter looked pained.

'Well obviously you'll always get the *wilder* characters . . .'

But I run a tight ship, was the subtext.

Markham felt sorry for the porter who suddenly looked old and frail in the half-light of the staircase.

He drew Stevenson away from staircase eleven back into third quad.

'As you say, Mr Stevenson, there'll always be students who kick over the traces,' he said soothingly. 'This could well be a sick prank, so we'll keep it to ourselves for the time being.'

The other drew himself up. 'I'll get back to the lodge then, Inspector.' Patting his regimental tie with headmasterly precision, he added: 'Can't leave the rest of them on their own for too long.' Clearly, as far as he was concerned, junior staff fell into the same category as students. The porter turned to go then hesitated. 'What's going to happen about the conference, sir?'

'I understand my colleagues will be decamping to St Ursula's, Mr Stevenson. It's literally round the corner, so they'll be perfectly comfortable.'

Something in the porter's demeanour made him add hastily, 'Not as comfortable as they would be *here*, obviously, what with Sherwin's legendary reputation for hospitality. But,' he smiled charmingly, 'any port in a storm.' The thought of the DCI safely stowed round the corner afforded some consolation. Bad enough having to deal with the likes of bursar Philip Greaves without having to fend off his own boss as well.

'Well, they won't be going without a cooked breakfast inside them.'

From his parting sally, it was clear the porter felt his college's honour was at stake.

Markham watched him out of sight and then returned to the trench at the bottom of staircase eleven.

Although the day was bright, the air of the stairwell was rank.

Markham felt sick at the thought of his vivid contemporary ending up in this mouldy hole. Snatches from the pathologist's initial report came to him as he stood there.

Bones found at a depth of around four feet . . . displacement of the skeleton . . . unusually small vertebrae . . . excellent state of preservation . . . young bones softer and more cartilaginous therefore disintegrate more rapidly . . .

His parting words to the head porter belied his own deep unease.

This was no prank.

A killer's hatred had boiled over into that vile graffiti.

As for the mocking floral tribute, it struck him as sacrilege. The murderer had deliberately returned under cover of darkness to defile the grave.

He wondered now about the noise Olivia had heard the previous night. Perhaps it wasn't the rustling of ivy after all . . .

'*Chuffing Nora.*'

Noakes had materialised beside him.

'Pol Pot in the lodge told me where you were.' He pulled a face. 'Blimey, it smells even worse than before. Enough to put me right off breakfast.'

'Somehow I suspect you'll force yourself, Sergeant.' But now Markham too was breathing through his mouth. 'Let's get some fresh air,' he said.

Out in the quad, they gratefully gulped it down.

'Talking of *fresh*, Noakesy, I trust you'll be having a wash and brush before we head down to St Aldates.'

Or go anywhere near the DCI, Markham said to himself, since the combination of ratty T-shirt, baggy knitted cardigan and sagging cords seemed positively calculated to make Sidney's eyes pop.

'I'm just doing the student thing, guv . . . *blending in* . . . Anyway,' he gave an aggrieved sniff, 'there weren't any hot water this morning. Probably Burton and Doyle used it all. *Selfish*, that's what I call it.'

'Method acting is all very well in its place, Sergeant. But we're a little long in the tooth to be channelling our inner student hipster. So for god's sake dig out a suit before we head down to Superintendent Charleson . . . And if the DCI's in the Great Hall this morning, I'd recommend you fade discreetly into the wall panelling.'

Another prodigious sniff.

'What's with the graffiti then?' Noakes said. 'Did Pol Pot know owt about it?'

'*Mr Stevenson* was as baffled as you and me. Random vandalism was his best bet.'

'Vandalism my backside . . . Whoever did that hated the lass.' The DS scratched his stubble. 'Could be they knew about the baby an' all.'

Markham's eyes were remote. 'Someone Catriona jilted, a one-time lover . . . That would fit with the rose . . .'

'What rose?'

Noakes hadn't peered into the trench, being only too keen to escape the noisome rot and fustiness.

'Someone had thrown a rose into the pit, Sergeant . . . It was ripped to shreds.'

My love is like a red, red rose, he quoted to himself. But this was a cankered blossom.

'Nasty.' Noakes said with feeling, squinting warily at staircase eleven. 'Like they're laughing at her not having a proper funeral or something.'

The shambling uncouth figure looked upset, and Markham remembered that he was the father of a daughter not much older than Catriona Rowlands at her death.

'*Christ*,' the DS continued. 'Sometimes it feels like we're always shovelling up corpses. An' for the lass to end up in a filthy tip like that . . . no respect . . .'

Markham famously loathed profanity but on this occasion uttered no reproof.

'Anyway,' Noakes added defiantly, 'it should have been basil.'

'*Basil*?'

'Yeah, that's the plant they say feeds on murdered folks' brains.'

'Where'd you hear that, Noakesy?' Markham was gentle.

'There's a painting,' came the unexpected reply. 'I remember it from the art gallery case. One of them weird Victorian ones with this longhaired drippy lass slobbering over a plant pot. Her lover was murdered, see, so she went an' dug him up an' stuck his skull in this tub of basil . . . kind of like a memento. Then she just lost the will to live an' died,' he declared approvingly as if the heroine of the tale had finished by doing the decent thing. 'Your Olivia,' a slight flush tinged the brawny neck, 'told me there's a poem about it.'

Despite his amusement, Markham could see this bizarre monologue represented his wingman's attempt to conceal strongly felt emotions.

'Basil flourishing on murdered brains,' he said musingly. 'How very sinister.'

Noakes recovered his composure.

'Well, it fits with that stinking compost heap back there,' he said. 'More than roses at any rate.'

'Let's get forensics to take a sample,' Markham instructed. 'See if there's any evidence on the petals.'

Noakes grunted then scanned the quadrangle.

'D'you reckon the killer lives in college then, guv?'

'It's possible, Noakes . . . Or they've got one of those fobs which opens the wicket gate.' Markham's gaze returned to staircase eleven. 'Do we have a list of people who lived on that staircase when Catriona Rowlands was an undergraduate?'

'Yeah, Burton sorted that. But it's no help, guv . . . all foreign postgrads. She's checking it out but doesn't look like any of them had a connection to our vic.' The DS was getting restless, massive head tilted towards the Great Hall as various savoury odours wafted towards them. 'She's doing one of her fancy spreadsheets an' all.' He forbore from comment, his views on Kate Burton's enthusiasm for data and statistics being no secret. 'But even if she works out exactly who was on all the staircases when the lass disappeared, that ain't going to tell us who did it . . . I mean, it's not like we can work out alibis. . . not after all this time.'

'True, but they'll still have to be followed up.'

One for the girly swot, Noakes decided.

Notwithstanding the lure of bacon and eggs, he looked back at staircase eleven.

'Did they find any of the lass's clothes?' he asked gruffly.

'Whatever she was wearing had disintegrated,' the DI replied. 'But they got a match from dental analysis, so we can be sure it's Catriona.'

'If she were pregnant, then she must have seen a doctor somewhere along the line — the uni health service or clinic or whatever . . .'

'I'm putting Kate and Doyle on it,' Markham said heavily, 'but I doubt it will give us the identity of the father or very much else for that matter.'

The DS ran pudgy hands distractedly through his hair, stiff porcupine quills giving him the air of a convict on the run. More Magwitch than Maigret, thought his boss despairingly. Better let him push off to breakfast. Given the speed with which Noakes shovelled down his food, there was just a chance he'd be out of the way before Sidney and the other grandees graced the dining hall.

'You get off to breakfast, Sergeant.'

'What about you, guv? You don't want to be facing Charleson and the St Aldates mob on an empty stomach. An' they do a mean fried egg here.'

The DI's stomach roiled ominously.

'I've had coffee,' he said. 'And anyway,' he felt a sense of relief, 'Here come the others.'

At least Burton and Doyle were appropriately suited and booted, the very epitome of keen young detectives. He was amused to see Kate's barely concealed horror at her grizzled colleague's 'sad dad' get up.

'Noakes will bring you up to speed with the latest development,' he said, noting how their eyes snapped with excitement at these words. 'And then we'll have a tidy-up,' with pointed emphasis, 'before seeing Superintendent Charleson.'

'We're all set to go, sir. The bursar agreed we can use his rooms as our base.'

'Excellent, Kate.'

'Batted your eyelashes, did you?' But Noakes's tone was affectionate and his colleague merely shrugged self-deprecatingly while Doyle grinned.

'After St Aldates, it's back here for a brainstorm and run-through of our key suspects,' the DI continued. 'We'll do formal interviews tomorrow morning in the Great Hall and then brief the principal.'

'Oh yeah,' grunted Noakes. '*Sir* Paul Mirfleet. Another stuck-up piece of work . . . looks at us like we're something he scraped off his shoe.'

Privately, Markham had formed much the same opinion of Mirfleet, however he said quietly, 'Well, it can't be easy having his college commandeered for a conference—'

'Even though they make a packet out of it,' Noakes growled.

The DI ignored this interjection.

'And now to have the body of a former student discovered on the premises . . .'

'Bad PR,' came the cynical observation from Doyle.

'Will there be a press conference, sir?' As always, Burton was thinking ahead.

'Most likely tomorrow, Kate.'

'What about the family?'

'They flew back yesterday evening.'

Noakes jerked his head towards staircase eleven and threw the DI a meaningful glance which the latter had no difficulty interpreting.

Nothing to say one of them couldn't have done the graffiti.

The vandalism was taking a risk, Markham thought to himself. But then whoever the killer was, they apparently had the confidence to prowl through Sherwin College, gliding invisible as a ghost along its dank cloisters.

The savoury smells of cooking were getting stronger.

'Off you go,' he said to his team. 'Back at the lodge for ten sharp please.'

Watching them go, Markham suddenly felt the nape of his neck prickle. As though he was being covertly observed.

His eyes raked the Elizabethan frontage of the quad buildings, inspecting the ivy-clad stonework and crenelated rooftops. But the ancient buildings met his gaze inscrutably, with no sign of a spy lurking behind mullioned casements or battlements . . .

Markham wandered towards the fellows' common room in first quad, grateful that he had somewhere to collect his thoughts before the meeting with Superintendent Charleson.

Lavishly appointed like the chapel, Markham delighted in the room's paintings of Tudor and Jacobean nobility looking down at him haughtily from over their ruffs. On one wall was a reproduction of the *Field of the Cloth of Gold* depicting the notorious extravaganza of Henry the Eighth and his French counterpart, with Disneyesque pop-up palaces and a great banner depicting a mythical creature — half dragon, half salamander — streaming across the sky. Disconcertingly, the sly pterodactyl eyes seemed to size him up with a mocking conviction that he was way out of his depth.

Catch Me Who Can . . .

With the defilement of Catriona Rowlands's grave right under their noses, it was as though their killer had thrown down the gauntlet.

Certainly, the case felt like no other they had undertaken.

For a start, they were out of their comfort zone, the rarefied environment of the university being so far removed from ordinary life that it might as well have been another country. The painting just about summed it up . . . thrones, dominations . . . a softer climate bathing a cluster of gilded spires . . .

And the inhabitants of this celestial city were unlikely to take kindly to any imputation that baser passions and motives seethed beneath its shining surface.

His team would have to tread carefully.

The principal and Sidney were no doubt already joining forces to repel any overzealous interrogation of college personnel. On past form, Sidney's ideal scenario would involve a sexually motivated attack by some anonymous drifter with no connection to Sherwin, but it looked increasingly unlikely that such was the case.

As a 'Sherwin man', he was presumably expected to observe the decencies and steer the investigation well away from the sacred college precincts. But he felt in his bones that the killer of Catriona Rowlands had to be Gown not Town . . . unless the answer lay closer to home in her family circle.

The local police posed another headache, likely to be touchy about an outsider being brought in . . . to say nothing of any suggestion that they had been negligent first time around.

And yet, he thought to himself, there *had* been negligence. That business with McMaster & Son for starters — imagine taking the word of those shysters at face value — and the assumption that Catriona had chosen to leave, that she wasn't murdered . . .

His lips tightened at the thought of *that* omission.

Even worse, he suspected a reverential deference towards the university authorities had played its part, like those Tudor servitors in the painting fawning over bluff King Hal.

Well, *he* was no stooge primed to save Sherwin from embarrassment or, as Noakes was wont to say, 'You can't polish a turd.'

The clock tower chimed a quarter to ten.

Time to beard Superintendent Charleson.

* * *

An hour and a half later, the team was back in the bursar's rooms brooding over the hostile reaction of their Oxford colleagues.

'Ole slab face ain't going to give us diddly-squat,' Noakes observed with gloomy relish as Burton busied herself at the Nespresso machine. 'You could tell he hated your guts, guv — jus' waiting for you to fall flat on your face. An' all that sarky stuff about him not having the right connections, made it sound like you were Little Lord Fauntleroy or something.'

It was true enough, thought Markham resignedly. Ian Charleson and his boot-faced cohorts had been superficially civil, but the whole scene had seethed with resentful subtext.

'They didn't like the idea their old guvnor might've screwed up,' Doyle put in laconically.

'Pity Carter and Mike Knight have snuffed it,' Noakes grunted, referring to the SIOs from the original investigation. 'An' as for the rest, you can bet Charleson's put the word out: no sharing information with the flash git from Bromgrove.'

Burton passed round their drinks.

'Blimey that's good,' Doyle said appreciatively after a sip of his frothy cappuccino.

'How the other half lives, Constable,' Markham said with a rare charming smile.

Noakes winked at the youngster. 'Wangle yourself one of them study leave thingies an' you can have this every day instead of the garbage they give us in CID.'

Burton was growing restive, shifting awkwardly in her chintz armchair as if deep in her soul she hankered for the utilitarian furniture of Markham's office in Bromgrove.

'We didn't learn much new at St Aldates,' she conceded wearily.

'Except that McMaster couldn't organise a piss up in a brewery an' the SIOs never bothered to check them out,' Noakes said breezily.

'At least we've got a list of the firm's employees — the ones who are still around — so I can follow up their statements,' Burton added.

Noakes and Doyle exchanged their usual semaphore.

Another fricking spreadsheet from the head prefect.

'Excellent, Kate.' Markham shot her colleagues a look that made them sit up straighter.

'Then there's the statements from people who may have seen Catriona,' Burton continued. 'Perhaps now her body's been discovered, it'll jog someone's memory . . . throw up something new.'

'Good idea.' The DI's gaze wandered to the pile of manila folders he had brought from St Aldates. 'Or there may be some discrepancy between their police statements and what our suspects tell us tomorrow . . . something we can use as a way in . . .'

'Who *are* the suspects, boss?' Doyle asked.

'The people in Ms Rowlands's immediate circle, her peers and college staff,' Markham answered.

Burton was ready. As Noakes often said, the woman was a walking rolodex.

'There's the two former boyfriends . . . Jon Warrender, the one she'd split up with—'

'The bloke who's a tutor here,' Noakes frowned in a way that boded ill for Warrender.

'Correct. Plus the other don Mark Drexler,' she went on brightly. 'Then we've got the bursar Philip Greaves —there was tension between him and Catriona when they were students, some kind of academic rivalry.' She turned to Doyle. 'Any sign of that piece she wrote about him?'

'Nothing doing but I haven't tried the students' union yet, they might know something.'

'Don't forget the pervy padre, Doctor Death,' Noakes grunted.

'Yes . . . Dr De'Ath has to be of interest given the rumours about him,' Burton continued, 'and there's the scout who may have had a grudge after being reported for harassment, Ray Cunliffe.'

'An' the folk who were students along with Rowlands.'

Unlike Markham, Noakes never had any compunction about referring to victims by their surnames. But Markham knew his number two meant no disrespect. One look at Noakes's face back on staircase eleven earlier had shown him that.

'Right.' Burton gave her mental rolodex a spin. 'Dr De'Ath's protégé Andrew Skeffington — the organist — he was a contemporary . . . And most probably there's staff in other colleges who crossed paths with her.'

'Yes,' the DI interposed quietly. 'From what Olivia says, I believe the dean and junior dean at Rochford College would have known her . . . Peter Hart and Margaret Payne.'

At the mention of Markham's lover, a spasm shot across Kate Burton's face, imperceptible save to Noakes whose compassion would have galled her had she been aware of it.

'How's Olivia enjoying the course?' she asked politely, her tone colourless.

'Oh, writing up a storm,' Markham said lightly. 'I don't want to destroy her street cred just yet, but I'll need to check out Rochford later this week.'

Burton smiled tightly. 'Good to hear! And finally, there's the family. Veronica and Sarah Rowlands.'

'Step relationships can be tricky,' Doyle put in.

'Hopefully I'll be seeing them tomorrow.' The DI loosened his Turnbull & Asser tie in a rare sign of lassitude. 'Sarah Rowlands is a teacher at Forty Martyrs Preparatory School here in Oxford.'

Noakes looked as if he was sucking a lemon, spooning up the foam from his drink with unnecessary vigour.

'How come she wasn't around when they found the body?' he grumbled. 'Schools don't normally break up till just before Christmas.'

'Sarah was escorting a party of students on a skiing trip,' Markham replied. 'After that, she met up with her mother, then she and Veronica flew back together.'

'Very cosy.' The DS's voice dripped sarcasm.

'You've forgotten the *Gaysoc* woman,' Doyle said with a wary eye on Noakes.

'Oh yes, sorry, Alice Matheson.' Burton decided to take the plunge. 'Possibly another romantic interest.'

'Some of them statements in there,' Noakes jerked a thumb in the direction of the manila folders, 'mentioned a girl with Rowlands on Cornmarket.'

For all his apparent laziness, Markham reflected, Noakes was like a truffle hog when it came to picking up the scent.

'Slim, tallish, dark hair tied back in a ponytail, specs . . . Mind you,' the DS puffed out his cheeks, 'prob'ly all them brainboxes looked the same.' He licked the foam moustache off his upper lip. '*Nah* . . . It's gotta be someone who was knocking off a slice.'

Markham purposely avoided looking at Burton.

'Where on earth do you get these dreadful expressions, Sergeant?' he asked, half-amused, half-exasperated. 'Presumably that's the vernacular for sex.'

Noakes was unabashed.

'She was pregnant, which meant a whole pile of trouble for the father, guv. Mebbe she even threatened to report him . . .'

'For getting her pregnant?' Doyle laughed. '*Get out of it*, sarge. They've moved on from *Brideshead*. It was the noughties, remember.'

But Burton's gaze was speculative.

'She could have threatened to report him for rape,' she said. 'That'd be a whole different ball game.'

Noakes shot Doyle a triumphant look.

'Anyway it makes more sense for it to be a bloke,' he resumed. 'A lass would give herself a hernia trying to pull that off.'

'Not necessarily,' Markham said slowly.

He walked across to the Nespresso machine, waving Burton back to her seat as she half-rose to fetch his refill.

Then, with deliberate lack of haste, he strolled across to the mullioned bay window which looked out onto the leafless shrubberies of Plessington College. Despite the lack of colour, there was something pleasant about the garden's neat parterres and geometrical patterns . . . an orderliness that helped him to arrange his thoughts.

'Killing Ms Rowlands on that staircase was a risk,' he said, turning back to the team. 'But it was the end of term . . . everyone intoxicated by a kind of summer madness—'

'You mean spliffs,' put in Noakes dourly.

The DI smiled.

'No, not drugs . . . More a sense of time suspended, a feeling that this moment would never come again and the normal rules didn't apply . . . liberated anarchy, if you like.'

Noakes's expression said very clearly that he *didn't* like.

He and the missus had been disappointed when their Natalie's A level grades weren't high enough to get her into university ('vastly overrated anyway,' said Muriel, quoting Princess Anne), but listening to the DI carry on like some mad Marxist made him quite glad she was safely tucked away in that salon back in Bromgrove. She had her head screwed on alright, and beauticians would never be short of custom.

'What I mean,' Markham came down from the heights, 'is that with all the fun and games going on, students congregating in the bar and on the lawns, well away from the college staircases, there was a window of opportunity. Ms Rowlands was slight, not to say tiny. If she was taken by surprise, it could have been over in minutes and the body tipped into the builders' slurry . . . there was a spade handily available along with various other implements and barrowloads of rubble.'

'Them dickheads,' Noakes rumbled thinking of McMaster's laxity.

The DI remembered his conversation with Olivia.

'Alternatively, Ms Rowlands could've been killed elsewhere and then transported across to staircase eleven by a wheelie suitcase, travel trolley, something like that . . . or even over someone's shoulder . . . someone who didn't realise they were carrying a dead body—'

'Because they thought Catriona was drunk.' As ever, Kate Burton was quick to catch on. 'And anyone who saw them would put it down to fooling around, some guy doing a *Me Tarzan* routine.'

'If that's how it happened, wouldn't they have come forward when Catriona went missing?' Doyle objected.

'Might have been afraid to,' Noakes said promptly. 'Or they could've been wasted,' he added darkly, 'an' not sure what the chuff actually happened that night. Mebbe they even worried *they* might have done something crazy. *Hey*,' he was struck by a thought, 'mebbe there *was* some kind of game going on an' then it got out of hand . . .'

'We can't rule anything out,' the DI said firmly.

They sat in silence for some minutes. But it was an amicable silence as they mulled the range of scenarios.

'What's with the dragon?' Noakes asked after a while, pointing at one of the impressive paintings on the wall behind the bursar's vast desk.

Like the *Field of the Cloth of Gold* in the fellows' common room, this one depicted another medieval gathering — a tournament this time, like something out of *Ivanhoe*, with squires in brightly coloured tabards and ladies in strange crescent-shaped headdresses all watching a joust from tapestried stands while a banquet was in preparation below. And once again, there was a kite or banner emblazoned across the left-hand corner of the picture with another fire-belching dragon scorching the sky.

'It's an emblem,' Burton told them. 'Henry Tudor — Henry the Eighth's father — was Welsh.'

Of course he was, thought Noakes with an inward eye roll.

Aloud, he contented himself with a muttered tribute, 'Oughta go on *Eggheads*. I reckon you'd wipe the floor with the lot of them.'

Doyle looked apprehensive, as though he feared they were in for a mini-lecture on heraldry.

But despite her sternly concealed pleasure at Noakes's compliment, Kate Burton had other fish to fry.

'It would have been useful to get the chaplain's take on things,' she said.

'True,' the DI agreed, recalling his frustration when it transpired that Sherwin's chaplain was unavailable for an advance briefing. Instead, they had been obliged to content themselves with the bursar and assorted minor functionaries whose lips were firmly zipped. 'At least he and Dr De'Ath are expected back from London some time tomorrow, so we'll have a crack at them then.'

Markham was starting to feel almost somnolent in the unaccustomed luxury of the bursar's rooms.

'Let's acquaint ourselves with the contents of the files,' he said briskly, gesturing to the buff-coloured paper wallets. 'Kate, would you divvy them up please.'

As she and Doyle bent over the papers, Noakes turned to his boss.

'D'you reckon heaven's like that?' the DS asked, his eyes wandering to the medieval picture. 'Parties an' feasting an' folk having a good time with their friends.'

Markham was startled. 'What makes you ask that?'

'Well, it's gotta be beautiful . . . The Bible's clear about that.' Sunday school had left its indelible mark on the DS. 'But if it's like church . . . all following the highest, like, an' no fun, it won't be what the lass was used to.' He cleared this throat. 'What you said back there about students thinking they were outside time an' kinda invincible, not having to follow rules an' that, well, if the lass went to heaven, she'd expect it to be like that . . .' The broken phrases petered out.

The DI found that he had a lump in his throat as he listened to George Noakes fumble through his ideas about the great mystery of the hereafter and what it might hold for Catriona Rowlands.

He sent up a fervent prayer. *Let heaven at least prove a kinder city than Oxford.*

Before he could formulate a reply, there was a knock at the door and the head porter appeared.

'Mr Stevenson. What can we do for you?' Markham enquired cordially.

'It's Ernie Braithwaite, Inspector . . . No one seems to know where he is.'

4. DE PROFUNDIS

The atmosphere in their temporary incident room was suddenly electric.

'Were you expecting Mr Braithwaite at work today, sir?' Markham asked the head porter.

'Yes, Inspector. He was on light cleaning duties once the students broke up for Christmas on the fifth.' The man was visibly agitated, his regimental tie askew as though from repeated tugging.

'You can usually set your clock by Ernie, so when there was no sign of him after breakfast . . . well, I thought there must be something amiss.'

'Here mate.' Noakes pressed him into an armchair and nudged Kate Burton. 'Sort him a hot drink will you, plenty of sugar . . . I'll only banjax that thing,' he added with a jerk of his head towards the Nespresso machine. With the quiet efficiency which characterised all her movements, his fellow DS hastened to comply.

Once the porter had taken a few shaky sips and composed himself, Markham asked, 'Have you called him?'

'Ernie can't be doing with mobiles, but we rang his place on the Cowley Road . . . there wasn't any answer. It's one of those phones where you can't leave a message.'

Noakes watched Stevenson closely. 'Has anyone checked out the address?'

'I got one of the junior porters to go round, but there was no one at home.'

Burton got out her notebook. 'Does he live with anyone . . . Is there a Mrs Braithwaite?'

'His wife died a while back. Cancer. No other family so far as I know.'

'He was pretty shaken up when that body turned up under staircase eleven,' Noakes said thoughtfully. 'Knew it had to be Catriona Rowlands even before the dental records confirmed it . . . mentioned a few names an' all . . .' Restlessly, he began pacing the Axminster before wheeling round on the porter. 'How'd he seem to you afterwards? Did he say anything?'

'He was a bit quiet, but it was only natural . . . I think it was the fact they found two sets of bones. He and his wife always wanted a family, but it just didn't happen. Knowing there was a child in there could've tipped him over the edge . . .'

Noakes stared at the porter.

'How'd he know about that? *We* only got the pathologist's report on Sunday.'

'Bill Knowles wasn't exactly discreet, Sergeant.' The man's lips thinned to a taut line. 'After finding the . . . skull . . . he took another look before the police arrived, said he was fairly sure he'd seen some smaller bones and thought a small animal must've got trapped in there somehow. Then someone said what if it's a baby.' Unhappily, he added, 'As you say, Sergeant, everyone had thought of Catriona Rowlands straight off . . .' An awkward clearing of the throat. 'I remember there were rumours she might have been in the family way.' The sallow face flushed. 'I don't like gossip, but you get to hear things.'

Noakes gave a soundless whistle. *Thanks a bloody bunch, Bill Bigmouth Knowles.*

The DI showed no sign of consternation, continuing in his light pleasant baritone.

'Mr Braithwaite shared some memories of Ms Rowlands and her fellow students with us,' he remarked easily. 'Did he mention anything about that to you, Mr Stevenson, or say anything that might have a bearing?'

Markham's air of calm authority had its usual tranquilising effect, the porter appearing less flustered now.

'I remember we were stood over by the lodge chatting just before Ernie finished on Sunday around five-ish — he'd helped us out with an extra shift what with the conference and everything . . . Anyway, suddenly, out of the blue, he kind of gave a little jump as if he saw someone he recognised—'

'Did you see who it was?' Burton asked quickly.

'No. They must have must have come out of one of the staircases and gone through the archway into second quad before I had a chance to clock them.'

Now it was Doyle's turn. 'Did Ernie say anything about it?'

'He just looked kind of thoughtful, and then it seemed like he was in a hurry to get off home . . .'

'Are you sure he didn't say anything, Mr Braithwaite?' Markham insisted. 'This could be important.'

'Hold on a minute . . . yes, there *was* something, but it didn't make much sense really.'

'Try us,' Noakes rumbled.

'Well, he was turned away from me as he said it, kind of muttering to himself.' They waited expectantly. 'He said something like he'd forgotten all about it until then, but he reckoned it must have been pretty much the last straw.'

'Was that all?' The DS was disappointed.

'Sorry, Mr Noakes,' the porter apologised. 'He's a bit of an old rascal is Ernie, looked a bit shifty, so at the time I figured he was up to some dodge or other and I'd be better off not knowing. It's only now I think again . . .' His voice tailed off.

'This thing he'd forgotten about . . . Something to do with a tutor?' Markham pressed. 'One of the fellows?'

Now Stevenson looked embarrassed.

'I could've got it all wrong and maybe he was one over the eight or something . . .'

'*One over the eight?*' Noakes was on the warpath.

'Ernie likes the odd tipple. No harm in that,' he added defensively. 'Anyway, he needed something for the shock after that drama with Bill Knowles and all the rest of it.'

'"Pass the Port" was it?' Noakes enquired with heavy sarcasm. 'Are you saying him an' the bursar had a bevvy?'

'Of course not.' The other was distinctly nettled. 'It was most likely medicinal . . . something for his nerves.'

And the rest, Noakes thought sourly. But at least the old prune-face bursar could probably be acquitted of letting Braithwaite loose in the college cellar.

'D'you think Mr Braithwaite just needed time by himself to make sense of it all?' Burton asked delicately.

'As in get rat-arsed.' No point beating about the bush, in Noakes's opinion.

Something about this full-frontal approach jolted the porter into frankness.

'Ernie's had a battle with alcohol,' he admitted, 'but he's worked hard for Sherwin down the years . . . You wouldn't find a more devoted college servant.'

'Could he have topped himself cos of this business with the lass?' Noakes's tone was softer now.

'No, I don't think so, Sergeant. I think deep down he'd accepted Ms Rowlands was dead . . . everyone had, to be honest. Bill Knowles's blather would have upset him, but he'd come through worse.' Now the man spoke with decision. 'There must have been something else bothering him.'

The detectives exchanged glances.

'If Ernie wanted to get away an' be by himself, mebbe sort things out in his head . . . where would he go?' Noakes asked. 'Is there anyone he usually hangs out with, goes down the pub with . . . ?'

'There's the British Legion. They've got a branch in Jericho . . . Ernie sometimes went up there for a chat about the old days.'

The DI nodded to Doyle who discreetly slipped into the adjoining room from where they could hear him making a call on his mobile.

The porter's face was tallow pale.

'D'you think Ernie may have known something about who killed Catriona Rowlands?' he stammered.

'It's possible, Mr Stevenson,' the DI replied. 'But we don't want to jump to conclusions. Nine times out of ten a missing person turns up safe and sound.'

Inside, though, he had a horrible feeling this would be the exception that proved the rule.

If Ernie Braithwaite had remembered something, had some secret knowledge about Catriona and her circle, he might have been tempted to capitalise on it with fatal consequences for himself . . .

Had he tried to blackmail a killer?

'Just one last question, Mr Stevenson,' he said, hoping the porter wouldn't see where this was leading. 'Can you tell us anything about Mr Braithwaite's personal circumstances. Was there any kind of financial difficulty that might have led him to . . . drop out of his life for a time?'

'Well, he wasn't a great spender, lived pretty frugally so far as I'm aware. The house is a two-up two-down, don't know if it's housing association or what . . . As for his pay here,' the porter hesitated, torn between honesty and college loyalty. 'It was . . . on a par with the sector and of course, there were increments for long service.' More defensively he added, 'I wasn't aware he had any complaints.'

'No indeed,' the DI said heartily. 'We just want to get the full picture.'

'Ernie having been at Sherwin so many years speaks for itself,' Burton said gently.

Mollified, the porter said, 'Yes, for more than thirty years. He's a bit of a father figure to the students.' A misty smile of reminiscence. 'There was one young lady kept managing to miss dinner in the Great Hall . . . Ernie'd always make sure to bring her some leftovers — a bit of mackerel from the starter or a nice helping of tapioca.'

Noakes's face suggested neither of these ranked high in his league table of tasty treats, but his voice was kind. 'Sounds like he was a soft-hearted ole bugger.'

The porter blinked at the description but nodded. 'A law unto himself, Ernie but loyal to the college through and through.'

Doyle had returned.

'The Legion put me on to one of his mates. He said Ernie likes the river, always goes that way when he's out of sorts.'

The DI summoned a reassuring smile.

'We'll head down there right away, Mr Stevenson,' he said. 'In the meantime, we'll leave you to take charge here. Not a word to anyone, please.'

The older man's nervous fingers fluttered about his trembling lips and he swayed slightly where he stood.

Noakes placed a steadying hand on his arm.

'We can thank our lucky stars we've got you at the helm, mate,' he declared. 'What with the conference having to shift down the road an' interviews for tomorrow morning, we're all-to-cock.'

It wasn't how Kate Burton would have put it, but she saw the bracing effect it had on the head porter and marvelled, not for the first time, how her uncouth, monumentally tactless colleague somehow managed to unsnarl nerves and pull off a weird kind of nirvana in the unlikeliest of circumstances.

'Right you are, Mr Noakes. I'll crack on here and make sure everything's sorted for those interviews tomorrow.'

Courteously, the DI escorted him to the door.

'Poor devil,' Doyle said once he was safely out of earshot. 'I thought he was going to keel over.'

'Them fellas always come up with the goods,' Noakes said. 'No way is Stevenson going to have anyone say he bailed out when the college needed him . . . might be a bossy ole git but I reckon he's salt of the earth.'

'Indeed he is,' Markham agreed. Then, 'Let's check out Christ Church Meadow . . . I don't believe Ernie will have gone too far from college, it's only five minutes away.'

'Are we talking blackmail, sir?' Doyle asked eagerly. 'Doesn't sound like Ernie's well off. If he had something on the killer, he might've decided to cash in.'

'He saw someone while he was talking to Mr Stevenson,' Burton mused, 'and it triggered a connection.'

Noakes was back to the hair-rumpling and pacing which invariably accompanied his cogitations. 'An' he talked about something being the last straw . . . mebbe he figured that's what tipped the killer over the edge.'

'Yes, I think Ernie may have had it in mind to try blackmail.' Markham's face was sombre. 'And as we know, that rarely ends well.'

'Mr Stevenson said Ernie was loyal to the college through and through,' Burton commented. 'So that might have been a factor too . . . I mean,' she contemplated the highly polished tips of her smart ankle boots, 'he might have *liked* this person, maybe even felt sorry for them.'

'I agree, Kate,' the DI said crisply. 'If the killer's connected to Sherwin College, that could have made Mr Braithwaite lower his defences and decide to go it alone.'

'They never see the bleeding danger,' Noakes growled. 'Even when they know some mad bastard's strangled a lass an' chucked her under a load of cement . . . they still reckon they can handle it.'

'Human beings are complex, Sergeant,' Markham said sadly. 'We're talking about a mixture of greed and deep-rooted allegiance to Sherwin.' No wonder Olivia had called the Oxford traditions feudal, he reflected. In Ernie Braithwaite's calculations, fidelity to his college trumped all else. Even murder. 'Right,' he said, 'let's get a move on.'

* * *

Christ Church Meadow presented such an idyllic prospect, that it was almost impossible to connect it with murder.

As they stood drawing in deep breaths of frosty air, savouring the exhilaration of being outdoors, the DI wondered if they were on the wrong track.

The meadow and woodland gleamed and sparkled, sloping down to softly fringed banks of sedge and smooth glassy water which reflected the December sunshine like a polished mirror. In the distance, the soft grey stonework of Merton College's chimneys and gables formed a graceful backdrop, nature and history fusing in an image of timeless harmony.

Perfect weather for rowing, he thought, though there were no boats out that day.

The Rochdale College boat house appeared to be open, however, with a dark-haired young woman standing next to the modest timber two-storey structure. She was examining a pair of sculls intently but turned round at his greeting.

No, she hadn't seen anybody hanging round the riverbank, she told them. One or two cyclists and a dog walker had gone by, but she hadn't paid them much heed. Sorry.

'No matter, we'll just follow the path for a bit,' the DI said. Sherwin's boat house was half a mile further down, round the next bend. He had an idea Ernie Braithwaite might have felt safest on his own college's premises as though its coat of arms above the lintel offered some guarantee of protection. He smiled at the student, who smiled shyly back. Noakes shook his head ruefully. The fact that Markham was pretty much oblivious of his effect on the opposite sex did little to reconcile Noakes to the unfairness of nature when it came to dishing out dashing good looks and effortless charisma.

The quartet rounded the bend and saw the muffled shape, trapped in a heavy tarpaulin canvas, half in and half of the water like some hideous giant cormorant that had met its end on the bank.

But this was no sea bird.

A short battle with the oilcloth disclosed Sherwin's longest-serving scout staring sightlessly upward, his snub-nosed features frozen in a ghastly rictus to rival the contortions of any gargoyle on the college battlements.

'*Beam me up, Scotty*,' breathed Noakes.

Even though they were expecting it, the stark reality was worse than anything they could have imagined as they took in the spectacle of the chatty bandy-legged little man, wispy grey hair clotted in stiff clumps around his livid forehead.

'Okay, I'm calling it in,' the DI said sorrowfully reaching for his mobile.

* * *

A short time later, the riverbank teemed with SOCOs and personnel, filling the chill still air with their hubbub and the noise of walkie-talkies. To Markham it felt like another desecration.

And then the ambulance was there, and Ernie Braithwaite's sheeted diminutive figure set out on its last journey through Oxford, the four detectives bowing their heads as he passed.

Jigsaw Man, as Noakes called him, brandished the bottle of anti-depressants found in Ernie's jacket pocket.

'He'd had a skinful,' was the blunt verdict, 'and with these on top . . .'

Markham disliked the man's brusque, clinical attitude and the pitiless conclusion.

Noakes felt a bizarre impulse to defend Ernie Braithwaite.

'He weren't just some dosser, y'know,' he said bullishly. 'Longest-serving scout in the university, everyone knew him . . . even the dons did what Ernie told them.' Markham was touched by the absurd hyperbole, recalling the regimental connection with his wingman's cousin Jack.

'Oh, right, a legend in his own lunchtime.' The owlish young medic looked sceptical.

Before Noakes could take up the cudgels again, Markham interposed.

'Can you give us any idea on time of death, doctor?'

The pathologist looked from one to the other.

'I should say early this morning,' he replied. 'Rigor had fully set in.'

Cause of death?'

'Initially I thought drowning while under the influence, Inspector, only . . .'

Markham pounced on the hesitation.

'You're not certain?'

'It *looks* as though he was blundering around on the bank and then somehow got tangled up in that sailcloth or whatever it is.'

'As in fell over and knocked himself out?'

'Correct, Inspector. Then he slid face down into the water . . . the effects of the booze and pills, plus the concussion, meant he couldn't extricate himself.'

'But you're not convinced by that scenario,' Markham stated flatly.

'It looks like there's some injury to the small of his back, but I have to rule out hypostasis and artefactual damage before I can be sure . . . lividity and external factors,' he translated. His expression was troubled as he added, 'And there's this.'

He held out a soggy pink scrap of paper in his gloved hand.

'It was clenched in his right fist,' the pathologist explained. 'Looks like the fragment from a fifty-pound note.' Something in Noakes's championing of Ernie Braithwaite must have had its effect because there was compassion in the man's tone as he said, 'I'm thinking your victim wouldn't normally have had that kind of money on him . . . That and the bruising make me wonder if this might not have been an accident after all.'

To the other's astonishment, Noakes stepped forward and gave him a bone-crunching handshake.

'Nice one, doc. Ta very much.'

The younger man visibly winced. 'Not at all . . . er, glad to be of help.' He turned to the DI. 'I'll be in touch later.'

'At least there isn't any family to tell,' Doyle remarked as they watched the pathologist tramp back along the towpath.

'Sherwin's his family,' Burton observed quietly. 'Poor Mr Stevenson will be devastated.'

Noakes's voice was thick. 'I'll break it to him,' he offered.

'Thanks, Noakesy,' the DI said simply. 'I'm sure he'll take it better coming from you.'

The DS looked embarrassed, chewing the ends of his horrible striped scarf in a paroxysm of awkwardness, but Markham could tell he was pleased nonetheless.

Burton contemplated the water wending its devious way alongside them, the day that had seemed so bright with crisp winter promise now suddenly dark and grey. 'What next, boss?'

His lean handsome face seemed somehow more lined and careworn, but Markham spoke with his customary resolve.

'Back to base for me and Noakes,' he said. 'Meantime, I want you and Doyle to catch up with the young lady we passed on our way down here. I sent a uniform to wait with her. Take a statement . . . the fact of a death may have jogged her memory.' He looked at the little coppices and clusters of brambles whose picturesque charm were now irrevocably tainted by murder. 'Then get along to the Legion. Apart from Sherwin, that seems to have been the extent of Mr Braithwaite's social circle.' He sighed. 'It may turn out to be a wild goose chase, but I want you to check if anyone from there spoke to him or saw him after he finished work yesterday.'

'D'you want me to bring the interviews forward, guv?' Noakes asked. 'I mean, it's not just about the lass now . . . we'll be wanting alibis for Ernie.' His underlip shot out pugnaciously. 'Cos don' let anyone tell me this ain't murder.'

'I'm very much of your mind, Sergeant.' Markham's tone was quiet as ever but held a steely determination familiar to his colleagues. 'To the casual observer, Mr Braithwaite may not appear to have had much of a life but in his own way, he was dauntless . . . soldiered on and made the best of the hand he'd been dealt. I think it's highly likely he was murdered, and we are going to catch whoever did this to him.'

'If it wasn't for that bit of paper, we'd likely have thought accident or some kind of half-hearted attempt at suicide,' Doyle mused.

'From what the doc said, Ernie was *shoved*,' Noakes said firmly.

Burton frowned. 'Forensics won't get anything useful from the tarpaulin.'

'But I'd be interested to know where it came from, Kate. See to it would you?' Markham knew she would gobble up all the tasks he could dish out, such was her zeal.

'To answer your question about next steps, we'll do the interviews tomorrow morning as planned, Noakes,' the DI continued. 'No point flustering Mr Stevenson with revised arrangements . . . He'll be in a bad enough state just hearing about Mr Braithwaite.'

Noakes nodded grimly.

'Do we tell Stevenson it's murder, guv?'

'For the time being, let's stick with "unexplained death".' Markham's mouth twisted. 'Obviously, I'll have to brief the DCI and the principal.' Needless to add that both these worthies would be focused on damage limitation and protection of the college's precious reputation, pressing him to rule out any connection with the discovery of Catriona Rowlands. God forbid the pristine name of Sherwin should be sullied by a serial killer . . .

A sudden chill struck him as he realised he had automatically assumed there would be more deaths.

One day at a time, he told himself.

The gleaming water meadows assumed a more sinister cast as he looked around him, wondering if a killer lurked somewhere in their ditches and dells.

He shook himself. It was time to return to Sherwin.

He turned back to his team. 'We've got a job to do,' he said.

Forty minutes later, back in the bursar's rooms, a call came from Doyle.

'The deputy manager at the Legion has just come on shift,' he said. 'She says she saw Ernie in the Lamb & Flag on Sunday evening.' The young DC was tripping over his words in his eagerness to get the story out. 'According to her, he acted like he was flush . . . said he was expecting a windfall and there'd be plenty more where that came from.'

So it *was* blackmail, Markham thought with a lurch of his heart. Ernie Braithwaite had gambled and lost.

'Well done, Doyle,' he said. 'See if there's anyone from the pub who can corroborate that and get statements. If Mr Braithwaite was in his cups, he may have let something drop to the clientele there . . . By the way, did Kate get anything from that student at the Rochford boat house?'

'Nada, boss.'

'Not to worry, it was always going to be a long shot.' He thought intently. 'Can you arrange for Catriona Rowlands's next of kin to come in tomorrow.'

'On it, sir.'

When he had rung off, Markham reached for the pile of manila folders.

Somewhere in the mound of paperwork there had to be some clue from the past that would put them on the trail of a killer.

The college clock tower struck the hour and the DI bent to his task.

5. WIDENING THE NET

'Well, I don't see any of them for it.'

It was early afternoon on Tuesday, 14 December and the team was sitting at one of the long benches in the Great Hall. The weather had taken a sudden turn for the worse, hail rattling like grapeshot on the flagged pavement of first quad while the trefoil stained-glass windows seemed to shiver in their embrasures. The electric lights in their wall sconces shone feebly on the linenfold panelling, almost as though the spirit of the place was cowed by nature's onslaught.

The team had spent the past two days interviewing Sherwin's personnel. The DI digested Noakes's disconsolate verdict on their interviews — he himself had remained discreetly in the background, circulating unobtrusively as he evaluated the pool of suspects or, as Noakes sarcastically termed it, 'the beauty parade'.

'I thought you were convinced we'd hit the bullseye with Dr Warrender, Sergeant.'

'Yeah, but he's worse than a wet weekend, guv . . .' the DS replied. 'Looked like it'd take all his energy jus' to get up of a morning.'

'We shouldn't judge by appearances,' Burton put in. 'He was a sportsman . . . got a blue for rowing.'

'*Eh?*' Noakes was a study in scowling incomprehension.

'A sort of university award for students who come top in competition,' she explained patiently.

'Well, why the hell can't they jus' say so instead of using daft lingo.'

His colleague decided against making any reference to the tradition of university colours, her enthusiasm for the sumptuous historic portraits surrounding them — the most magnificent being the Virgin Queen in all her periwigged splendour — having already met with a decidedly lukewarm reception. 'Too many folk from olden times in silly frocks, plus they've stuck Maggie Thatcher in that poky corner where no one can see her . . . They need to get their priorities straight.'

Burton suppressed a sigh and returned to the matter in hand.

'Dr Warrender was an all-round athlete,' she continued, 'which means he was no slouch back when he and Catriona were students.'

It was true, Markham thought. In the case of the tall fair-haired don with blue poached egg eyes, he suspected that appearances might be deceptive. The tutor must have been very handsome in his undergraduate days, with a come-to-bed voice that lost nothing from a slight speech impediment, the occasional hesitancy only contributing to an overall impression of charming diffidence. With thinning hair and the hint of a paunch, the man's glory days were clearly behind him, but Markham could see that at one time he might have cut quite a swathe through Sherwin's female population.

Though Warrender made no overt sign of recognition, Markham detected a certain wariness about the other's expression when he introduced himself as a former contemporary. As the interview went on, the years fell away and an image flashed into his mind — Warrender and a group of sportsmen lurching around Sherwin's front quad one night after a long boozy dinner. The machismo had been almost palpable, boisterous shouts ringing out in the darkness.

His wingman wasn't impressed by the don. 'Bug-eyed ponce,' was his withering pronouncement.

'You know, he didn't sound too fussed when we asked about his relationship with Catriona,' Doyle observed.

'Hmm.' Markham was thoughtful. Warrender had certainly shown no sign of discomfort — in his words he felt 'it was time to move on, no hard feelings, we were young and it was just a boy-girl thing . . . still good friends' — but was there perhaps something too glib, too well-rehearsed, about the insouciance with which he batted away questions about his romantic connection to the girl found under staircase eleven.

It was only when Markham raised the subject of Catriona's pregnancy that he stiffened.

'I heard the rumours,' he said, 'but she never said anything to me about it. We'd broken up by the time the story was doing the rounds. For all I knew, it was idle gossip. She certainly didn't look pregnant at the time.' The admission was frank enough, but Markham couldn't help but wonder. Was this the real reason for the couple's break-up? Had Warrender suspected her of two-timing him with another man?

'The doc says Ernie snuffed it around five a.m. an' wanky wonder boy says he didn't get up till eight. But he could have snuck out to the river without anyone seeing him an' still made it back in time for his muesli.' Noakes clearly didn't see Warrender as a trencherman.

'That's true for all the Sherwin lot, sarge,' Doyle pointed out mildly. 'The night porter heard the wicket creak a few times but didn't think anything of it.'

'What about Dr De'Ath?' Noakes retorted, drawing out the vowels as though to demonstrate his contempt for all apostrophised surnames. 'We know he was back in Oxford around three on Sunday afternoon.'

The DC nodded. 'Yeah, that's right, cos De'Ath got a lift back with his friend while the chaplain hung on and came back on Monday.'

'So Doctor Death could've done for Ernie,' Noakes declared triumphantly. '*Hey*, mebbe it was *him* Ernie saw in college Sunday afternoon just before he clocked off, during that chinwag with ole Stevenson when he remembered something.'

The DI's mind wandered to the Reverend Dr Royston De'Ath. Certainly the man struck an imposing figure, as far removed as possible from the clerical letch of college rumour. Tall and distinguished looking, with a fine head of silver hair, patrician features and deep-set eyes behind half-moon spectacles, he bore a distinct resemblance to a painting of Cardinal Richelieu that Markham had admired in the fellows' common room. His voice matched his appearance, being commandingly resonant and charged with authority.

'Students saw me as a sort of father confessor,' he had confided during his interview this morning in a manner which almost suggested he expected the detectives to kneel for a blessing.

'The lasses an' all?' Noakes had demanded in a hostile tone meant to signal his imperviousness to any priestly blandishments.

De'Ath had been unperturbed. 'Oh, I was a "safe" male on whom they could practise their wiles, Sergeant,' he said with a benign chuckle. There was the odd schoolgirl crush, but that's an occupational hazard in my line of work.'

Noakes's voice broke into the DI's thoughts, returning him to the present.

'De'Ath's a conceited git. Fancies himself the bee's knees.'

'Well, you have to admit he's not your average vicar,' Burton ventured. 'Looks like an older version of Richard Chamberlain in *The Thorn Birds*. He must have been a bit of a hunk back when Catriona was here.'

'He seemed on the level,' Doyle put in.

But Markham had seen a flicker behind De'Ath's hooded eyes. It was gone so swiftly, he might almost have imagined it. For all the suave urbanity, something was bothering De'Ath.

The man made all the right noises about the 'appalling tragedy' of Catriona Rowlands's murder and 'the loss of a life that was really starting to blossom', yet something rang hollow.

'The chaplain's right under De'Ath's thumb.' Doyle continued to review the *dramatis personae.*

'I don't think we need to waste too much time on Mr Gardiner,' Markham said as their thoughts turned to the college's insignificant sandy haired 'pastoral lead'. 'Quite apart from the fact that his Oxford antecedents don't go back as far as 2000, it would have been impossible for Gardiner to have killed Ernie Braithwaite.'

'Skeffington's another one under De'Ath's cosh,' Noakes mused. 'Kept looking around to check where he was . . . like he was asking his permission or something.'

It was a fair summary, the overweight dough-faced organist with his pudgy fingers being an unprepossessing foil for De'Ath to whom he obviously deferred.

'You could tell he thought we were thick as mince,' Noakes groused. 'Talking extra slow and loud as if we were special needs or deaf.'

Markham chuckled grimly. 'I've no objection to Andrew Skeffington under-estimating us, Sergeant. It might prove useful.'

'What's the deal with him and De'Ath then?' Burton pondered.

'A case of "You scratch my back and I'll scratch yours", most likely,' Doyle suggested sagaciously.

'As in doing favours . . . keeping secrets,' Noakes pounced on this. 'Yeah, he looks the type.'

'Could they be lovers?' This was Burton.

Her fellow DS mimed being sick, but she persisted. 'There was something intense going on with him and De'Ath.'

'Wasn't he thinking of becoming a Catholic priest?' Doyle said.

'Who, Skeffington? Right up his street then,' Noakes shot back. Then, apologetically in response to a look from the DI, 'I'm jus' *saying.*'

'There was no visible reaction when you mentioned Catriona, sir.' Burton sounded puzzled by the lack of affect. 'I mean, you'd think he could at least have faked being sorry about what happened to her.'

'Not if he's autistic or one of them Asperger types,' Noakes said, cheerfully mixing diagnoses.

Markham sighed, realising that recent diversity seminars about the evils of stereotyping had fallen on deaf ears.

Doyle too clearly felt this was dangerous ground and moved onto their next suspect.

'Well, it was obvious the bursar, Philip Greaves, couldn't stand Catriona . . . even after all these years,' he said.

That was true, thought Markham. There had been a kind of honesty about the bursar's response. The man was so cold he was like ice that burned when you touched it.

'Any luck finding that satirical piece she wrote about him?' he asked Doyle.

'Nothing doing, boss,' came the reply.

Burton screwed up her face. 'I wonder what it was.'

The DC hazarded a guess. 'Something he didn't want anyone to know. Something embarrassing.'

'Bad enough to make him top her?' asked Noakes.

'Could be,' came Doyle's laconic reply. 'Don't they say, "the pen is mightier than the sword"?'

The DS looked suspiciously at Burton as though he suspected her of filling the lad's head with pretentious nonsense, but she looked innocent of guile.

'Mark Drexler's a better bet,' she said.

Noakes was quickly diverted.

'God yes,' he said feelingly. 'The other boyfriend. Warrender an' Drexler, what a pair . . . *Shits R Us*.' He kicked an ornately carved table leg in frustration. 'The lass had *terrible* taste in blokes.'

On the face of it, Drexler was just your typical Oxbridge swordsman, thought Markham.

The Modern Languages tutor was short and stocky with curly black hair shot through with grey, an olive complexion and black eyes that suggested Italian ancestry rather than the Teutonic origins denoted by his surname. A gravelly smoker's voice added to his charisma.

But what to make of him?

The don had demonstrated a sexual callousness that fully justified Ernie Braithwaite's description of him as a 'tosspot' and nearly led to a nasty moment with Noakes when he informed them, 'Yes, I got it on with Catriona while she and Warrender were still an item. I didn't mind his leavings . . . gave the thing extra spice.'

'Have some respect,' the DS had growled. 'The lass ended up in a frigging tip cos someone strangled the life out of her. She weren't no prostitute neither.'

It was the parent in him speaking.

'Catriona wasn't Mother Theresa, Sergeant,' Drexler had countered baldly. 'She liked to party, ended by getting out of her depth.'

Markham had then joined the conversation, hard put to hide his distaste. 'Are you saying she was promiscuous, Mr Drexler?'

'She was up for a good time just like the rest of us. No crime in that.'

'There chuffing well is when it ends with her getting shoved under a pile of cement,' Noakes said hotly.

Drexler's expression was hard, closed off. And yet Markham sensed his DS had struck a chord.

'It was all so long ago,' the tutor had said defiantly, a muscle leaping at the corner of his jaw. And then, with unmistakeable bitterness, 'Women are nothing but trouble. My divorce taught me that.'

He appeared unfazed by the issue of Catriona's pregnancy. 'She and Warrender had a fight about it. The stupid bastard probably decided it was mine. As if *that* was good enough reason to pass up a regular shag. And anyway, Catriona didn't seem to care which of us it was.'

'Bad husband material,' was Burton's conclusion after the interview.

She and Noakes were agreed on this point at least. 'God help the poor cow who ends up with that fella,' he said glowering at the don's retreating back.

Now, as they conducted their review, a thought struck Markham. 'Is Warrender married?'

'He mentioned a partner.' It was Burton's turn to check her notebook. 'He has rooms here, but they mainly live out in Woodstock, the stockbroker belt.'

The DI levered himself out from his seat at the trestle table and paced the length of the dining hall. There had been no abatement in the downpour outside and the long narrow refectory felt oppressive, its great framed portraits coldly indifferent to meteorology and murder alike.

Kate Burton watched him closely. Unlike Olivia, she never questioned her own reactions to the City of Dreaming Spires, simply drinking in its turrets, domes, alleyways and parks as though she could never get enough. If she envied anything, it was the way that Markham seemed perfectly of a piece with the antiquity of his surroundings whereas she knew herself to be an outsider.

Noakes, of course, wore the chip on his shoulder almost as a badge of honour.

'My bum's getting numb sitting on this fricking bench,' he grumbled. 'It's like something out of *Oliver Twist*—'

'Or Hogwarts,' Doyle put in.

Markham laughed.

'They've laid on sandwiches in our incident room,' he said. 'I suggest we fuel up and then head out to Rochford College for a word with the dean.'

Noakes had brightened up at the mention of food. 'Oh yeah, there's a couple of 'em were here the same time as Rowlands, right?'

'Correct, Sergeant.'

'We might see your Olivia an' all.' As always, a certain bashfulness stole over the bulbous features at the mention of Markham's lover.

'I'm afraid she'll be off in a creative writing seminar, Noakesy.' Seeing how the other's face fell, he added, 'But never fear, you'll see her at the memorial service for Ms Rowlands on Saturday.'

'Where's that happening then?'

'Here in Sherwin's chapel.'

Noakes looked outraged. 'De'Ath's not doing it, is he?'

'No, Mr Gardiner will be taking the service. It's to be very low-key, what the family want, apparently.'

'Talking of the family,' Doyle flipped over another page in his notebook. 'They can't come in till tomorrow morning. Is that okay or do you need them sooner, guv?'

'No, that's fine Doyle.' Markham thought hard. 'I'd like you and Kate to do some research on them while Noakes and I get the lie of the land over at Rochford.'

He saw the shadow of disappointment pass across Burton's face. It was impossible to explain to her that he was counting on Noakes's unrivalled genius for getting under people's skin to throw Rochford's dons off-kilter. But perhaps she understood. As she cast a swift sidelong glance at her belligerent colleague, he felt that she followed his reasoning.

'You're with me for the family tomorrow, Kate,' Markham said. Using Noakes to rattle the dons at Rochford was one thing, but it would be kid gloves for Catriona Rowlands's step-relatives. Burton flashed him a bright look of gratitude that reminded him not to take her for granted. Whenever she did decide to move on from his team, her tact and acumen would be sorely missed. He wanted a woman in the unit, but the thought of inflicting Noakes on some hapless rookie didn't bear thinking about . . .

His bête noire was growing restless. 'Are we gonna get them sarnies or what?'

'Right you are, Sergeant. With you around, there's no danger of my forgetting that an army marches on its stomach.'

'What about the woman from *Gaysoc*, sir?' Burton asked as they prepared to depart, reminding the team that they hadn't yet exhausted their list of suspects. 'Alison Matheson, the one who, er, fell out with Catriona.'

'See if you can track her down, Kate . . . and that scout who went rogue, the one they accused of harassment.

'Ray Cunliffe, boss.'

'That's him. Matheson and Cunliffe both had motive.'

Along with just about everyone else . . .

The rain-lashed first quad was dank and slippery and deserted. As he looked back at the Great Hall, Markham fancied the lights flickered.

It felt like a warning.

* * *

'What did you reckon to them two, then?'

Noakes and Markham sat in the DI's car on Little Clarendon Street some time later, having just interviewed the dean and junior dean of Rochford College.

The rain had finally stopped, but it was already growing dark, streetlamps illuminating the quaint row of gift shops and cafés that had given up on the late afternoon trade and were winding down for the day. It didn't feel particularly busy for the Christmas season, Markham reflected, but then that was Oxford . . . visitors and tourists came and went, but the city's ancient tranquillity and age-old rhythms remained somehow inviolate.

Murder changed everything, however, and there were now two victims to be avenged.

He dragged his thoughts back to Rochford College.

'They seemed like your average academics,' he said wearily.

'Yeah, out of touch with bleeding reality,' the DS said. 'An' no common sense.'

Markham chuckled.

It was true that Peter Hart and Margaret Payne — the dean and junior dean — had come across as wrapped up in their work and each other to the exclusion of pretty much everything else.

The dean was a handsome black man with an engaging manner and mellifluous speaking voice. It struck Markham his lectures must be a pleasure to attend.

Margaret Payne put the DI in mind of Alice in Wonderland, with simply styled wavy mouse-brown hair held back by a hairband and wearing a floral maxi dress that swamped her diminutive frame. She wore no makeup, but a clear complexion, regular features and intelligent dark eyes saved her from absolute plainness. She spoke with a soft accent that he couldn't quite place, though it held the same musicality as her husband's. More reticent than Hart, she unbent when Markham disclosed that he was a Sherwin alumnus. 'Not one of the smart set,' he hastened to add.

'Oh, me neither,' came the reply. 'We used to call them the "Okay Yahs",' she added at which they both laughed.

Noakes looked as if he didn't care to comprehend the joke.

'D'you remember him, luv?' he enquired, jerking his thumb at Markham.

'Yes, I believe I do,' she said slowly. 'You matriculated the year after me, Inspector.'

Something in the DS's truculent expression got through to her.

'It's just a ceremony for when you arrive at university,' she explained.

'Very *Da Vinci Code*.'

But Noakes's tone was indulgent. These two weren't up themselves like that lot at Sherwin. Full of daft speak and all that nonsense, obviously, but alright with it. Seemed pretty lovey-dovey into the bargain, which made a nice change after the likes of Drexler. The study they shared was cluttered and homely, its walls hung with striking seascapes. A vase holding winter jasmine and roses sat on the top shelf of the country-cottage bookcase.

'I seem to recall we auditioned for OUDS at some point,' Markham smiled charmingly. 'But it turned out we weren't in the top rank of thesps.'

They had laughed at this, moving on to share some light-hearted reminiscences about Sherwin College to which Noakes listened with less impatience than might have been expected.

Looking back on the fruits of their interview, however, the two men contemplated each other glumly.

'When it came to remembering Rowlands, they weren't much cop,' Noakes said. 'She musta been — what did the lass call it? — one of them Okay Yahoos . . .'

'Okay Yahs, Sergeant.'

'Whatever. Any road, it don't sound like they moved in the same circles. You can tell them two are nerdy types. Y'know, burning the midnight oil in the library an' swotting every spare minute while Rowlands was a party animal.'

Catriona Rowlands might have been safer if she'd stuck with the 'nerds', Markham reflected sadly.

'That blonde piece who barged in at the end was a cracker,' Noakes continued. 'Looked jus' like Princess Di an' had one of them posho names too.'

'Hmm. Perdita Cargill-Thompson,' the DI mused. 'I didn't get the impression Ms Payne was too keen on her despite them all having been at Sherwin together.'

'Probably got her eye on Hart . . . they both teach Classics an' you could tell she fancies her chances.'

'Mr Hart was uncomfortable about something, Noakes, but I don't think it was that.'

No, Markham thought, he was willing to bet something about Catriona Rowlands had stirred unwelcome memories . . . It was there in a sudden clenching of the man's jaw before he recovered himself.

'Odd that Princess Tippy Toes didn't remember Rowlands,' Noakes commented. 'She looked like the type to hang out with the fun people, so you'd think the name would ring a bell.'

'Oh, I think Ms Cargill-Thompson *did* remember Catriona, Sergeant. She struck me as a little too keen to place herself away from Sherwin, down at the students' union with the political crowd.'

'Yeah, thass true. To hear her go on, you'd think she *slept* there.' Noakes frowned.

'Well, I seem to recall her as being quite earnest back then,' Markham said thoughtfully. 'Certainly something of an activist.'

'Blimey, I can't imagine her being the grungy type.'

Markham laughed. 'Oh, she was never that, Sergeant.'

'Tippy Toes had no trouble remembering *you*, boss,' Noakes observed slyly. 'Looked like it rattled her.'

'Visits from the police tend to focus people's minds,' came the laconic response.

'I reckon she's hiding something, guv.'

'It could be she's just reluctant to get dragged into a murder investigation,' Markham pondered. 'Or she could know something.'

'The way she kept clutching them pearls and fiddling with her hair . . .'

'Go on, Sergeant.'

'Well, she was like a cat on hot bricks . . . *frightened*.'

'Yes, that's true,' Markham said quietly.

'An' there was the way her eyes slid away from the others as if she didn't want to look at them directly, kind of sneaky . . . *Yeah*,' Noakes was gaining confidence now, 'she was giving it all that with the expensive clothes an' sticking her chest out at us, but you could tell she jus' wanted to get away . . .'

The DI gazed thoughtfully back at the high walls of the college.

He recalled Olivia describing Rochford as being like a favourite great-aunt — benign and reassuring — whereas Sherwin was more like something out of the Brothers Grimm.

Apart from some ugly Lego-like extensions, bulging out over the surrounding streets like a crass modernist afterthought, the main buildings certainly had a gracious charm which soothed the eye and put him in mind of an unpretentious country home.

But standing in Peter Hart's comfortable study — despite cosy clutter — he had felt it.

Something *off*.

Only he couldn't put his finger on what it was.

Noakes's voice recalled him to the present.

'And they remembered Ernie alright,' the DS said approvingly.

It was true that the scout saved choice titbits from supper for the favoured few, Margaret Payne told them with a rueful smile. 'He used to come over with one of those huge cloche serving dishes and whip off the lid . . . made quite a little ceremony of it. Of course, if you were under the weather, the last thing you wanted was some smelly rollmops or halibut but everyone was so fond of him, they played along.' Her lips were pressed firmly together as though to suppress laughter, but it broke out anyway. 'I'll never forget the day Ernie caught me in my curlers — he looked at me like I was something from outer space.'

Peter Hart joined in. 'They don't make them like that anymore. One of a dying breed, Mr Braithwaite.' It was an unfortunate choice of words in the circumstances, but Hart was quite unaware since the detectives had refrained from mentioning the scout's demise, simply referring to the college servant as someone devastated by the discovery under staircase eleven. Markham had adroitly elicited the couple's morning routine, establishing that they took an early morning jog round the University Parks just north of the city centre, setting off around six a.m. and returning in time for breakfast.

'No one saw them so I s'pose they could've gone down by the river an' done the business with Ernie,' Noakes said doubtfully. 'But it don' seem likely. I mean, they seemed fond of the guy . . .'

Markham felt despondent. 'Yes, Rochford's looking a bit of a blind alley.'

'Still, at least the library woman's promised to ask around,' Noakes rallied him. '*Hey*, bit of a coincidence her being Payne's sister. Talk about keeping it in the family.'

Ruefully, Markham recalled Olivia's comments on Oxbridge nepotism.

'She an' Payne are twins ain't they . . .' Noakes was reflective.

'Non-identical twins, Sergeant.'

'Well, I reckon *she's* the one got the looks.'

Sheila Payne's still curvy figure, thick brunette locks and friendly manner had met with the DS's approval. Dropping in on her sister and brother-in-law, she seemed perfectly at ease and oblivious of any undercurrents. 'I'm one of the red-brick mob,' she told them cheerfully. 'Did my degree at Liverpool. Mags had the brains in our family.'

Now Markham said, 'I'll get Kate to do some digging . . . see what we can turn up on the Rochford people and any other alumni floating about.' He pinched the bridge of his nose in a characteristic gesture of fatigue. 'As things stand, I don't see a connection and fancy the answer lies at Sherwin . . . But we need to cast our net wide.'

Suddenly, his mobile trilled and he turned away to answer it.

'Doyle's got some intel on the family,' he reported after the brief exchange.

'Something tasty?' Noakes enquired hopefully.

'He seems to think so.'

Markham started the engine and pulled away from the kerb, their car disappearing into the murky twilight.

6. SHOT WITH ARROWS

As they turned into the lodge at Sherwin and got out of the car, Noakes's mobile sang out the 'Mexican Hat Dance'. Deducing from the DS's sheepish expression that this was a call from his wife, Markham moved discreetly away so his wingman could commune freely with She Who Must Be Obeyed.

The head porter murmured a polite greeting, looking as though he had aged a hundred years in the course of the last twenty-four hours. Markham's heart ached for the man as he twiddled his Sherwin College cufflinks and twitched his blazer so that it sat straight on the skinny shoulders. He could tell Stevenson was burning to ask if there was any news on Ernie Braithwaite, restrained only by his consciousness that it somehow wasn't fitting to pester the police.

'Thank you for setting up the hall for us earlier, Mr Stevenson,' he said gently. 'The hot drinks and biscuits were a godsend with it turning so chilly.'

The kind words helped.

'It was my pleasure, Inspector.'

Markham noticed the porter's hand was shaking as he smoothed down his grey short back and sides.

'Hopefully I'll be able to tell you something more regarding Mr Braithwaite very shortly, sir . . . after I've checked in with my team. Of course, I know I can count on your discretion.'

At that moment, they were interrupted by a commotion from the back office.

'I'd better see what they're up to back there.' His bearing ramrod straight after Markham's compliment, the porter disappeared into the recesses of the lodge.

Markham moved out into first quad, watching how the college ramparts glistened with their characteristic clammy condensation as though afflicted with a bad case of catarrh.

Give me Sherwin over Rochford any day, he thought, surveying the grey stone Elizabethan architecture with satisfaction. Its compact watchfulness and self-containment suited him far better than any rambling mellow-toned country house set-up.

It occurred to him that this preference for starkness — squat dark walls, stone canopies and vaguely menacing cobbled alleys — could somehow be a reflection of his own personality . . . reserved, chilly and aloof towards all but a very few.

Kate Burton considered Sherwin College cosy and almost homely, he recollected, rating its medieval facade as far superior to the polychrome brickwork of St Ursula's Victorian Gothic or the Renaissance-style staircase towers of Mater Ecclesiae.

Where *he* saw constriction and secrecy, Burton found enchantment, leading Noakes to predict gloomily that she would be 'sounding off nonstop like some ruddy guidebook'.

He grinned at the memory.

In the event there had been no time for tours of 'dreary chapels an' dusty ole museums' but, privately, he was hoping to take in the prehistoric exhibition at the Reynolds Museum. This currently boasted a reconstruction of the famous Newgrange passage tomb, with its mysterious roof box perfectly aligned to catch the light of the winter solstice, which had captured his imagination ever since he saw it featured in the brochure provided for the delectation of visitors to the police conference. Always intrigued by necropoli, this cathedral to the dead built by incestuous Irish chieftains had made a powerful impression on him, its primitivism a reminder of man's essential darkness. Olivia teased him for his 'Fred Flintstone fetish', but he only knew that he felt uncannily at ease in anterooms and winding passages, as though they offered a clue to the primordial self . . .

Noakes was back, wearing the furtive expression that generally signified some ambush by his better half.

'Muriel well, I trust?' the DI enquired politely. That should flush it out.

'Er . . . the missus fancies a day trip — cultural, like . . . Wants to see all the places from *Morse* an' have afternoon tea at the Randolph.'

Markham's lips twitched.

'I tole her there's been a second murder an' I'd need to check with you, boss.' The DS looked self-conscious. 'I thought mebbe she could look in on your Olivia in case we're tied up . . . Y'know, they could do girlie stuff,' he finished hopefully.

Girlie stuff! God, Olivia would crucify him for this.

But somehow, looking at Noakes's half-shy, half-eager expression, Markham could not bear to squelch him.

'I don't see why not, Sergeant. When did Muriel have in mind?'

'Saturday, boss.'

'Well, she could do her own thing in the morning, meet up with Olivia, if she likes, then come to the memorial service for Ms Rowlands in the afternoon.'

'An' tea at the Randolph?'

Clearly this was the crowning attraction.

'We could do that after the service, if Muriel's agreeable to Olivia and me joining you.'

The suggestion was a mark of respect to his sergeant. Muriel Noakes's shrill '*Gilbert*' affected him like nails scratching a chalkboard, but the outing would win Noakes extra brownie points at home, and he had no objection to that.

He guessed that in the wake of the Bluebell case there had been rocky times chez Noakes and wanted to shore up his sergeant's amour propre. As far as Olivia was concerned, he knew her fondness for Noakes would carry the day and she would submit to being patronised by the redoubtable Muriel albeit with gritted teeth and a rictus smile.

'Will Natalie be joining Muriel?' he asked.

He couldn't imagine Noakes's perma-tanned hair-flicking progeny relishing Muriel's *Morse* tour of Oxford, while Olivia's patience would certainly be sorely tested.

'Saturday's her busiest day at the salon,' the other replied proudly. 'Allus fully booked.'

'Ah well, another time then,' the DI murmured with a guilty feeling of profound relief.

'I c'n jus' see our Nat in a place like this,' his DS said, revolving on his heels, paunch thrust out, for all the world like a connoisseur of academe.

Markham tried not to boggle.

'If she'd kept at the books, it'd have been a walkover. But she were that popular . . .'

His boss was well aware that the proud father's concept of popularity did not remotely resemble his own thoughts on the subject of Natalie Noakes's 'people skills'. 'The girl's a man-eater,' was Olivia's verdict and, having watched 'our Nat' put the moves on DC Doyle at last year's shindig in the Grapes, he was inclined to agree. On the other hand, that was before her ordeal in the Bluebell investigation, so perhaps her priorities had changed for the better . . .

He became aware that the DS was watching him expectantly.

'The world's her oyster, Noakes,' he said clutching at the cliché. 'And a job like that will take her anywhere.'

It was a satisfactory answer. 'Thass what the missus says,' the other replied happily.

Markham felt a wave of affection rush over him. It took so little to give the man pleasure, his devotion to that big brassy daughter and the wife who ordered him about like a drill sergeant bestowing a grace that somehow transfigured him.

'Come on, Noakesy, let's see what Kate and Doyle have got for us.'

* * *

'Jigsaw Man says Ernie was definitely murder,' the DC greeted them without preamble.

Clearly Noakes's sobriquet for the pathologist had caught on.

'How's that then?' Noakes asked eagerly.

'Well, once he'd ruled out a bunch of stuff and whatever it was that began with an "H"—'

'Artefactual damage and hypostasis,' Burton amended primly.

'That's it,' Doyle said cheerily, not at all discomfited. 'Anyway, after discounting everything else, he was ninety-nine percent positive.'

'That'll do me.' Noakes sank into an armchair. 'Any chance of a cuppa?' he enquired of no one in particular.

With what Doyle termed her 'early Christian martyr face', Kate Burton trudged to the Nespresso machine.

Markham took the sofa. 'Did you get anything from the Lamb and Flag crowd, Constable?'

'Turns out that manager from the Legion was right about Ernie giving it large down the pub. The barman and two of the regulars heard him at it, bragging about a change in his circumstances. It must've been blackmail, sir.'

'Any clue who might have been the target.'

'Nix.' The DC lost some of his fizz. 'Apparently he clammed up when someone asked what he meant . . . just tapped the side of his nose and looked shifty.'

Oh, Ernie, Markham thought sadly, picturing the little bantam of a man enjoying his last hurrah.

'How about the tarpaulin, Kate?' he said, flashing her a grateful look as she brought over drinks for him and Noakes.

'Just standard rigging . . . all the boat houses use it.'

Damn and triple damn.

'Anything from the SOCOs?'

'Nothing that gets us any further, sir . . . trace evidence is virtually useless given the body was so waterlogged. And anyway, it seems like virtually everyone in the university's been down that towpath at one time or another.'

'While you're on your feet, luv, can you turn the radiator down or open the window or something,' Noakes grumbled wrenching at his tie. 'It's like bleeding Center Parcs in here.'

Burton shot him another 'what did your last slave die of' look but nonetheless cranked open a window casement before taking a seat to hear what had transpired at Rochford.

Doyle looked disappointed. 'It's odd that they don't remember Catriona.'

'Well, it's not so much that . . . I mean, *I* don't remember her all that well either, even though we were here at the same time,' the DI said. 'But there was definitely tension in the air. They were uncomfortable about *something*.'

'Might be worth cultivating that librarian, Sheila Payne,' Burton said thoughtfully. 'She did her degree at Liverpool but didn't you say she mentioned coming up to see her sister in Oxford, sir?'

Markham sipped his frothy beverage appreciatively before replying.

'Correct, Kate. Plus, she's Rochford's development officer — handles fundraising and events for alumni, so I imagine she's in the know.'

'Less dippy than her sister an' the brother-in-law,' Noakes grunted. 'Easy on the eye too,' he added, winking at Doyle.

Both Markham and Burton affected not to hear.

'I'll check out Perdita Cargill-Thompson as well, sir. Maybe if I can speak to her away from Rochford . . . somewhere on neutral territory . . . she might open up.'

Or slip up, Markham thought grimly.

Doyle suddenly sat up. '*Christ!*'

The DI shot Doyle a chilly look.

The young DC caught himself hastily. 'Sorry, sir. I mean, I forgot all about it . . .'

'Forgot about what?' Noakes sucked up the last of the froth from his mug, contemplating his colleague with beady eyes.

'You know you asked me and Burton to suss out Rowlands's family, sir . . . Well, I tried pumping the bursar and he told me Catriona's stepsister Sarah had something going with a don at Rochford . . . said the bloke ended up as dean.'

Noakes scowled. 'Why the chuff didn't you mention it before — when the guvnor told you about us seeing Hart?'

'I didn't make the connection, sarge. Greaves didn't give me his name — fed me some baloney about data protection. I've only just twigged that's who he meant.'

The DI took pity on his hapless subordinate.

'That's useful to know, Constable.'

Was it some kind of diversionary tactic by the bursar, he wondered. A ploy to turn their attention away from himself without being too obvious.

'When did Hart and the sister cop off then?'

Burton didn't turn a hair at Noakes's inimitable phraseology.

She turned to Doyle. 'Presumably this was before he married Margaret Payne . . . when they were students, right?'

The DC flicked through his notebook. 'Sarah Rowlands went to Oxford Brookes,' he said.

'That used to be a polytechnic, didn't it?' Burton mused. 'Before becoming one of those "new universities".'

Noakes gave a snort of derision. 'Emperor's new clothes,' he muttered.

'Not as clever as Catriona, then,' Burton went on. 'Interesting . . . means there could've been some sibling jealousy.'

'Yeah, I reckon so, sarge.' Doyle was anxious to redeem himself. 'Greaves kind of implied they were competitive .

. . said something about Catriona making off with all the prizes.'

'Including her sister's boyfriend?' the DI enquired drily.

'Hart said he didn't remember Catriona,' Noakes joined in. 'But he coulda been lying through his teeth.' His tone implied that to think otherwise would be a triumph of hope over experience.

'We don't know that Catriona swiped Peter Hart from Sarah,' Markham observed. 'But if you put sexual jealousy in the mix with intellectual envy.' He whistled softly. 'That's a potent combination.'

He got up and moved across to the bay window.

From here he could see into the garden of the of the neighbouring college, Plessington, whose shrubberies looked ghostly, floodlights lending them an eerie insubstantiality as they dripped softly in the evening drizzle. Beyond Plessington lay Lincoln College and the High, with the top of Carfax Tower just visible in the distance.

The perspective somehow unspooled some of the busy turmoil in his brain and helped him focus once more.

'Hart didn't admit to knowing Catriona,' he said, turning back to his team. 'But that could have been through embarrassment or awkwardness . . . After all, he's happily married now, and maybe he just doesn't want to be drawn into a murder investigation.'

'Or mebbe he *knows* something . . . Like Princess Tippy Toes.'

'Noakes means Perdita Cargill-Thompson,' Markham clarified, looking at the mystified faces of the other two. 'Teaches Classics at Rochford. She's possibly what Margaret Payne would call an "Okay Yah".'

'An' shifty too.' Bromgrove CID's Panzer was taking no prisoners. 'She were dead twitchy . . . Kept yakking on about the students' union like she didn't want us to think she spent any time at Sherwin.'

'But they were *all* at Sherwin,' Burton said slowly. 'Peter Hart, Margaret Payne, Perdita and Catriona.'

'Yes,' Markham said slowly. He had placed them all — the bookish couple with their interest in amateur dramatics, the Sloaney social climber and Catriona. Smart, beautiful Catriona who'd seemingly had the world at her feet.

Noakes scowled.

'An' now them three are settled all nice an' cosy . . . feet under the top table at Rochford an' the sister teaching posh kids round the corner while what's left of Rowlands is shoved in a container down the morgue like some sodding puzzle box.'

The room fell silent at his outburst, a gentle hiss of rain beyond the window the only sound to break the hush.

Then the DI spoke again.

'Anything else on the Rowlands family?' he asked levelly.

'There were issues between the stepmother, Veronica, and Catriona,' Burton replied.

'Issues?'

'The usual kind of thing, boss,' she continued. 'They didn't get on. Catriona resented her father marrying again while Veronica didn't like the closeness between father and daughter, tried to keep them apart. There were some pretty fierce fights by all accounts.'

'What sort of a woman is she?' Markham asked.

'Imperious . . . Very much the you-fetch-this-fetch-that type. The family solicitor was happy enough to talk given it's a murder enquiry.' Burton consulted her notes. 'Things weren't helped by Gerald Rowlands changing his will shortly before his death, leaving the bulk of his estate to charity. Veronica and Sarah were decently provided for, but it was nowhere near what they expected. Apparently, Gerald and Veronica were headed for divorce when he died. He got it into his head that his remarriage was somehow to blame for what happened to Catriona — that she would never have gone off the rails and put herself in danger if she'd been happy at home. He was a sick man and brooded about it.'

The DI pondered this information. 'They didn't contest the will?'

'No point . . . He wasn't incompetent or anything like that and it was all above board.'

'What did the solicitor think of Veronica?'

'I got the feeling he'd rather take up residence in a crypt and cuddle up to one of the coffins than spend much time with her.'

'Hey, that's quite good!' Noakes guffawed at this unexpected flash of wit from 'ole sobersides'. Burton's mouth twitched.

The DI returned to the sofa, crossed one long pinstriped leg over the other and steepled his fingers meditatively.

'So, there's the family,' he said. 'Veronica and Sarah Rowlands both had reason to dislike and resent Catriona.' Possibilities danced through his mind like bubbles. 'Then there's the Rochford connection. Peter Hart was definitely involved with Sarah and possibly Catriona too, and we've got Perdita Cargill-Thompson who came across as thoroughly uncomfortable with the whole subject of Catriona. Plus Margaret Payne and her sister Sheila, who might know more than they were letting on.'

'Sherwin's a better bet.' Noakes was bullish, stubby fingers raking his hair till it stood wildly askew. 'You've got Greaves an' the creepy twins De'Ath an' Skeffington. But my money's on Warrender or Drexler . . . one of them two got the lass pregnant an' then killed her. They didn't fancy playing Daddy or freaked out in case her being up the duff ruined their precious careers . . .'

'But it was 2000,' Doyle protested. 'Getting a girl pregnant wouldn't have been the end of the world even back then.'

'Could be there was more to it,' his colleague said darkly. 'Mebbe the lass was holding summat over 'em.'

'Like what?'

'I dunno . . . but whatever it was, they'd be screwed if it came out.'

The DI became conscious of a dull headache beginning to form, just behind his right eye.

Noakes was right about the room being stuffy and overheated. He had a sudden urge to plunge into the cool damp air of Plessington's garden next door.

Or perhaps it was a sense of all the suspects being like so many snakes, coiled up together in the recesses of his mind, ready to spring out at him the minute he took his eye off the ball . . .

Talking of snakes, right on cue, Burton sprang the coup de grace.

'Oh, by the way, sir, the DCI wants a briefing first thing tomorrow morning. Nine a.m. in the principal's lodgings.'

Markham's gaze wandered to Noakes whose attention was suddenly riveted by the carpet pattern.

'Sorry, Noakesy,' he said, 'you're on that with me.'

'Burton'd do it better,' the DS said.

It was undoubtedly true, but Noakes's particular blend of chippiness and dumb insolence would throw Sir Philip Mirfleet off guard. And when people were rattled, there was a chance they might let things slip.

He'd had that effect on the Rochford group, the unnerving scrutiny of those piggy eyes and point-blank refusal to be overawed by his surroundings, combined with his guile, somehow betraying them into talking too much and revealing what lay behind the mask.

'Kate's doing the family,' Markham pointed out. Turning to Doyle, he asked, 'What time are they coming in?'

'Around eleven, boss.'

The DCI's mauling should be concluded by then, the DI thought grimly. Even Sidney couldn't sustain a rant for two hours.

'Then there's Alice Matheson.'

'I've spoken to her on the 'phone, boss.' Burton was pleased to have something positive to report. 'She can come in tomorrow.'

'Excellent, Kate. Let's have her in for twelve noon after I've spoken to the family.' He got up from the sofa. 'What did you make of her?'

'A cool customer, sir . . .' Burton spoke with her customary deliberation, conker-brown pageboy hair swinging as she bent over her notebook. 'Seemed very relaxed. No sign of strain. If she's faking it, she deserves an Oscar.'

'Don' they all,' was Noakes's dour verdict.

The splitting headache had begun.

'Right,' Markham said, endeavouring to speak briskly. 'The timetable for tomorrow is as follows. I'll brief the DCI at nine a.m. with Noakes, after that, interview the family at eleven with Kate. Then Noakes and I will see Alice Matheson.'

'Anything else you need from us, sir?' Burton, as ever, was bristling with executive efficiency.

'Yes. Keep looking for Ray Cunliffe. I want to get to the bottom of that harassment business.'

'What do you want us to do about Ernie, sir?' Doyle asked. 'Should we come clean to folk about it being murder?'

At that moment, the bell in Sherwin's clocktower tolled seven o'clock.

It might have been the death knell at a funeral, so bleak and tomblike was the sound.

'I'll speak to Mr Stevenson,' the DI said quietly. 'Something to the effect of its being treated as suspicious.'

'He'll spread the word,' Noakes said with satisfaction. 'Means we won't have to do an announcement or owt like that.'

'We've put back the press conference, sir, what with us finding Ernie.' Burton jiggled her foot in its patent leather ankle boot. 'Was that right?'

'Absolutely, Kate.' No doubt Sidney would cover the PR angle tomorrow. He shuddered to think how the DCI was going to spin the double homicide . . . Surely to god he wasn't going to adopt his default position of the 'bushy haired stranger'? The principal would love it, naturally, but all the evidence pointed to this being a university murder.

After the team had dispersed for the night — Noakes and Doyle to the Frog and Firkin and Burton to the Phoenix

Picturehouse to sample 'some cripcrap with subtitles', as Noakes put it — Markham continued to sit in darkness, trying to still the clamour that resounded in his head.

Finally, he got to his feet, thinking through the morrow's agenda.

The DCI, then the family followed by Alice Matheson.

In a swift call to Olivia, he had promised her a promenade down by the river the next day. There was to be some sort of sprint regatta in the afternoon and he vowed they would be there, carve out some time together free of bodies and suspects and murder.

Carefully, he closed the window and took one last look at the ghostly shrubberies then headed for his own quarters.

* * *

Ten a.m. on Wednesday morning found Markham and Noakes licking their wounds in the fellows' common room.

Noakes, predictably, didn't have much time for the 'Field of the Cloth of Gold' or any of the other Tudoresque paintings which adorned its walls. 'Wouldn't get much fighting done with them puffy sleeves an' all the fuss an' feathers,' he pronounced, squinting at the retinue of servitors snaking its way across the canvas.

On the other hand, a reproduction of Mantegna's 'Saint Sebastian Shot with Arrows' clearly fascinated him, especially the saint's head which appeared to be impaled on a javelin. 'Looks like it's made the lad's eyeballs swivel,' he said with ghoulish relish. 'You gotta hand it to them holy painters, they really know how to do gore.'

Shot with Arrows.

It was an apt description of how Markham felt after the meeting with DCI Sidney and Sir Philip Mirfleet.

Sated with artistic S&M for the time being, Noakes plonked himself down on an overstuffed armchair.

'You could tell Sir Pip thinks one of the Sherwin lot did for the lass,' he said cheerfully. 'Thass why he joined in with

Sidney's bollocks about the Oxford drug scene an' it most likely being some lowlife from one of them Jericho squats.'

Bollocks was the operative word, thought Markham gloomily thinking back over the encounter.

Noakes had indeed got under the rubicund principal's skin with repeated insinuations that Oxford colleges were little better than knocking shops. And when Sidney attempted to close him down, he simply changed tack, bobbing and weaving with a dexterity that elicited the DI's reluctant admiration.

Eventually Mirfleet snapped.

'I suggest your enquiries would be more profitably directed at the university's *subversive* element rather than distinguished academics,' he said with tight-lipped rancour. 'I understand there's a character from *Gaysoc*,' he put inverted commas around the word, 'you should be looking at . . . The woman has a history of stalking and was involved with Ms Rowlands at one time.'

The subtext was unmistakeable. If the police insisted on looking at Gown rather than Town, a lesbian agitator on the fringes was less of a potential embarrassment to Sherwin than the arrest of a college fellow.

It was a narrative that appealed to Sidney.

'As a Sherwin man and guest of the university, I know you can be counted on to respect academic sensitivities, Inspector,' he said with thinly veiled menace. 'No call for flights of fancy.' Ho. 'Good solid coppering's what we want.'

In other words, make sure nothing leads back to Sherwin or any of the higher echelons.

Ernie Braithwaite got short shrift from the principal: 'A loyal college servant who never really got over the death of his wife . . . a troubled soul, I fear.'

Sidney chimed in with, 'Superintendent Charleson is inclined to think there may have been an altercation with a vagrant or some such.'

'I believe Mr Braithwaite's and Ms Rowlands's deaths are linked, sir,' was Markham's quiet response. 'Not only was he Ms Rowlands's scout but, according to witnesses, he boasted of having financial expectations, which points to the possibility of him attempting to blackmail the killer.'

'Oh, by all accounts Braithwaite was a Walter Mitty character,' Sidney shot back in a tone of voice that suggested his recalcitrant DI was just such another. 'You wouldn't want to invest too much faith in causal pub talk out of some *romantic* sympathy with the man.'

Now Noakes said, 'Sidney made it sound like you were some dippy daydreamer.'

'More like a glory-hunter looking to make a name for himself with a nice juicy college scandal,' the DI observed resignedly.

'Interesting about the dykey stalker.'

'*Noakes.*'

'Don' worry, guv, I know how to talk to 'em these days. Burton's allus bending my ear. Gay rights this, LGBT that . . .'

'Well, I'd be grateful if you could put all your new-found diplomacy into practice when we interview Ms Matheson. No minority-baiting, understood?'

''*Course*, guv. Like I said, it's all about making the right noises.'

The DI supposed he would have to be satisfied with that.

'Whatcha going to do about this drugs an' vagrants malarkey?' the DS asked. 'Mebbe Burton c'n bung Sidney an' prune face some of them spreadsheets an' graphs . . . throw statistics on potheads an' nutters at 'em.'

'Sounds like a plan, Noakesy. At least there's no press conference till Friday, which buys us some time for . . . creative blindsiding.'

There was a knock at the door and a junior porter appeared.

'Your visitors are in the lodge, Inspector.'

'Thank you. We'll be with you in a minute.'

'Right, Sergeant. It's time to meet Catriona Rowlands's family,' Markham said.

The two men left the common room, watched by the saint writhing in his gilt frame.

7. ANOTHER DEATH

Veronica Rowlands was every bit as uncongenial as Kate Burton's report had suggested.

A striking looking woman sporting a beautifully styled platinum bob, her face had a hooded hawk-like look that repelled; likewise her voice with its strident undertone suggesting a strong sense of entitlement.

However, she answered their questions frankly enough.

Yes, she and Sarah had arrived home from Lech on Sunday at around midday and then spent the rest of the day quietly at the flat in Abingdon.

With no witnesses to their movements, this meant either or both had an opportunity to pay a visit to Sherwin and leave that graffiti.

Tactfully, Burton elicited the information that they had a lie-in the following morning, which made them each other's alibi for Ernie Braithwaite's murder.

Then the focus shifted to Catriona.

'Look, what you have to understand is that my stepdaughter's capacity for manipulativeness was quite frightening,' Veronica Rowlands said in a lazy drawling voice — vowels an optional extra — which would have set Noakes's teeth on edge. 'She looked like butter wouldn't melt, but my god she was a piece of work . . . really venomous.'

Under further gentle pressure from Burton, the woman admitted that family bonds had been severely strained by the time Gerald Rowlands died.

'My husband had a stroke and was never the same after that,' she said bitterly. 'He developed an obsession with Catriona's mother, the sainted Monica. Suddenly I was the wicked witch responsible for breaking up the family, even though he'd been screwing around for years before I met him. It must be in the genes, Catriona was just the same . . . had several boyfriends on the go.' She laughed, a harsh discordant sound. 'Used to rank them as if it was some kind of trap draw . . . you know, like they do with greyhounds.'

It was an extraordinarily vivid image.

'Veronica was jealous of Catriona,' Burton pronounced afterwards. 'Deeply jealous.'

'Yes, and not just because of the way Gerald Rowlands canonised his first family,' Markham said thoughtfully. 'There was sexual competitiveness too.'

Burton was startled. 'What . . . do you mean as in them going after the same bloke, sir?'

'I don't know, Kate, but there's something . . . *rapacious* . . . almost feral about Mrs Rowlands underneath all that expensive Home Counties grooming.'

Sarah Rowlands was a different proposition. Very attractive, she was well-groomed like her mother, with honey blonde hair drawn into a low chignon, a style which set off her startlingly blue eyes. A grey cashmere maxi dress, suede boots and Oliver Bonas geometric statement earrings had made Kate Burton feel suddenly dowdy and unsophisticated by comparison.

But Burton had to admit, Catriona's stepsister was not remotely standoffish or defensive. Indeed, there was something positively endearing about her frank admission that Catriona had carried off the academic laurels.

'Cat got her dad's brains,' she said wryly. 'I chanced my arm at Oxbridge entry but didn't have what it takes. Plus,' she grinned, 'I wasn't prepared to knuckle down the way she did. A dedicated couch potato, that's me.'

Burton could see that the DI, too, was disarmed by Sarah Rowlands. Shades of that blonde psychologist from their Newman Hospital investigation, she thought sourly. She wondered, not without a touch of vindictiveness, what Olivia would make of it . . .

Now he asked, 'Were you and Catriona competitive with each other?'

'Oh sure.' The question didn't appear to rattle her. 'But I was a late developer whereas Cat . . .'

She opened her hands wide then let them drop helplessly by her sides in a gesture that was poignant in its wealth of unspoken meaning.

'No falling out over boyfriends?'

'Well, Cat always had her pick.' The mobile lips quirked. 'And I did pretty well scooping up her rejects.'

'We understand you . . . went out with Peter Hart,' Burton prompted, inwardly cursing the working-class prudery that made her uncomfortable when it came to broaching the issue of sexual relations.

Sarah Rowlands was unperturbed.

'Yes, that's right. We met volunteering on a prehistoric dig out at Eynsham. After that, we were in a relationship for about eighteen months . . . Then it fizzled out.'

'He didn't throw you over for Catriona then?' the DS pressed.

Their interviewee's look of surprise appeared to be unfeigned.

'Not at all,' she answered. 'What makes you think that?'

'It sometimes happens with sisters,' Burton improvised swiftly, earning an approving look from her boss.

'Oh, I see what you mean.' A self-deprecating shrug. 'I imagine she could have had him if she wanted, but he was too serious for Cat.' She chuckled. 'Too serious for me too in the end . . . As they say in the horse-riding world, I wasn't up to his weight. But Margaret Payne — that's the one he married in the end — was perfect . . . you know, kind of sat at his feet and worshiped him like he was the Pope.'

The sparkiness and a certain ironic inflection reminded Markham of Olivia's irreverence. He suspected there was far more to Sarah Rowlands than met the eye. For all the humorous self-denigration, the woman was no Sloaney air-head. And she might have been a late developer, but this was someone who had grown into her skin, confident and assured — altogether light years removed from the gauche student of yesteryear.

'Amazing she's turned out so normal with a mother like that,' was Burton's blunt verdict when the interview was finally over. 'Veronica's a grade A bitch,' she added in case there was any doubt as to her opinion.

'Well, I doubt she wasted many tears on Catriona,' the DI said. 'Whereas Sarah, on the other hand . . .'

Beneath the light, clipped tones of the well-bred girl about town he had detected an undertone of genuine emotion . . . commingled envy, sadness and regret.

'She reminded me of Sheila Payne,' Burton continued. 'No raging inferiority complex about always coming second to a brainbox sister.'

'Hmm. Well, I'm not sure they didn't choose the better part in the end,' Markham said, thinking of Catriona's jumbled remains under staircase eleven and Margaret Payne's subdued demeanour.

'It doesn't look like anything happened between Catriona and Peter Hart, sir. Sarah seemed surprised when I suggested Catriona might have pinched him off her.'

'True.' A line appeared between Markham's brows. 'But in that case, why was Peter Hart so uneasy when we turned up at Rochford asking about Catriona?'

'Could be he just didn't want to be reminded about when he was a student especially if he *did* make a fool of himself. Maybe had a crack at Catriona and got turned down.'

Burton spoke with unusual feeling. She still occasionally writhed with embarrassment when recalling her own student knock-backs.

Markham saw her logic. 'Yes, I suppose it could have stirred up unwelcome memories.'

'Then there's prejudice,' Burton continued.

'How so?'

'Well, racism could have played a part, sir . . . You can just imagine how Veronica Rowlands would've reacted to a black boyfriend.'

'Sarah Rowlands didn't come across as racist,' Markham said thoughtfully. 'On the other hand, we're talking twenty years ago. Back then, she and Catriona could unconsciously have internalised Veronica's "family values", seen a black lover as unacceptable in the long run.'

Burton bent over her pocketbook.

'It's Alice Matheson next, boss . . . with you and DS Noakes.'

Her tone was doubtful. It seemed to say: *Do you really want to let George Noakes loose on this one?*

The DI chuckled.

'Your colleague assures me you've dragged him into the twenty-first century, Kate, so he's fully up to speed with LGBTQ protocols.'

She looked pleased and apprehensive at the same time.

'Seriously, Kate, don't worry. Horses for courses. Your skills at patting things down were perfect for Veronica and Sarah. With our next interviewee, an element of the unexpected might be called for . . . *edgier*, if you get my drift.'

'Of course, sir.' She smoothed down the lapels of her Hobbs trouser suit, almost as though mentally smoothing away her concerns about Noakes's interviewing techniques. 'I'll see whether Ms Matheson's in the lodge.' Punctiliously, she added, 'Do you want me to sort drinks, sir?'

Veronica Rowlands had visibly shuddered at the notion of any beverage *from a machine*, but Sarah happily accepted a cappuccino.

'Noakesy can do the honours, Kate. Can you roust him from wherever he's lurking? In the meantime, I'd like you and Doyle to see if we're any nearer locating Ray Cunliffe.' The renegade scout had apparently gone to ground, but Markham was keen to hear what he had to say. 'A round-up of information on Oxford's drug dealers and drifters would be useful . . . DCI Sidney believes we should be focusing on local flora and fauna rather than the university.'

Her heart sank like a stone.

Oh god, that's all she needed . . . the usual dummy set of statistics and 'actioned tasks' to keep Sidney off their back.

But then Markham smiled at her. The smile that transformed his austere features so that they seemed lit from within.

The moment of amused complicity made it all worthwhile.

'I'm on it, sir,' she said.

Waiting for Noakes, the DI reflected on the Oxford 'bubble' — the hermetically sealed world that was its own microcosm, strangely detached from everyday concerns since all that counted was living in the moment behind the ramparts of ancient custom and privilege . . . an enchanted Elysium that he would never be able to explain to outsiders.

Gilded Youth.

Golden lads and girls all must, as chimney-sweepers, come to dust.

'So, nothing doing with Lady Muck then?'

Noakes's voice rudely interrupted his thoughts.

'I saw her nibs and the daughter leave,' the DS continued. 'Me an' Mister Stevenson were having a chat when she swept out. Looked like a bitch on wheels.'

Noakes and Kate Burton were on the same page when it came to an assessment of Veronica Rowlands.

Markham swiftly briefed the DS on the outcome of interviews with the family. Surveying Noakes's wardrobe for the day, he could only thank his lucky stars he had chosen Burton to conduct the questioning with him. What 'Lady Muck' would have made of the mismatched green sweater, fawn cords and superannuated black leather biker jacket was anyone's guess.

'The daughter looked well cheesed off,' Noakes said. 'Like she wanted to clobber Mum.'

'Well, let's just hope she postpones thoughts of matricide to a more convenient moment . . . ideally when we've solved the murders of her stepsister and Ernie Braithwaite.'

But it was an interesting observation. *Why had Sarah been so angry?* Markham wondered. Furious at her mother's 'lady of the manor' routine or something else?

Noakes guffawed at the boss's pleasantry.

'You didn't get any vibes from Sarah then, guv? Apart from Mum being a pain in the backside?'

'She seemed a well-adjusted affable woman,' Markham replied. 'Catriona may have had the potential to attract calamity, but Sarah has her head well screwed on . . . clearly enjoys her job at Forty Martyrs—'

'Oh yeah, teaches Lord Snooty an' his pals, right?'

'Get rid of that chip, Noakesy. If you mean she's a member of staff at a highly respected independent school, then correct.' He had enjoyed Sarah Rowlands's mischievous riff on her pupils' illustrious double-barrelled antecedents. 'She's paid her dues . . . did a stint in the state sector before they poached her.'

'Oh aye.' Noakes was clearly sceptical about any socialist credentials.

'Anyway, Alice Matheson will be joining us in a minute, so let's turn our minds to what we know about her.'

'Tree-hugger,' the DS said. 'Keen on demos about climate change an' gay rights an' . . .' He had nearly said 'all that garbage' but, conscious of his status as a freshly minted connoisseur of equal opportunities and of Markham's steely gaze, hastily amended this to 'student stuff'. A sickly smile made it clear what he thought of Alice Matheson's CV, but at least he wasn't overtly hostile.

In the event, a dispassionate observer would have been amused by Noakes's attempts to signal non-partisanship. He fetched tea for the three of them and even managed not to blench at the woman's candid admission of her feelings for Catriona Rowlands.

'Which weren't reciprocated, Inspector, though we managed to stay friends.'

'How come?' Noakes asked in genuine mystification. 'I mean, how'd you cope with seeing her cop off with blokes an' all that?'

The thick-set woman, stocky as a pit pony, tossed a lock of shaggy brown hair out of her eyes and contemplated the DS steadily.

Whatever she saw in his face seemed to reassure her.

'I was prepared to settle for what I could get, Sergeant. If that was platonic, so be it.'

An image of Olivia Mullen's face flashed before Noakes's eyes.

He kind of got what Matheson was saying but he wondered if he would ever really understand it. Like Burton said, it was all about *inclusivity* and being a *rainbow nation* and whatnot these days. After the team's New College Close investigation, he had felt more confused than ever and now here it was again . . . the gender thing.

He became aware that the DI's eyes were upon him.

With considerably less finesse than Burton, he went through Matheson's alibis for the graffiti incident and Ernie Braithwaite's murder.

Home alone. It meant she couldn't be ruled out.

The principal's allegation that Alice Matheson was a stalker turned out to be a damp squib, however.

'I slapped my girlfriend after a row,' she said. 'Cassie spun the police a line about harassment to get back at me, but the charges were dropped. Storm in a teacup, believe me. The local rag got hold of it and slanted everything. Gay-bashing under cover of journalism.'

There was a meaningful pause.

'Don't tell me' she laughed. 'It was Sir Philip Mirfleet who pointed you in my direction.'

'Yeah,' Noakes said. 'Mister double chin seemed to think you're trouble, luv.'

'He would,' came the bitter reply. 'When it comes to LGBTQ rights, it's like the sodding Dark Ages with that lot.'

Keen to move forward, Markham cut to the chase. 'Who do you think killed Catriona Rowlands, Ms Matheson?'

'She was so charismatic, Inspector . . . drew everyone into her orbit.' Her tone was wistful. 'I've always assumed it was a *crime passionnel,* something with one of her boyfriends that got out of hand.' She paused. 'The break-up with Jon Warrender was messy.'

'Thass not what *he* says, luv.' Noakes was on it like a flash. 'According to him it was all dead civilised.'

The woman looked like she was on the point of saying something then thought better of it.

Her expression hardened. 'The truth is, even though we were friends, I stayed well out of Catriona's personal life after she gave me the old heave-ho.' Now there was raw pain in her eyes. 'I was out of the loop . . . But all the same I'm pretty sure it got ugly with one of her boyfriends. That was the problem with Cat . . . she got in too deep.'

It was an echo of what Mark Drexler had said.

'Did you know any of her boyfriends?' Noakes asked.

'Not really.' Her guard was up now. 'Like I said, I was out in the cold, on the margins. Cat dropped in and out of my life on her own terms.'

Try as they might, she wouldn't be drawn further on the subject of Catriona Rowlands's circle.

After Alice Matheson had left, Markham slumped on the sofa with a sigh.

'Could she have been the dark-haired girl witnesses saw with Ms Rowlands on Cornmarket?' he ruminated.

'She's eaten a lot of pies since then, guv,' the DS observed ungallantly.

'Go back twenty years, Noakes . . . It could have been her.'

'Could've been any of the girls, boss. Even the fair-haired lass, Sarah, her stepsister. They all change hair colour as often as they change their underwear these days.' A clearing of the throat. 'Any road, that's what our Nat says.' Clearly 'our Nat's' pronouncements were gospel to Noakes.

The DS stood and padded over to the tray of chocolate hobnobs that the head porter had considerately provided.

'He's a diamond geezer that Mister Stevenson,' he mumbled through a mouthful of biscuit. Then, 'Matheson were dead keen to put us onto the boyfriends . . . Only she didn't want to be too obvious about it.' He munched away. 'D'you reckon what she said were true, guv . . . all that about staying out of Rowlands's life once the lass ditched her?' He answered his own question. 'She didn't look the type to take rejection lying down specially if the lass . . . led her on an' messed her about.'

'Yes, I wondered about that. She played it down, but the incident with her girlfriend gave me pause for thought.'

There was a knock at the door and Burton appeared closely followed by Doyle.

'The Thames Valley mob have located Cunliffe,' the DC said without preamble. 'He was hiding out in a squat on Stratford Street.'

'Excellent, Constable. Let's get him in this afternoon.'

The other was just reaching for his notebook when Markham's mobile rang.

He listened carefully, his face darkening perceptibly though all he said was, 'Right away, sir.'

'What is it?' Noakes demanded when he had finished.

'It appears there's been another murder . . . a woman . . . down at the Reynolds Museum.'

* * *

Later, it struck Markham as a horribly eerie coincidence that their third victim should have been found at the Reynolds.

Close to University Parks, the museum was a strange modernist building that looked like a cross between a NASA facility and an urban shopping complex. Visitors received an overwhelming impression of glass, steel and concrete in a grid layout, though the brutalist impact was offset by hedge-lined walks and arboreta. Markham had always wondered if the architect had intended some sort of ironic comment on Oxford tradition, so different was the museum from most other buildings in the city. Certainly it could not have been in greater contrast to the classicism of Lady Margaret Hall on the other side of the Parks.

As they arrived, the sky was overcast and swollen with rain, though the threatened downpour was holding off.

Markham contemplated the very English gardens characterised by a preponderance of yew hedges.

Yew, he thought. The Tree of Death in Celtic folklore whose antiquity dated to the Picts and Druids, maybe even to Pontius Pilate if the legends were to be believed.

Inside, the building had the more usual neo-Gothic museum ambience with dim hushed exhibit rooms and large oak display cases.

A paper-suited SOCO escorted them to the first-floor gallery which housed the prehistoric collection, now cordoned off and guarded by several uniformed officers.

'One of the security guards found her in this Stone Age tomb thing . . . kind of like a reconstruction. You know, a burial mound like they have on *Time Team*. Schoolkids go wild for it.'

The Newgrange exhibit took up a whole wing at the far end of the gallery, the entrance guarded by life-size Neolithic chieftains. Markham noticed that Noakes gave these mannequins a wide berth, inching crab-like along the wall, though Burton and Doyle were clearly intrigued.

The replica was a kidney-shaped cement megalith roofed over with turf and surrounded by standing stones with a huge boulder to the right of the entrance. Markham judged that the whole display must have occupied a couple of hundred square feet.

'That rectangular space over the doorway acted like some sort of solar calendar,' the SOCO told them. With a wry smile, he continued, 'The likes of you and me would be more interested in all the artefacts and history.' He pointed to the glass cases, huge information boards and interactive digital consoles that ran along the walls. 'But apparently this is a big draw for youngsters, especially when they do the whizzy special effects stuff all about ancient astronomy and the rising sun.'

'Fricking creepy,' was Noakes's verdict.

'I suppose it is a bit,' their guide replied. 'Anyway, you can go inside. There's a passageway and central chamber with three smaller ones leading off it.'

'And she's in there, right?' Doyle asked, and there was a noticeable tremor to his voice. Now it came to it, he also seemed a little wary and reluctant.

'Yes, in the central section.' The SOCO hesitated. 'On one of the basin stones.' Seeing that further explanation was required, he added, 'It's where they put the bones of the dead.'

With that, he led the way into the edifice, the detectives following close behind.

And suddenly, they were inside a corbelled vault illuminated by electric lights where Noakes's 'Jigsaw Man' stood next to a large hollowed-out chiselled stone bearing a corpse curled on its side in the foetal position.

The DI realised with a shock of recognition that he had encountered the person before.

'It's the young woman from outside the Rochford boat house,' he said. 'The dark-haired student we met when we were looking for Ernie Braithwaite.'

'Oh yeah.' Noakes moved in closer. 'The one you asked if she'd seen anyone hanging about.' The one who made sheep's eyes at the boss, he thought with a sharp spasm of regret.

The slight figure was presented to them like some sort of virgin sacrifice.

'Who is she?' Doyle demanded impatiently.

'She had a student ID card in her jeans back pocket,' the pathologist told them.

The detectives looked at him expectantly.

'Belinda Lycett, a postgraduate at Rochford College.' Then, taking in their blank expressions, 'I can see the name doesn't mean anything to you.'

Markham asked, 'How did she die?'

'A massive blow to the back of the head which shattered her skull.' The pathologist flexed his gloved hands as though mentally recreating that explosion of violence. Then he bent down and gently tilted the woman's head to expose the cranial trauma.

Burton swallowed hard as he repositioned the head, taking care not to dislodge the clotted mass of blood and bone.

'What was the weapon, doctor?'

'I would say a hammer or chisel,' he replied. 'I can't be certain till I've done the PM but it's consistent with the trauma to her head.'

'Time of death?' the DI asked.

'Very recent . . . sometime this morning. But you'll appreciate I don't want to commit myself just yet.'

They never do, thought Noakes crossly.

'How come nobody saw anything?' Doyle sounded bewildered. 'I mean don't they bother to patrol this Stonehenge mock-up or whatever it is?'

'You'll want to speak to the director,' Jigsaw Man said. 'I gather with it being so close to Christmas there were hardly any visitors.'

'But don't people have to sign in or something like that?' Burton pressed.

'Admission's always been free. Oxfordshire County Council owns the museum. It's a public resource, though obviously students and researchers from the university use it a lot.'

'What about CCTV?' Noakes jerked a thumb behind him. 'All that Indiana Jones treasure back there has to be valuable, right?'

'They're reviewing the footage for you now, Sergeant.'

Burton turned to the DI.

'CCTV won't cover this area,' she said. 'I can't see any cameras.'

Markham followed her gaze around the room. No CCTV.

He nodded at her. 'It was a clever move luring her inside the installation but hopefully the CCTV from the previous room will have caught them in action.'

They all gazed back at the body.

'Right, I must get back to the John Radcliffe, Inspector, but I'll be in touch. I take it we can take her away now?'

'Yes, thank you doctor. I'll wait to hear from you.'

The pathologist led them out of the monument. Silently, they watched as he issued instructions to his colleagues who were waiting with a stretcher.

Shortly afterwards, Belinda Lycett was carried out of the building, the team and SOCOs respectfully acknowledging the little procession as it passed.

In that instant, it seemed to Markham the very air around the passage tomb seemed to darken.

His eyes wandered to one of the glazed noticeboards.

'Newgrange is known as a brugh, or *brú*, from the old Irish for "womb",' he read. 'Many archaeologists believe the tomb's design depicts the female reproductive organs as part of the worship of Mother Earth or a maternal life-giver.'

But it was death that came to Belinda Lycett in that mysterious cairn, not life. And the winter sunrise, venerated since prehistory, would never shine on her again . . .

'We need to find out if next of kin have been notified,' he said.

'I'll sort that, boss.'

Burton ducked under the police tape and spoke to one of the uniforms.

'They're trying to track down the family, boss,' she said on her return. 'They'll let us know as soon as they've made contact.'

A man, portly and bespectacled, appeared at Markham's side.

‘DI Markham?’ he asked, extending a pudgy hand. ‘I’m Dr Michael Carruthers, director here at the museum. Would you care to come to my office? I can show you the CCTV footage.’

Markham roused himself from his increasingly dark thoughts to shake the director’s hand before gesturing to his staff to go ahead.

With one last look at the floodlit replica, he followed the director from the gallery.

8. NARROWING THE FIELD

Before adjourning to the director's office, Markham made a call to Olivia, cancelling their plans for a riverside stroll. As he did so, it occurred to him that the dead girl had doubtless planned to take part in the rowing event later that day . . . before fate had intervened.

'How awful,' Olivia murmured after he described what they had found inside the replica passage tomb. 'Like some kind of heathen ritual.'

It was true, Markham reflected as he made his way to the administrative block, there *was* something ritualistic about the way the body had been posed . . . as though it answered a deep need in the killer.

Belinda Lycett must have been lured to the scene, since it would have been too risky by far to carry her lifeless body there.

Did the Newgrange exhibit hold some personal significance for the murderer? Was it connected to their work? Or was the museum simply a convenient rendezvous, offering Belinda the reassurance of meeting in a public venue while enabling her attacker to exploit the pre-Christmas lack of traffic through the building?

'She was reading Classics and Ancient History,' Carruthers, told them. 'Came in here quite a lot and helped out sometimes with events. She was very interested in the Newgrange replica, she was hoping to do a PhD in megalithic tomb orientation.'

'Whass that when it's at home?' Noakes grunted, determined not to be impressed.

Carruthers smiled benignly. 'Basically, the reasons why prehistoric peoples chose particular sites to bury their dead.'

Noakes looked as though it was beyond his comprehension why anyone would find this a useful field of endeavour.

'Presumably, she was looking to make an academic career in anthropology and ethnography.' Burton said politely.

Carruthers looked at her gratefully while Noakes shot Doyle a glance full of longsuffering forbearance at their being saddled with someone who had swallowed a dictionary.

Anthropology and Neolithic customs. Suddenly Markham remembered Sarah Rowlands telling them how she had met Peter Hart while they were both volunteering on a prehistoric dig out at Eynsham. Was Belinda Lycett's passion for antiquity a link to her killer?

'Do you know if Ms Lycett had been accepted to do a PhD?' he asked.

'Upgrade from an MPhil. to the PhD is decided by a college's research committee,' Carruthers told them. 'She hadn't been successful first time around, but that's quite common. Usually, it's a case of the candidate tweaking his or her research proposal and resubmitting it.'

'Who was on this research committee thingy?' Noakes asked. 'I mean, sounds like it's a big deal.'

'I believe at Rochford it's chaired by the dean, Professor Hart.' A fussy clearing of the throat. 'Obviously, he takes advice from the candidate's supervisor and other subject specialists.'

'Do you happen to know who Ms Lycett's supervisor was, sir?' Markham asked.

'I think she'd got through a couple . . . currently Ms Cargill-Thompson was doing the honours.'

Burton's head came up. 'When you say she had got through a couple of supervisors, Dr Carruthers, do you mean there'd been problems with people in her department, personality clashes for example?'

'It's not that unusual, Sergeant. Students often chop and change before they find the right "fit".'

'But you weren't aware of any flare ups at Rochford. Any,' Burton hesitated over the word, '*unpleasantness*?'

'Oh no, nothing like that.'

But the man looked uncomfortable, causing Markham to wonder whether he was in fact privy to tensions at Rochford. If so, Carruthers wasn't telling.

An apprehensive looking security guard knocked at the door and wheeled in a trolley with a VCR.

'We've got her on tape coming through the entrance lobby,' he told the director.

'Excellent, Mike. Can you show the inspector, please?'

The next few minutes were spent checking the somewhat grainy footage of the entrance hall and principal galleries.

'Seen enough, officers?' The burly guard was clearly keen to get to back and share the drama with his colleagues.

'I bet this is the first bit of excitement they've had here in decades,' Noakes murmured to Markham sourly, so only he could hear. Difficult to get excited about a load of old coins and pottery even if they *did* date back to when folk were hunting woolly mammoths . . .

The DS had only the vaguest conception of prehistory, his notions of the ancestors deriving mainly from *One Million Years B.C.* and pleasurable recollections of Raquel Welch modelling a fur bikini. Any minute now Burton was bound to start rabbiting on about one of those boffins from the telly . . . David Attenborough . . . Or was it David Leakey . . . David something or other any road . . .

But once the door had closed behind the security guard and Dr Carruthers, Kate Burton was all business.

'You can make out Belinda arriving alright,' she said. 'But that's only because we know what she was wearing. The picture's such poor quality it's virtually useless . . . and I guess there's no chance of enhancing it.'

'Agreed,' Markham said quietly. 'In any event, our killer no doubt adopted some sort of disguise.' His frustration was so acute, it made the blood sing in his ears. 'Did you recognise any of our suspects on there?' he asked the team. They shook their heads. 'No, me neither.'

'Don't help that the image kept freezing an' jumping,' Noakes said tetchily. 'There weren't that many folk wandering around the place, but the picture's so bleeding patchy one of them chieftain dummy wotsits could've come to life an' done a war dance an' we wouldn't know owt about it.'

The vision conjured up was so ludicrous, that Markham had to smile.

'Why'd they have such duff security?' Doyle burst out.

'Well,' Burton sighed. 'Let's face it, we're not talking high-end here. The museum's council-owned, catering to a niche market.'

Definitely not *Thomas Crown* territory, thought Markham ruefully.

'Plus, there's nowt worth nicking,' Noakes growled.

'It's not so much that,' she countered. 'The artefacts in here don't have much commercial value in themselves. But in research terms . . . well you can't put a price on that.'

Her colleague's sniff was eloquent in its scepticism.

'Anyway, you heard the director say they've only had a handful of incidents over the years,' Burton continued, 'so hardly worth splashing out on state-of-the-art gadgetry.'

'Ole Carruthers looked properly spooked, though,' Noakes said. 'Betcha he gets on to the council an' bends their ear about an upgrade.' He sniggered. 'No chance of *him* featuring in a Stonehenge remake!'

Doyle turned to Burton. 'He got a bit shifty when you asked if Lycett had made waves at Rochford, sarge.'

'Yes, it felt like the temperature suddenly dropped several degrees,' she agreed. 'He obviously didn't want to go there.'

'Why not, I wonder . . .' Markham looked thoughtfully around the well-appointed office then wandered over to the large double height window that overlooked a neat quadrangle bordered by cypresses.

Cypresses for mourning. He remembered Olivia saying they were a symbol of immortality in both Muslim and Christian iconography. But on this occasion, the reflection brought him no comfort.

The sky was more overcast than ever, dark clouds massing in the distance like attacking armies.

And now the rain began to fall, softly at first then more insistently until the museum resounded to its tempo like some vast kettledrum.

He turned back to his team.

'Dr Carruthers told us that Peter Hart is chair of the research committee which approves applications to transfer from the MPhil. to a PhD,' he said. 'But for some reason it was decided that Ms Lycett hadn't made the grade . . . perhaps because of rows with the college hierarchy.'

'Lycett ended up with Cargill-Thompson,' Noakes said eagerly, 'so happen there was summat going on there.'

'Clearly Perdita Cargill-Thompson will need to be interviewed,' Markham said, 'seeing as she was Ms Lycett's current supervisor.'

'What about the prof?' Noakes's iconoclasm was rearing its head. 'Sounds like *he* might've had a down on the lass if she were allus making waves.'

'Yes, we'll need to speak to Peter Hart again too.'

Markham's temples were beginning to throb to the rhythm of the tempest. The austere features were taut with strain.

'There's no obvious connection between this victim and either Catriona Rowlands or Ernie Braithwaite,' he said.

'Perhaps she saw who killed Ernie,' Doyle suggested.

'Possible but unlikely,' the DI replied. 'She would have told us when we met her down by the river.'

'Mebbe she only figured it out afterwards.' Noakes took up the baton. 'Remembered summat she didn't realise was significant at the time.'

Burton looked dubious. 'I don't see her trying blackmail or anything like that,' she said. 'Way too risky.'

'She could've let summat slip,' her fellow DS persisted stubbornly. 'An' for some reason it made the killer think she were on to 'em.'

'Or it could be this murder's got nothing to do with the other deaths,' Doyle surmised. 'Perhaps it's completely unconnected.'

Noakes scowled. 'Come off it,' he rumbled. 'You're not telling me it's a coincidence one of Hart's students turns up with her head stoved in jus' when we're looking at him an' the rest of 'em for Rowlands an' Ernie . . . There's him, his missus, her sister an' the double-barrelled one for starters.'

'I thought your money was on Sherwin College, sarge,' Doyle pointed out slyly. 'One of the boyfriends, you said, or one of those other creepy blokes sniffing around Rowlands.'

'That were before *this* happened.' Noakes was not the man to back down. 'Lycett's a Rochford student,' he tousled his hair so vigorously it seemed as though he must tug it out by the roots, 'so stands to reason them lot are in the frame.'

Burton looked discouraged by the way the pendulum was swinging back and forth between the two colleges.

'What do you want us to do, sir?' she asked Markham.

'For now . . . we regroup,' the DI said. 'I want in-depth suspect profiles for everyone in Sherwin and Rochford — the family and Alice Matheson as well.' He suppressed a groan at the thought of what lay before them. 'The field's too broad. We *have* to narrow it down.'

'What about the sex pest scout, Ray Cunliffe?' Doyle asked.

'We'll deal with him tomorrow,' Markham said. 'In the meantime, get the local police to hold him on something: illegal squatting . . . trespass . . . whatever buys us some time.'

Doyle rubbed his temples. Clearly even the gangling young DC was baulking at the tasks ahead. 'What about the museum staff, boss?'

'I need you and Kate to check them out too, Constable. Did they see anything, hear anything, recognise anyone from Sherwin or Rochford? Did they notice anything off-kilter with any of the visitors or see Ms Lycett talking to someone?' His face clouded and he frowned. 'We've established that the CCTV footage is next to useless and only covers certain areas in any event. But it's possible staff may have spotted something that struck them as being out of the ordinary.'

'I'll have a word with Sheila Payne, sir,' Burton said crisply, scribbling in her notebook. 'She may have done outreach events at the museum along with Belinda.'

'Good idea, Kate . . . See what she has to say about that research committee and Peter Hart. Also, I want you and Doyle to do some more digging at Rochford. If Ms Lycett got bolshie with somebody, I want to know what went on.' His eyes wandered to the window and the rain-thrashed cypresses. 'And lean on Perdita Cargill-Thompson . . . See if you can find out whatever it is she's not telling us.'

'All the sodding women on this case,' Noakes grumbled. 'They're all the same if you ask me. Bloody sneaky.' His pouchy features looked more pug-like than ever. 'Plus I can't get 'em all straight in my head.'

'It's just Margaret Payne — Hart's wife — her sister Sheila, the librarian, and Perdita Cargill-Thompson,' Burton said reasonably. 'That's the Rochford lot at least.'

'Proper little harem,' her fellow DS groused. 'An' Hart as top dog running the show.'

'To be fair, Sergeant, he seemed perfectly civilised,' Markham commented. 'Not exactly anyone's idea of a sinister Svengali.'

Noakes's scowl deepened. It was clear he wasn't sure who Svengali was, but he was damned if he was going to ask the guvnor in front of Kate Burton.

The DI's lips twitched. 'It means the kind of man who plays mind games with impressionable young women, Sergeant.'

‘Well, Hart’s wife looks like she wouldn’t say boo to a goose,’ came the mulish response.

‘Oh, I don’t think Margaret Payne’s totally under her husband’s thumb, Noakes.’ Markham smiled as he recalled her comment about Oxford’s ‘OK Yahs’. ‘It seemed a partnership of equals to me.’

‘Even if she reckons he’s next best thing to the Pope,’ Noakes muttered.

The DI laughed. ‘It was his sister-in-law Sheila said that, remember. I think a touch of the green-eyed monster reared its head when she discussed their relationship.’

‘Either way, I don’t trust him.’

Doyle looked at him curiously. ‘D’you really see *him* for the murders, sarge?’

‘It felt like he was hiding summat.’

‘Christ, they’re *all* hiding something if you ask me.’

Doyle caught Markham’s eye and blushed. ‘Sorry sir, but Rochford feels like a dead end . . . Okay, Belinda Lycett didn’t get on with everyone, but *so what*?’ He shrugged his shoulders expressively. ‘You get that kind of thing in any academic institution, especially with all those mighty intellects and egos knocking about.’ He shook his head. ‘She had to have been killed because of something to do with Catriona Rowlands and we haven’t turned up anything to show Peter Hart was involved with Catriona or that she stole him from Sarah Rowlands.’

Markham nodded. ‘Okay, who’s your money on then, Constable?’

‘I don’t know, sir, and that’s the honest truth.’

Noakes looked smug.

Doyle seemed to think some explanation of his position was in order. ‘It’s just with there being so many . . . *cliques*,’ he said. ‘Wheels within wheels. It’s like the university is some kind of secret society with its own rules, closed to outsiders.’

‘The guvnor’s not an outsider,’ Noakes pointed out with an insufferably omniscient air.

Markham ignored him. With a kind expression, he turned to his constable. ‘I know what you mean, Doyle.

There's that feeling of everyone closing ranks against interlopers. After so many years away, *I'm* now an outsider too.'

No, you belong here, Burton thought as she observed the handsome face with its shade of melancholy and the austere, almost medieval features that seemed to belong within the frame of a dusky Old Master rather than CID . . .

She felt a sharp pang of regret for the Markham she would never know. The clever undergraduate, familiar with these rarefied college cloisters, towers and parks. The young man who slipped through narrow archways and past creeper-covered chapels, who strolled along cobbled streets in summer with a girl on his arm, poised to pluck the glittering prizes that were his for the taking . . .

She sensed that the DI's youthful past was his secret property, all hung about with *No Trespassing* signs. She was hungry to know more, she yearned to turn the pages of that forbidden book, but his impenetrable gravity somehow repelled any attempt at familiarity . . .

Oh god, Noakes was wearing that sardonic little smile he sometimes adopted. The one that made her feel like some sort of grubby eavesdropper peering through the keyhole of a locked door. Suddenly, she wished fervently that she could wrap herself in the armour of indifference where her boss was concerned. As things stood, her fellow DS evidently regarded her as being like a pathetic little schoolkid with a crush on the sixth-form prefect.

Snap out of it, she told herself. He's with Olivia Mullen and that's that. It was enough to know he valued her as a colleague and member of his team.

And yet, deep inside she felt a pang for the way that Oxford had somehow magnified the gulf that lay between them. In that stuffy room, skewered by Noakes's knowing stare, she felt tears threaten, pricking behind her eyes.

But, in the end, it was the old warhorse who saved her from embarrassment.

'If them two are busy with Rochford,' he jerked a thumb at Burton and Doyle, 'what's the plan for you an' me, guv?'

'We need to brief the DCI and principal,' Markham said firmly, ignoring the way Noakes's expression congealed at his reference to those worthies. 'But it can wait till tomorrow seeing as it's Sidney's keynote speech at the conference this afternoon.' Deadpan, he added, 'No doubt he's fine-tuning the soaring rhetoric even as we speak.'

'There's the press conference on Friday, sir.'

'So there is, Kate.' A line, faint as gossamer, appeared between Markham's eyes. 'We'll convene at four p.m. tomorrow to take stock and decide what we can safely release to the press.'

'And don't forget, we've got dinner in the Great Hall at Sherwin on Friday evening,' she continued.

'You *what*?' Noakes looked distinctly put out. 'No way am I sitting with a crowd of boring old farts listening to them bang on about a load of dead folk.' He looked at Dr Carruthers's bookshelves for inspiration. 'Julius Caesar an' the Romans an' stuff like that. 'Sides,' he added plaintively, 'it's *Friday Night Football* at the pub.'

'Stow it, Noakes,' Markham rapped. 'It's a chance to see the Sherwin suspects together in their natural habitat.'

'I ain't got the right clobber,' his wingman said truculently.

'Everyone wears gowns,' the DI said thoughtfully. 'We can't disguise you in one of those, Sergeant, but I'm pretty sure a darkish suit will do. And don't say you haven't got one,' he went on, fixing Noakes with a deadly stare, 'because I happen to know you've got some formal gear and you'll be wearing a lounge suit to Catriona Rowlands's memorial service on Saturday.' He was on the point of mentioning the necessity of suitable apparel for their outing to the Randolph Hotel, but an imploring look from Noakes halted him in his tracks. Mrs Noakes's partiality to a cream tea was doubtless best kept private. Besides, he had a feeling Kate Burton might be hurt by further evidence of her exclusion from the inner circle.

Scrutinising Burton's earnest little face from beneath lowered lids, Markham determined afresh that once this investigation was behind them, he would steer her towards new opportunities. Noakes was just making mischief when he talked about her alleged 'crush', but he feared her devotion to him and the team could become a career stumbling-block. He owed it to her to make sure that didn't happen.

* * *

Thursday and Friday passed uneventfully.

As Markham confided to Olivia on Friday afternoon over a hastily snatched snack at The Rose on the High Street, it felt like an eerie lull before the storm.

'How did the press conference go?' she asked, tucking into the toasted cheese sandwiches that were the little café's speciality.

'Well, it's a better class of vulture than Gavin Conors and that lot back at the *Gazette*.'

Olivia grinned at the allusion to Noakes's bête noire, said Conors being his least favourite journalist, so much so that they had even come to fisticuffs on one infamous occasion.

Markham spread butter on a scone, not so much because he was hungry as to conceal his dispiritedness from Olivia.

'Catriona Rowlands plus two more victims and not a clue as to the murderer,' he sighed. 'But at least we managed to damp down any speculation about serial killers by saying we haven't established whether the deaths are connected. Then we gave it the usual about respecting the privacy of the families blah blah.' His face bleak, he added, 'Belinda Lycett's parents were killed in a car crash when she was a child. There's a brother and sister living in the States. I broke the news to them by Zoom yesterday. I don't think they were able to take it in. The earliest her brother can get over here is Boxing Day.'

'God, how awful.'

'Sidney and the vice-chancellor between them seem to have done a deal with the local press. Somehow we managed to keep a straight face while Sidney intoned about Oxford's squalid underbelly. Let me see, how did he put it,' Markham's tone was disdainful. '"Even the dreaming spires are not immune from the random criminality that afflicts all great cities and seats of learning."'

'Bloody hell,' Olivia's fork was arrested in mid-air. 'Did he really say that?'

'Oh yes,' came the grim reply. 'He then bored them into submission by reciting great chunks from his conference speech, rounded off with a smorgasbord of statistics helpfully provided by Kate Burton . . . By the end of it, the poor sods were desperate to get away.'

'Sounds like a masterclass in misinformation.'

'Well, you know Sidney. No way is the trail going to lead back to an Oxford college if he can help it.'

Olivia's expression said this was par for the course. 'How did they react at Rochford when you broke the news about Belinda?'

'I left that to Burton and Doyle. Time to bring Kate on, get her ready for her own command team.'

Seeing that he appeared somewhat self-conscious, Olivia thought to herself, he's woken up to the problem with Kate . . . and not a minute too soon!

Aloud, she said, 'Presumably it caused shock waves.'

'Well, not as much as if this had happened during term time. Kate said the atmosphere was subdued. Everyone reacting pretty much as you'd expect and very close-mouthed about the late lamented.'

'The "she didn't have an enemy in the world" bullshit?'

'Yep.' Now Markham was crumbling his scone distractedly. 'To hear them carry on, you'd think Belinda was the most outstanding postgraduate of her generation when in fact the research committee had turned her down for a PhD.'

'How'd her supervisor take it?'

'Ah, Ms Perdita Cargill-Thompson.' Markham became aware of the mess on his plate and pushed it away. 'Kate said her response was very flat . . . she didn't show any reaction at all.'

'Odd.'

'Not necessarily. Shock takes people in different ways. Kate got the impression she was concerned for Peter Hart: he was the one who seemed most upset.'

'Pangs of conscience over not approving her for the PhD or something else?'

'At the moment it's anybody's guess,' Markham sighed. 'Somehow we just can't get a handle on these dons.'

'What about Catriona Rowlands's stepsister . . . Sarah, isn't it?' Olivia's tone was intentionally casual. 'I hear she's very attractive.'

'Yes, she is . . .' Markham smiled. 'But I'm hopelessly addicted to redheads these days.'

The jealousy subsided, and she pressed his hand.

'Ms Rowlands was shopping with her mother when Belinda was killed,' he said heavily. 'Forty Martyrs has broken up for Christmas, so she was apparently dedicating herself to "retail therapy". Kate and Doyle are trawling alibis for everyone at Rochford and Sherwin, but so far nothing useful. People were in their rooms, the library, having a late breakfast, with their partner, out jogging — take your pick — and as things stand, we can't prove otherwise.'

Having polished off the toasties, Olivia turned her attention to other edibles on the cake stand in front of her. 'This place has to do the best afternoon tea in Oxford,' she said happily, looking around the vintage teashop with its shelves of quaint crockery and curios.

'Better than the Randolph Hotel?' Markham asked teasingly.

'That'll be all stiff and starchy,' she retorted. 'But ever so *refined* . . . which means Muriel can do her gracious lady bit.'

'Don't forget, it's a three-line whip for you, me and Noakes tomorrow after the memorial service.'

'As if I *could*! The only consolation is at least I don't have to schlep round the shops with her in the morning.'

'I believe she wants to look out some locations from *Inspector Morse* — the Bodleian Library and that kind of thing.'

'That's just her cover story,' Olivia grinned. 'John Lewis more like.'

'Well, whatever Noakesy's lady wife gets up to, let's keep our end up come teatime.'

'Sure thing,' she replied amicably. 'Anything for George.'

Markham leaned back in the surprisingly comfortable wicker chair and contemplated her affectionately over his coffee cup reflecting that she looked hardly older than a student herself, the russet hair spilling out of its braid and the grey-green eyes sparkling with enthusiasm.

'Did the museum staff come up with anything useful?' she asked, slathering a fruit scone with butter and jam.

'One of them *thought* she saw Belinda with someone but whoever it was had a limp, which doesn't seem to fit . . .'

'Man or woman?'

'She couldn't say. They were wearing a duffel coat, jeans and some sort of beanie, was all she remembered. No real clue about age or sex. Our informant struck me as a bit of an attention-seeker, so it could be just hot air.'

'Any luck with the pervy scout?'

Markham stirred his cappuccino thoughtfully as he recalled his unsatisfactory interview with the rat-faced college servant that had been sandwiched between the discovery of Belinda Lycett's body and the press conference.

'Hmm, Ray Cunliffe . . . An unsavoury character alright and definitely had a grudge against Catriona for being one of the group who got him the sack but he's potentially off the hook for both Ernie and Belinda. He hasn't got the strongest alibis in the world, but in any event, I don't see him as our killer.'

Olivia raised her eyebrows interrogatively.

'He's the kind of sneaking character who does other people's dirty work but I think he'd stop short of murder.'

'You think he did dirty work for someone at Sherwin?'

'The head porter said he used to run errands for some of the fellows . . . was pretty thick with Dr De'Ath—'

'The slimy chaplain?'

'Chaplain emeritus actually, but the current incumbent's pretty much a cipher.'

'What sort of errands?'

'Mr Stevenson wouldn't say, but it was clear from the set of his lips he disapproved of the set-up. But it wasn't just De'Ath . . . apparently Cunliffe was well in with the bursar and college organist as well.'

'Maybe he spied for them,' Olivia suggested thinking of the army of informants at her own workplace.

'More than likely,' Markham agreed thinking of how the man's eyes slithered away from his own. 'But whoever his protectors may have been, it didn't stop him getting the sack for bothering female students.'

Olivia turned her attention to a chocolate brownie. Blessed with an enviable metabolism, she ate like a horse without ever putting on a spare ounce.

'Do you think he knows anything about the murders, Gil?'

'I think he may know a bunch of stuff about different fellows . . . may even have supplemented his income by trading secrets . . . But I'd swear what happened to Ernie and Belinda was news to him.'

The motherly waitress came over with an offer of more drinks.

'No thanks, that's my lot,' Olivia said waving her away with a smile. 'It's all been delicious.'

She laid a hand on Markham's.

'I've enjoyed this, Gil.'

'Sorry we missed our riverside ramble,' he replied. 'But I'll make it up to you.'

'Hush,' she said raising a finger to his lips. 'More important by far to recover that poor girl.' She tensed suddenly. 'It's really *wicked* the way she was left in that installation. As though the killer was making some kind of sick point.' A shudder. '*Meet the Ancestors.*'

Tapping into the centuries-old inheritance of lethal violence, thought Markham.

Olivia paled as a thought occurred to her.

'That tomb replica thing was really popular with kids, right. What if a *child* had walked in on it . . . or found the body?'

'They chose their moment well, Liv. There were very few visitors to the museum . . . no schools or families with it being so near Christmas. The staff were all demob happy and nobody was paying much attention. It must have been easy to lure Belinda inside — the novelty of meeting like that may even have appealed to her — and then it was the work of minutes to strike her down.'

'Wouldn't they have been covered in blood?'

'There wasn't much blood spatter — the blow was carefully aimed — but under a duffel coat or an anorak . . . with the dim lighting in there, who would notice? If they had a bag or rucksack, a change of clothes in the loos would take care of any tell-tale stains.'

She shivered again and glanced out of the window.

It was cosy inside the little tea shop, but soon they would have to head out into a sleety drizzle.

'Enough of murder,' Markham said firmly. 'I'm all agog to hear how the creative writing's going? What news of your magnum opus?'

With a shy smile, Olivia proceeded to tell him.

* * *

Later that evening, Markham and his team sat stiffly at 'High Table' in Sherwin College with a sprinkling of dons and college personnel. It felt chilly and exposed on the raised dais at that end of the Great Hall . . . as chilly, indeed, as the expression on the face of the Virgin Queen who presided from her massive, framed canvas in pride of place beneath the golden apse emblazoned with the college's coat of arms.

Only one of the six tables, ranged two by two in three long columns in the well of the hall 'below the salt', was occupied by junior fellows and their guests, giving the whole affair a rather forlorn aspect.

At least Noakes was appropriately clad, albeit his suit had a distinct whiff of an undertaker about it. Burton and Doyle sat on either side of him, the trio having declined to be split up.

It was for the best, Markham concluded grimly. The fellows weren't ready for a blast of unfettered Noakes. Judging from the dark expression on his face, the DS was not enraptured by either the bill of fare — mushroom soup, Goosnargh chicken and fruit salad — or the donnish discussion going on around him.

Markham wasn't particularly enamoured of the proceedings either. His feet were cold (why the hell did tradition seem to preclude decent heating?), while the begowned fellows struck him as resembling black crows.

Left to himself, he would have opted for whisky, the radio and an early night.

As it was, he was in for what Olivia had mockingly called 'mouldy futilities'.

He braced himself for a long evening, the high-pitched baying voice of Andrew Skeffington on one side of him only marginally more bearable than the arch twittering of some female academic on the other.

The claret jug was just out of reach.

Time to zone out.

Then suddenly he was aware of a minor commotion. There was the crash of a bench being overturned followed by the sound of angry voices and running feet.

Turning around, since he was seated with his back to the lower portion of the hall, Markham caught a glimpse of two figures in academic gowns heading for the exit as their fellow diners watched in consternation. With a shock of recognition, he caught the eye of one of the female guests. Sheila Payne, Rochford's librarian, grimaced awkwardly as though her own evening had just gone from bad to very much worse.

But then the moment was over, and the stultifying eddies of Sherwin's dinner-table talk swirled about him once more.

Sandwiched between Burton and Doyle, Noakes cheered up as he witnessed the sideshow.

Nothing like a bit of aggro to loosen tongues, he thought.

Something was definitely up.

9. AND BREATHE

The morning of Saturday 19 December was crisp and bright, determining Markham to treat the team to breakfast at Browns on the Woodstock Road for their morning briefing.

In the sharp, clear air he felt stung to life after the fug of dinner the previous evening.

As they passed Blackfriars Priory on St Giles, its honey-coloured facade glowing softly in the sunshine, he wished he could make a detour into the cool vaulted interior of the church.

But he could tell Noakes was already keenly anticipating the delights of a full English as opposed to more spiritual nourishment. In the circumstances, it would be unfair to make him wait. Not least as the DS had acquiesced meekly, with only a token protest, to donning his lounge suit once again for the rigours of Catriona Rowlands's memorial service followed by afternoon tea at the Randolph. The porcupine quills appeared to have been gelled into place and eau de mothballs overlaid with something more fragrant, leading Markham to conclude that Doyle had risen to the occasion and lent a hand with his mentor's grooming.

Browns stirred memories of queueing on the pavement outside with a gaggle of friends on various special occasions.

A wave of nostalgia hit him, surging up from somewhere deep inside, making him catch his breath like a runner suddenly winded.

Markham looked around at the students sauntering ahead of them along St Giles, their cheery voices ringing out.

Lucky, lucky youth just starting out . . . all the 'highlights' of life still to be relished and savoured. As though the grim reaper was a storybook phantom who could never breach the golden forcefield around them.

He could almost see the ghosts of Catriona Rowlands and Belinda Lycett on the fringes of that laughing group, muffled in college scarves, their faces upturned to bantering swains, aglow with hope and promise . . .

Breathe, Markham, breathe.

He beat down the nostalgia. You could never go back. The past was a foreign country, they did things differently there.

'You alright, guv?' Noakes nodded casually at Blackfriars. 'If you fancy popping in for a quickie . . . er, a *prayer* or something,' he added clocking Doyle's grin, 'it's no bother. We can wait.'

The DS knew the boss was Catholic, with a thing for old churches. Moreover, he had the faraway look that meant his mind was likely running on all those murder victims they had been unable to save down the years. As if he was some frigging pied piper and they trailed round after him like the undead. If that meant the DI needed a word with the Almighty, fine by Noakes.

Markham was touched.

'Far be it from me to keep you from the Browns special, Noakesy,' he said lightly. 'The Dominicans can wait.'

Noakes was hard pushed to hide his relief. He hadn't realised the place was run by monks. Ever since the St Cecilia's investigation, he hadn't felt comfortable around anyone in a habit.

They passed under the distinctive awning and into the brasserie.

It hadn't changed much, Markham thought. Still the same preponderance of wood and leather together with smartly dressed waitresses and the bizarre addition of a jazz pianist rattling away in the corner.

In no time at all, their orders were taken: the gargantuan traditional breakfast for Noakes and veggie equivalent for Burton, while Doyle opted for eggs Florentine and Markham chose scrambled eggs and smoked salmon.

'Champion,' Noakes sighed happily as a tray of frothy cappuccinos arrived. He eyed the occupants of a neighbouring table in horror as they tucked into honey granola, beetroot hash and kale smoothies with every appearance of enjoyment. As he saw it, they might as well be eating animal feed.

The DI's lips twitched. 'I take it this makes up for last night's disappointment, Sergeant?'

'*Too right!*' Surreptitiously, Noakes loosened his belt in preparation for an assault on the viands. 'Sherwin's a rich college, right? Well, you'd think they could've come up with summat better than that crap. It were like eating *Pedigree Chum* an' they were dead stingy with the potatoes.'

'I think dinner in the hall is supposed to be a feast for the mind, Noakesy . . . brilliant conversation, stimulating debate, that kind of thing.'

'That weren't much cop neither,' the DS grumbled. 'A load of dried-up ole bookworms chunnering on about whose footnotes were the best. That skinny woman with the specs an' the awful shrieky voice kept eyeballing me the whole time, like she were checking to see I was still awake. An' the witchy one with the long grey hair gave me the heebie-jeebies . . . I mean what the chuff's a *pansexualist*?'

Burton looked pained. Markham imagined the previous night had been a sort of purgatory for Noakes's fellow DS, but meeting his eye she smiled weakly and buried her nose in the coffee.

Doyle grinned. 'At least the cabaret was good,' he said. 'Folk kicking off definitely wasn't in the script.'

'Yeah.' Noakes brightened up. 'Watcha reckon to *that*, guv?' he said eagerly. 'Ole mister double chin tried to smooth it over afterwards, but you could tell he were embarrassed.'

Sir Philip Mirfleet had certainly looked ill at ease, Markham reflected, but then it was hardly surprising given that two of his dons had got embroiled in some unseemly argy-bargy right under the noses of the police.

'Do you know what happened exactly?' Burton enquired. 'Mirfleet spun coffee out so long that there was no sign of them afterwards.'

'I cornered one of the kitchen staff,' Noakes said. 'It were Warrender an' Drexler having a barney . . . One of the others on the table said to take it outside so they buggered off.'

Markham was interested. Having been detained by the principal in interminable conversation until long after his team had made tracks, he had given up hope of getting to the bottom of the fracas. 'Did your informant say what the fight was about, Sergeant?'

'Summat to do with a group or a club they belonged to when they were students.'

'A dining club?' There had been several of these around in Markham's own undergraduate days, ranging from distinctly seedy to highbrow intellectual. Exclusive societies like the Bullingdon and Piers Gaveston were rather passé these days, but there had been a time when they possessed considerable cachet.

'Dunno.' Noakes replied. 'Sounded like some fancy outfit, though . . . an' whatever it was, summat bad happened.'

'Something to do with Catriona Rowlands?' Doyle pressed eagerly.

'Sounded like it,' Noakes told them. 'The lad thought someone at the table said her name but he couldn't remember who it was. Then one of the other waiters told him to get out of it an' stop earwigging.'

'Sheila Payne was on that table,' Markham said thoughtfully. 'It didn't look like she was having a good time.'

'She had a bandaged ankle, sir,' Burton pointed out. 'Must have sprained it or something.'

'Vino an' painkillers,' Noakes was censorious. 'Not a good combo.'

'Come off it, sarge,' Doyle laughed. 'The vino wasn't exactly flowing . . . except towards the principal—'

'An' the bursar,' Noakes amended. 'I bet it weren't the gnat's piss the rest of us got served.'

The DI smiled. 'Perks of the job, Sergeant.'

'You're telling me.' Then a thought struck him. 'That dough-faced Skeffington were putting it away alright.'

'Yeah, I noticed that,' Doyle chipped in. 'His eyes were glassy by the end and he was slurring his words.'

Burton cast her mind back. 'Dr De'Ath was looking daggers at him.'

'Probably nervous in case doughboy's tongue ran away with him an' he blurted stuff,' Noakes said.

But *what* stuff? Markham wondered.

At that moment, their food arrived, calling a temporary halt to the theorising.

Markham's scrambled eggs were excellent and the beatific expression on Noakes's face indicated that the traditional breakfast was a hit. Burton and Doyle too ate with gusto — unsurprising, really, given their substandard fare the previous night.

'D'you reckon Sherwin grub's as bad as that all year round?' Noakes returned to the subject while he was getting his second wind. 'They do a decent breakfast, but you'd expect them to make a bit of an effort for dinner. I mean, that's when they get out all the posh silver an' say the fancy Grace.'

'Dinners during the conference weren't too bad,' Markham pointed out, 'but college is winding down for Christmas so maybe the catering's getting a bit lax.'

Actually, the food at Sherwin these days was a vast improvement on the nursery stodge he remembered from his student days. It had been so bad, that it was one reason for trying his hand at amateur dramatics: at least OUDS lay on a good spread post-performance.

'No sign of Mister Stevenson,' Noakes observed, his tone implying that standards would have been higher had the head porter been at the helm.

The DI let his team finish their meals before he returned to business.

'So, Warrender and Drexler had a fight which quite possibly had something to do with Catriona Rowlands,' he mused. 'Did you see who their guests were?'

'Sheila Payne looked like she was with Warrender,' Burton answered. 'But there wasn't anyone else from Rochford. Fellows probably have to show their faces in hall every once in a while, so it was most likely a duty dinner, doing a favour to staff from other colleges.'

'Some favour treating them to that crap,' Noakes snorted. 'They'd do better going to Nando's.'

'Let's not allow Sherwin's mediocre cuisine to become a running grievance eh, Noakesy,' Markham interposed hastily.

For answer, the DS merely sucked in his cheeks and rolled his eyes, giving a very passable impression of a TB patient afflicted with goitre, before helping himself to more toast.

'Do you reckon Sheila Payne has something going with Warrender then, guv?' Doyle took advantage of Noakes having his mouth full.

'As in romantic?' Markham asked. Then, as the DC nodded, 'I'm not sure, Constable . . . When we spoke to her, she mentioned visiting her sister at Sherwin on a regular basis, so presumably she came across him then.'

'Warrender's got a partner,' Burton observed.

'*Huh*, as if that counts for owt.' Now Noakes was the voice of the moral majority. 'Places like this, they're all at it like rabbits.'

'I don't think that's true of her sister,' Markham commented thinking of Margaret Payne's solemn earnestness that reminded him of Kate Burton.

'No, she an' Hart looked well loved-up,' Noakes admitted. 'But they might've jumped in an' out bed with other people back when they were students.'

'Hmm.' The DI looked doubtful. 'I was inclined to believe them when they said they hung out with the nerds . . .'

'You'd be surprised at the folk who turn out to be swingers.' Noakes always had to have the last word.

'Well, they'll all be at the memorial service, so let's keep an eye out for giveaway body language,' Markham instructed. 'And I want you to keep close tabs on the family too.'

A black-stockinged waitress came over to enquire if they wanted more drinks. Markham noted with amusement the disapproving look Noakes shot Doyle as the young DC engaged in the flirtatious banter that was practically de rigueur for diners at Browns. The old monster was such a strange mixture, he reflected . . . an absolute Neanderthal in some respects but oddly chivalrous in others. Certainly there was no questioning his devotion to Muriel Noakes who was doubtless even now terrorising shop assistants somewhere in Oxford . . .

Olivia, for example, was fascinated by the transformation that came over the Noakeses on the dance floor when the ill-assorted pair appeared miraculously light on their feet and moved like a dream. 'It's quite poignant,' was her verdict at the end of one evening when they had been dragooned into attending a ballroom competition event. 'It takes decades off them . . . and she smiles at him like a young girl.'

Markham could only hope she still felt as charitable about her by the end of the day.

* * *

The omens were not good.

'*WTF!*'

Olivia boggled as she caught sight of Muriel waiting for them in the Sherwin College chapel.

Mrs Noakes had clearly pulled out all the stops when it came to millinery, an elaborate confection of gauze and what looked like outsize cherries perched atop a freshly lacquered bouffant that appeared to have been modelled on Nancy Reagan's. His gaze travelling downwards, Markham took in a riotously floral knitted jacquard two-piece that would not have looked out of place at a royal garden party.

Spying them skulking at the back of the chapel, Muriel fluttered her fingers at Markham in a coquettish greeting which left them no choice but to sidle down to the middle block of choir stalls where she reigned resplendent.

'*Gilbert!*' It was the usual arch whisper which invariably made Markham feel as though he was starring in a bad melodrama. A proprietorial hand on the arm and Colgate smile managed to exclude Olivia entirely.

'Muriel, how delightful you look.' The DI's old-world courtesy would never permit him to slight a lady even without the added inducement of Noakes's megawatt beam of pride at the stupendous impression produced by his other half.

Mercifully, there was no time for small talk, Sherwin's William Drake organ swelling to the strains of 'Jerusalem' as Catriona Rowlands's family and assorted dignitaries filed into the chapel and took their places in the reserved seats at the front. With a swift turn of the head, Markham established that the other two members of his team had melted discreetly into the background, waiting in the little vestibule beneath the organ at the back of the chapel.

The DI hoped fervently that Kate Burton had her wits about her, since he always found himself challenged on such occasions by the way mourners seemed to merge into a homogenous whole.

Vaguely aware of the organist embarking on some sort of coda to the entrance hymn, Markham once more savoured the chapel's strangely intimate ambience, locking eyes with Mary Magdalen and St George as if they were old friends.

The mahogany woodwork and floor tiling gleamed and two towering arrangements of lilies stood on either side of the intricately wrought reredos in front of the altar. Medieval saints shone like jewels in the stained-glass windows on either side of the choir while plaques along the narrow chapel walls displayed the names of long-dead principals who slumbered in the crypt beneath the chequerboard aisle. Atop the pilasters to the left and right of the altar, marble seraphim stood poised as though to whirl the worshipers' intercessions upwards.

The service itself was anodyne and uninspiring, though saved from utter obscurity by the inclusion of John Donne's 'A Hymn to God the Father', badly mangled though it was by Andrew Skeffington's lacklustre delivery. Observing how the winter sun struck bright gleams out of the stained-glass windows like fragments of heaven, Markham found himself praying that somewhere outside time and space a similar radiance enveloped Catriona Rowlands, Ernie Braithwaite and Belinda Lycett.

There was no eulogy, just a simple commendation read by the head porter whose voice remained clear and steady.

Before Markham knew it, the Reverend Mr Gardiner was intoning the recessional antiphon.

They that wait upon the Lord shall renew their strength; they shall mount up with wings as eagles; they shall run, and not be weary; and they shall walk, and not faint.

Would Catriona Rowlands rise incorruptible, or was she destined to oblivion?

Veronica and Sarah Rowlands in their couture mourning were the picture of restrained elegance. The fellows too struck a dignified note, though Jon Warrender and Mark Drexler sat as far away from each other as possible and avoided eye contact. Royston De'Ath, leaning on an ebony-headed cane, looked as though he was thinking how much more impressive the service would have been had *he* presided over proceedings, while Andrew Skeffington appeared to be battling the effects of a bad hangover.

The Rochford College group formed a tightly knit phalanx in sub fusc, nobody standing out from the crowd. All of them had denied knowing Catriona Rowlands. And seeing them here today made Markham start in surprise. Perhaps some inter-college diplomacy had been exerted, he reflected, in order to ensure a respectable turnout. Or possibly simple curiosity had drawn a crowd.

He noticed Sheila Payne, white-faced and strained, shooting uneasy glances around the congregation as though she would sooner have been anywhere else. Margaret Payne and Peter Hart stood very close, their shoulders touching, absorbed in their own private thoughts. Sherwin's bursar nearby was wrapped in thin-lipped saturninity, while across the aisle Alice Matheson was wedged next to assorted college personnel. The dumpy brunette looked brittle and miserable, as though it would take very little for her to burst into tears. Perdita Cargill-Thompson, on the other hand, was all swan neck and sleekly waving blond hair, the impressive cleavage showcased by a fitted cashmere sweater and charcoal jacket which perfectly matched her long pencil skirt and suede ankle boots.

As the congregation filed out of the chapel, mourners were reflected in the large side-view mirrors mounted on either side of the organ. Watching the queue that snaked behind him, Markham saw Perdita Cargill-Thompson reach out tentatively to touch Peter Hart's sleeve. But Rochford's dean appeared not to notice, his face as remote and impassive as the wood carvings on the chapel reredos.

There was a buffet laid on in the principal's lodgings, but for once Noakes was unconcerned about 'eats' given the imminent delights of afternoon tea at the Randolph Hotel. At a murmured hint from Markham, the Noakeses headed off with Olivia in the direction of Beaumont Street. 'I'll be along in a minute,' he told them, watching with some amusement as the cherries bobbed their way towards the notables, Noakes and Olivia trailing along behind like two errant children.

The DI, Burton and Doyle politely expressed their condolences to Veronica and Sarah Rowlands. 'You two can show your faces at the principal's reception,' Markham told them as they lingered in the chapel for instructions. 'Check out the dynamics . . . make a note of anything unusual or out of place.'

'Anyone in particular you want us to target, boss?' Doyle asked.

'Perdita Cargill-Thompson looked like she was trying to attract Peter Hart's attention back there,' the DI replied. 'See if you can find out what that was about. It could have been a gesture of solidarity, or there might be something else . . .'

'Will do, sir.'

'And see if you can find out more about that bust-up between Warrender and Drexler,' Markham added. 'It would be useful to know more about that dining club or whatever it was they belonged to.'

Burton nodded crisply. 'Alice Matheson might be in the mood to talk,' she said. 'The woman looked pretty wretched in there and she kind of cringed away from Warrender when everyone was walking out.'

'Excellent,' Markham approved. 'Do what you can by way of mingling and then take the rest of the afternoon off.'

Doyle visibly brightened at the prospect of a few beers and *Match of the Day.*

'I think I'll call in at the Ashmolean,' Burton said. 'They're running a Caravaggio exhibition.' The DS smiled shyly, her snub-nosed little face suddenly transformed so that it was almost pretty. 'I saw the Derek Jarman film about him at the Phoenix,' she explained. 'More like a mafioso than a great painter, so kind of intriguing.'

Doyle looked appalled.

'Don't worry,' she reassured him. 'I'm not expecting you to come with me.'

'I'm more for contemporary stuff than those big sprawling canvases,' the DC said hastily, fearful lest the boss conclude he was a complete philistine. 'Er, Lowry, Rennie Mackintosh, Graham Sutherland . . .' he elaborated, snatching wildly at star names he remembered from the team's murder investigation at Bromgrove Art Gallery.

'Each to their own,' the DI said easily, with a conspiratorial glance at Burton.

Phew. Might just about have got away with that, thought Doyle whose idea of a fun afternoon did not include listening to Burton banging on about some Italian geezer's brush strokes.

'There was something *off* back there in that chapel,' Burton said unexpectedly. 'Something . . . hateful.'

Markham looked at her enquiringly. It wasn't like his down-to-earth colleague to succumb to ESP.

The DS blushed. 'Oh, I know it was a beautiful setting with the stained glass and the choir stalls . . . I just had the feeling someone was pretending to be sad but actually *gloating* over what happened to Catriona Rowlands.'

Burton could just imagine what Noakes would make of this when it was relayed to him by Doyle, but bravely persevered. 'When the chaplain talked about Catriona being like a flower cut down in full bloom, I heard a hiss. It was very faint . . . almost like a catching of breath but,' with a defiant glance at Doyle, 'I *heard* it.'

'Maybe someone thought all that stuff was cheesy,' the DC said. 'I mean, it sounded like the padre had dug out his Big Book of Clichés to be honest.' He grinned. 'Veronica Rowlands looked like she wanted to puke.'

'Well, there was no love lost between her and Catriona,' Burton retorted.

'Did you notice where this sound came from, Kate?'

'That's just it, guv . . . my attention must have wandered and then the noise kind of jerked me back to reality.'

'Could be autosuggestion, sarge,' Doyle said cheerfully, 'what with that weird painting of Adam and Eve on the wall at the back . . . the serpent looked more like a bloody great cobra from where I was standing.'

'It's a William Blake reproduction,' she said slowly. '"The Temptation and Fall of Eve."'

'William Blake . . . *Right* . . . Isn't he the bloke who gardened in the nude or something?'

It was remarkable, Burton thought savagely, how Doyle and Noakes invariably latched on to the more salacious biographical details.

'He was a radical visionary,' she said repressively. 'Anarchic.'

Doyle looked unconvinced.

'But you might have a point,' she admitted wearily. 'I *was* struck by that painting, so maybe I connected the serpent with negative emotions . . . envy and jealousy . . . and it translated to a hissing sound . . .'

The DI observed her crestfallen demeanour.

'It's a compelling painting, Kate,' he said. 'And a compelling chapel for all its small size.'

Kate looked both embarrassed and resigned. 'Forget I said it, guv.'

'No,' the DI said slowly. 'I *want* you and Doyle to tap into the vibes. Whatever malignity lurks in the shadows, we *have* to bring it into the light.'

* * *

As he headed across to the Randolph Hotel, the image conjured up by Kate Burton remained with Markham, so that it seemed a slithering snake coiled and uncoiled itself on the pavement, undulating alongside him as he traversed Beaumont Street.

Entering the hotel drawing room ('Trusthouse Forte meets *Country Life*', as Olivia described it), he found Muriel Noakes holding court. Observing Olivia's distinctly glazed expression, he gathered that there had already been a whistle-stop résumé of Oxford's top attractions courtesy of *Inspector Morse* and *Endeavour*. Indeed, as he arrived, Mrs Noakes was in full spate about an episode of *Morse* ('The Wolvercote Tongue') which had actually been set in the Randolph. From the beady way her small black eyes darted around the room, it was apparent she was half expecting Simon Callow or some floppy-haired Hugh Grant lookalike to pop out from behind a chaise longue as if on a Merchant

Ivory film set. Markham found the spectacle both ludicrous and touching, not least as Noakes looked fit to burst with gratification at the way his 'missus' put everyone else in the shade . . . though from the way one or two solitary tea-goers sheltered resolutely behind their newspapers, as though re-enacting Rorke's Drift, it would appear this assault on the Randolph was not universally welcome.

Tea was good, though, and Markham did full justice to the dainty sandwiches, petit fours and Victoria sponge, observing with amusement that his wingman was giving it the full *Downton Abbey*, even to the extent of crooking his little finger, a feat which nearly resulted in him pouring tea all down his front.

'He was trying so hard,' Olivia rocked with laughter afterwards at Noakes's notions of gentility. 'Did you see how he got the twin lasers when he was sawing away at those scones. And there was a dodgy moment when he nearly asked for a builders instead of Lapsang Souchong!'

But Markham found something gallant about Muriel Noakes and her determination to scale the pinnacles of bourgeois respectability. He sensed vulnerability behind all the affectation and the gruesomely girlish mannerisms . . . as though she sought endlessly to graft high romance onto the humdrum reality of her life. As 'Gilbert' — Noakes's tantalisingly inaccessible boss — he belonged to that alternative landscape and, even though it occasionally made him feel light-headed, he played the part assigned to him.

He knew too that the Noakeses had their poignant hinterland and Muriel would die a thousand deaths rather than her husband's boss should ever know her early history and the secret of Natalie's parentage. And so, he listened with grave courtesy as she held forth on how said daughter had thought about 'putting in for Oxbridge', when his experience of the young lady strongly suggested that *Love Island* was her more natural habitat.

Muriel was clearly fascinated by the Rowlands family, *Hello!* magazine having armed her with the necessary background information.

'Such a charming woman,' she gushed about Veronica Rowlands.

Carefully avoiding Olivia's satirical eye, Markham murmured something non-committal.

'Terribly tragic when family members fall out like that,' Muriel pronounced. And with an irritable glance at Olivia, 'Of course that daughter from the first marriage was the *skittish* type . . . *wayward* . . . trouble with a capital T . . . Bad blood, you see,' she added with all the confidence of an aristocratic horse breeder evaluating equine pedigree. 'A lovely creature, though,' she went on with a sidelong glance at Markham expressive of profound sympathy for his having been caught in the toils of a calculating siren. 'Must have made other girls feel positive *wallflowers* by comparison.'

'God, Gil,' Olivia burst out afterwards when they had finally extricated themselves from the Randolph. 'If I'd had to listen to any more of those barbed insults, I think I would have exploded.'

'She's an unhappy woman, Liv,' he said quietly. 'Confused. But underneath it all, I think she loves Noakesy.'

'He looks at her like she's sodding Cleopatra.'

Markham chuckled. '"Age cannot wither her, Nor custom stale her infinite variety,"' he teased.

'Stuff the bard, Gil. *I'm* finding Muriel pretty stale, believe me!'

'Interesting what she said about women being the best haters,' he mused.

'Typical. Always hardest on her own sex.'

'Enough of gender wars,' he laughed. 'Let's go back to Sherwin.' He hesitated, 'By the way . . .'

'Oh no,' she groaned. 'Don't tell me I'm on duty with Muriel again tomorrow.'

'No, nothing like that . . . Noakesy's putting her on a train later.'

'What then?'

'There's the college Christmas service tomorrow evening. If you can bear it now your course has ended, I'd like you there.

It'll be a relatively quiet affair on account of the murders, but even so . . .'

She slipped a hand into his.

'I can do festive fa-la-la-ing with the best of them, Gil.'

He drew her to his side.

'It'll be a holiday from murder, my love,' he told her.

But even as he spoke, Burton's serpent slithered into his thoughts.

Envy and jealousy and hate.

The demons were abroad.

10. CONFIDENCES

Sunday 20 December was fine and clear, the wintry morning air invigorating Markham as he waited for Kate Burton outside Folly Tower in the grounds of Latimer College.

Perched on rising ground, the eighteenth-century tower looked as though it had been modelled on some baroque basilica from the annals of Christianity, with a few flourishes reminiscent of the Taj Mahal, before the college authorities suddenly got cold feet or ran out of money. A copper domed belfry topped a graduated layer-cake structure in Portland stone whose three tiers jutted out above an octagonal column with a sturdy oak door at its base. Weathered steps fanned out on either side of the column in a seashell effect, enclosing a crypt at the base of the edifice.

The bells were long gone from the belfry, but there was an ancient blackened clockface with verdigris mermaids either side and a narrow stone balustrade beneath. To left and right of the clock were two gilt arches with life-size statues standing in front of them: St Frideswide on one side in her abbess's habit with the crown of an English princess and St Eanswythe, another scion of Anglo-Saxon nobility, on the other.

Markham had always liked the monument, especially its statues and the over-the-top brickwork of the crypt, which conjured the picture of a maverick architect following his own whim. Along with Keble College's 'holy zebra' architecture, it was always a hit with tourists though somewhat off the beaten track, situated as it was in Latimer's parkland on the north-east side of Port Meadow.

It seemed like a good place to talk to Kate, be brought up to date on her work and perhaps discuss her future in the force.

'Quite something isn't it, sir?'

Absorbed in contemplation, he hadn't heard Kate approach.

'It's got a certain . . . character,' he smiled.

Burton gazed up at the clock, caught up in a reverie as Markham watched her curiously.

'When I was little, I was mad for *Trumpton*,' she said unexpectedly. 'You know, the TV series.'

'I would have thought that's a bit before your time, Kate.'

'My aunt was brought up on it. She got me the DVDs and I watched them for hours. There was this clock . . . It had little arched doors on either side with painted roller shutters. When the clock struck the hour, these shutters went up and there was this tinkly music and two figures came out with funny jerky little movements. I think one was a knight and the other a princess with a pointy headdress. The princess had a bell and the knight struck the time on it with a hammer. Then they went backwards through the doors and the roller blinds came down again.' She smiled at the memory then recollected herself with an embarrassed start. 'Sorry, sir, I didn't mean to babble on.'

'Not at all.' He was amused and oddly touched by this glimpse into Burton's childhood.

Knights and princesses. He could see how that would appeal to his history-loving sergeant.

'It's just . . . all this reminds me,' she said with a wave of the hand. 'Like those statues up there could start moving if they wanted to and walk back inside the clock.'

'I know what you mean,' he said. 'I've always thought they're pretty lifelike, not a bit like the usual eighteenth-century kitsch.' He contemplated St Frideswide's haughty aquiline features. 'Almost as if the artist modelled them on people he knew.' And in the abbess's case, didn't particularly like.

'The one on the right's much prettier,' she ventured shyly. 'The nun looks snooty, like she doesn't approve of her.'

He laughed. 'I can see what you mean . . . The pretty one's St Eanswythe, a princess who went off to become a nun. Quite a popular career choice in those days,' he added dryly.

'Isn't she the one whose bones turned up recently behind the wall of a church?' Burton asked excitedly. 'In some sort of casket . . . They had to hide them during the Reformation when all the monasteries were being pillaged.'

'I do believe you're right, Kate. Somewhere in Kent.'

The reverence accorded to the saint's bones was in poignant contrast to the neglect of Catriona Rowlands's jumbled remains.

He looked again at the dark-haired statue which reminded him vaguely of Sheila Payne. It didn't correspond remotely to Noakesy's idea of a nun, he thought with an inward chuckle, recalling his wingman's horror of the species during the St Cecilia investigation.

Burton's attention had turned to the crypt.

'Is anyone buried in there?' she enquired, scrutinising the sinister iron wrought double grille that extended across the front. 'It looks like it's sealed up.'

'That was the college mausoleum for a time. They put former principals there before discontinuing the practice in the early nineteen hundreds.'

'Did you ever get to see inside, sir?'

'I did. When I was an undergraduate, the college held an open day so visitors could have a look around. We went in through that door in the octagon. There's steps up to the belfry and downstairs a kind of rotunda — lead-lined stone coffins on shelves branching out from the centre . . . lots of marble and a statue of Hugh Latimer watching over the dead.'

'Oh right, the bishop who was burned at the stake by Bloody Mary,' she said eagerly. 'Wasn't he the one who wrote a confession to save himself, then changed his mind and put his hand into the fire first . . . cos he wanted to punish himself for being a coward?'

The DI smiled.

'That was Thomas Cramner,' he said. 'Latimer had more guts — died bravely . . . told the fellow being burned with him to "play the man".'

Burton flashed an impish grin. 'Noakes would like that.'

Markham grinned back at her. 'The bishop preached some colourful sermons too . . . about how we play card games with Satan.'

Burton shivered.

'It feels like the devil holds all the tricks right now, boss,' she murmured.

Markham motioned her towards a bench at right angles to the crypt.

'You sound discouraged, Kate,' he observed gently. Then, 'How did it go yesterday?'

'I went for a coffee with Sheila Payne,' she said. 'In the covered market.'

'Ah, Ben's Cookies.' The DI smiled. 'The best in Oxford . . . I developed such an addiction to them, it nearly cost me my seat in Sherwin's First VIII.' He scanned Burton's downcast face. 'I take it you didn't get very far with our friendly librarian.'

'Well, she was willing enough to talk, sir, but I just can't see where it all leads.'

'Go on.'

'There *was* bad feeling between Belinda Lycett and Peter Hart over her not getting to do a PhD. Belinda apparently lost her cool and threw a few scenes and tried to involve the director from the Reynolds . . . ran her mouth off about Hart being chauvinistic and a bully, that kind of thing.'

'And was there any truth in it . . . I mean, about him having a down on her?'

'Sheila didn't seem to think so, sir. She said Belinda was quite neurotic and highly-strung . . . brilliant but couldn't always come up with the goods. Apparently, Professor Hart built that department up from nothing. Classics and Ancient History was the poor relation until he came along so he's choosy about who they take onto the PhD program.'

'Sounds like Ms Payne is in Hart's corner,' Markham ruminated.

'She said he'd made a play for Catriona.'

'*Ah* . . . Maybe not then.'

'She seemed to think we already knew.'

'Was this while Hart was seeing Sarah Rowlands?'

Burton frowned. 'Sheila suddenly clammed up when I asked . . . like she realised she'd been indiscreet.'

The DI's gaze wandered to the garlanded stone nymphs in their twin niches on either side of the crypt entrance. In their cool inaccessibility, they reminded him of Catriona's slim blonde stepsister.

'Sarah didn't seem to think there was anything going on between Hart and Catriona,' Markham said, 'but it might have been an act. Or maybe she really didn't know?'

'If Hart *did* get up to something with Catriona and he got knocked back or it ended badly, then that gives him motive.'

'It could give Margaret Payne motive too if she knew about it or she and Catriona were rivals.' Markham thought hard. 'Did Sheila say anything about that?'

'No . . . but Classics is a four-year degree, unlike the other undergraduate courses which are three years. Apparently, Hart and Margaret only began seeing each other in their final year whereas Catriona disappeared in her third year. So it's not like Catriona was muscling in on Margaret's territory or anything like that.'

'Hmm . . . I wonder, did Peter Hart keep schtum about his involvement with Catriona Rowlands to avoid embarrassment or was it because he had something to hide?'

'I'd say he just didn't want to rock the boat, guv. Especially if it wasn't common knowledge. Plus, he and his wife make a good team, he wouldn't want us raking up some student fling from twenty years ago.'

Markham considered this. 'Surely he must have figured we'd find out eventually, though . . . After all, his sister-in-law knew about it.'

'He probably hoped she'd forgotten or that she'd have the sense to keep her mouth shut,' Burton said wryly. 'But then I plied her with Ben's Cookies and the game was up.'

The DI's eyes travelled back to the crypt and its over-ornamented brickwork bordered by what appeared to be more nymphs. Only these were different from the priestess-maidens presiding aloofly in their niches. Instead, there was a procession of dryads dancing, twanging harps and brandishing goblets, as though the architect had suddenly tired of dignified classical icons and chose to divert himself with sirens at some bacchanal.

'What do you make of Sheila Payne?' he asked Burton abruptly. 'She struck me as quite a different proposition from her sister.'

'Yes, Margaret's the serious one,' she replied. 'But she and Sheila seem to have a good relationship — not like Catriona and Sarah Rowlands. Philip Greaves said *they* didn't get on, remember.'

'Though I'm not sure I'd trust the bursar as far as I could throw him,' Markham observed caustically.

'Sheila is friends with Jon Warrender.'

'In the biblical sense?' The DI gestured expressively. 'Let's not forget that Noakesy seemed to think bed-hopping was the order of the day. But then he invariably takes a depressingly low estimate of human behaviour.'

This elicited a chuckle.

'I couldn't say, sir, but she obviously likes him. Incidentally, she told me he and Drexler belonged to the Culpeper Society—'

'*Culpeper* . . . Wasn't that the randy young courtier who messed about with one of Henry the Eighth's wives and got himself executed?'

'Correct, boss. Wife number five, Catherine Howard . . . Both of them were beheaded, along with Jane Boleyn, also known as Lady Rochford, who helped them carry on right under Henry's nose.'

'Ah, my Tudor history is coming back to me, Kate . . . Jane married into the Boleyns but then betrayed her husband George Boleyn, Viscount Rochford, and his sister Anne Boleyn . . . accused them of incest as I recall.'

'Yes, Jane was poisonous.' Burton's eyes glowed with antiquarian enthusiasm. 'Stuck on the margin of other people's lives . . . weaving webs like a spider.'

'But at least part of the illustrious family title lives on.' Markham's tone was ironic.

'Yes, Rochford College was founded by descendants of the Boleyns,' she told him. 'That's how it got its name.'

'Indeed . . . You're a mine of information, Kate,' he said. 'But to return to this Culpeper Society . . . I'm presuming with those colourful Tudor antecedents it was a drinking club as opposed to anything of a scholarly nature.'

'That's right, sir. Posh boys whooping it up.'

Or what Margaret Payne had termed the 'OK Yahs'.

'I don't recall it from when I was a student,' the DI said thoughtfully.

'Apparently it was all very secret squirrel.' Burton's tone was faintly disparaging. 'Code names, special rituals, passwords and stuff like that.'

'You make it sound like a Boy's Own caper.' He paused. 'But I have a feeling it was nothing so innocent, correct?'

'Sheila was quite cagey about it. She said there'd been times when Warrender and Drexler "went too far".'

'What does that mean? Was she there?' the DI asked quickly.

'It's all-male, but Sheila said they felt bad later about incidents with women.'

'Was Catriona Rowlands one of them?'

'Sheila pointed the finger at Drexler . . . said that something happened between him and Catriona but it was all hushed up.'

'An assault? Rape?' Markham's voice was sharp.

'If you believe her, it was a game that got out of hand.'

'And *do* you believe her?' Markham's eyes were intent on her face. 'Or was she trying to steer you away from Warrender?' There was repressed urgency in the DI's tone. 'You said it yourself, Kate . . . An allegation of criminal behaviour would mean instant disgrace and curtains for decent career prospects.'

'Motive for murder,' she said quietly.

'If Catriona held it over her assailant, easy to see how they might have snapped,' he said. 'And then the other murders . . . to stop it all coming out. Maybe Ernie Braithwaite made the connection with Culpeper . . . perhaps *that* was it.'

'And Belinda Lycett?' Burton sounded dubious. 'I can see Ernie trying to cash in on secrets, but I don't know about her . . .' Aware of Markham's frustration, she added, 'I've got Doyle pumping Ray Cunliffe. *He's* the type to convert secrets into cash.'

The two detectives sat in companionable silence for a time, both thinking hard, before Burton broke the silence.

'Is it *really* like that at Oxford, sir?' she asked shyly. 'I mean,' with a deepening colour, 'to hear them all, it sounds like some kind of sexual merry-go-round.'

'The dreaming spires aren't all they're cracked up to be, Kate.' The DI's tone was unusually gentle, almost tender. 'Beneath all the hype, it's just young people struggling to forge an identity . . . the same as anywhere else.' A hollow laugh. 'God knows, *I* didn't take a ride on that particular merry-go-round.'

Burton felt as if she had been entrusted with a precious insight, so rarely did the boss allude to his personal life.

'I used to make stuff up when I was at uni,' she confided.

'How so?' Markham was intrigued.

'When I went home to Mum and Dad. I never had anything exciting to tell them . . . but I could see they kind of *expected* something.' The brown eyes were fixed on the slope which rose behind the folly. 'So I made up this social life, pretended I was part of the "in-crowd".' The rosy hue on her cheeks deepened. 'I even had a make-believe boyfriend.' She bit her lip. 'They were so pleased for me. Before I knew it, I was in too deep to tell them the truth . . . that I was Billy No Mates.'

'We've all been there, Kate.'

Her earnest gaze met his in a moment of absolute candour.

'But it wasn't like that for you, sir. *You* could take it or leave it.' A deep breath. '*I* never got the chance to turn down the smart set. A brown smudge, that was me.'

The DI turned to face her.

'That's not how I see you, Kate. You're anything but a "smudge" to me.'

Her voice was dreamy. 'I used to sit with dad in the hen house — that's his hobby — and spin him these stories about how popular I was.' She seemed almost oblivious of Markham. 'There was this particular hen, Sophie, who used to perch there looking at me like she knew it was all bullshit. I can still smell the stench from that shed. It used to make me feel sick — all those birds clucking and gobbling — but dad was happy as Larry listening to me talk about the parties and painting the town red . . . all the fun he and Mum never had . . . and it was just moonshine.'

'I promise you, we all do it, Kate, believe me. We all big ourselves up . . . At least it gave your mum and dad some innocent pleasure.'

Markham's throat was tight at the recollection of the mother and stepfather who had cast him adrift after a decade of abuse when he was barely out of his teens. Listening to Kate Burton, he felt his guts twist with something close to longing as she described that warm shed where she played Scheherazade to her dad and an audience of poultry.

The bleak expression on her boss's face finally registered with Burton.

'Sorry sir,' she said, 'I'm rambling again.'

'It's interesting to hear another perspective on,' with heavy irony, '"the best days of our lives".'

'You won't tell Noakes will you, guv?' She chewed her lip again. 'He'd laugh himself silly at me.'

'Actually, Kate, I don't think he would.' Markham paused. 'Has he ever said anything to you about the Bluebell case?'

'No, sir.' Carefully, she added, 'None of my business anyway.'

Now it was the DI who looked introspective.

Noakes had killed a man. All under cover of the police playbook, of course — defence of the public etcetera and he was eventually cleared by the IOPC — but the DI knew the red mist had descended and what happened was personal. He suspected he would never discover what had passed between Noakes and 'the missus' on the subject of the Bluebell — perhaps a veil had fallen never to be lifted — but in the final analysis George Noakes was more intimately acquainted with human frailty than of yore.

'Noakesy learned something about himself during that investigation, Sergeant.' No need for specifics. 'He might surprise you.'

Another companionable silence ensued. Oddly peaceful.

'How was the Ashmolean, Kate? Did Caravaggio live up to expectations?'

'Well, after the art gallery case I thought I'd never want to set foot in one of those places again.'

Markham nodded sympathetically. He still had nightmares about the loss of a friend during that particular investigation.

'But it was brilliant. Caravaggio was big on martyrdoms and beheadings. Sinister as hell but I felt safe with it being up there on the wall inside a frame.'

The DI recognised this displacement behaviour, since he too was simultaneously fascinated and repelled by lurid Old Masters and their depiction of human depravity, as though the huge canvases somehow *contained* violent emotions that would otherwise run rampant.

'The museum was so quiet. I had it all to myself and there was a nice security man who let me take pictures on my mobile.'

'Good. We all needed some time away from the case, Kate . . . to let our ideas "incubate" if nothing else.'

'Trouble is, I'm fresh out of ideas, sir,' Burton said glumly. 'Belinda Lycett's murder came out of left field.' She hesitated, marshalling her thoughts. 'The way she was posed at the Reynolds in that prehistoric exhibit . . . it feels like something an *academic* would do . . .'

'A don?'

'Yes . . . And it got me thinking about Peter Hart. If Belinda had a grudge against him for blocking her PhD, then she could have tried to force his hand somehow. Maybe she found out about a liaison with Catriona Rowlands and threatened to make trouble for him with the police unless he allowed her onto the programme.'

'If she really believed he was a killer, then wouldn't that have been extraordinarily foolhardy? Remember, you said she was savvy, Kate. That implies a strong sense of self-preservation.'

'She might *not* have believed he was a killer though, boss. She might just have thought he would baulk at having his past pawed over by the police . . . not a good look if he's hoping to become Rochford's first black principal. She could have reckoned he'd be keen to dodge the scandal of having his collar felt.'

Burton sighed. 'Or maybe Doyle's right and Belinda's death has nothing to do with Catriona Rowlands . . .'

'Hmm.' Markham's tone was dry. 'I take it Doyle had an enjoyable evening's "incubation" in the Frog and Firkin.'

'Bromgrove Rovers slipped to bottom of the league,' she grinned. 'But a few pints of Ruddles eased the pain.' Tone carefully neutral, Burton added, 'Did Mrs Noakes have a chance to see much of Oxford?'

For a moment, Markham wondered if she had spotted their little group at the Randolph. After all, the hotel was directly opposite the Ashmolean.

On the other hand, Burton had been interviewing Sheila Payne at around the time they were sampling the petit fours, so unless she hot footed it up to Beaumont Street straight afterwards it was unlikely.

Burton's solemn little face was guileless. It was merely polite interest that prompted the question, he decided.

'Muriel's a great admirer of *Inspector Morse* and *Endeavour*, so Noakesy will have taken her around a few landmarks,' he parried diplomatically.

If Burton knew he was being evasive, she didn't show it.

'One of the detectives in *Endeavour* turns out to be a ballroom dancing champion,' she laughed. 'A great big, battered, bear of a man . . . the least likely twinkle toes you could imagine . . . unless you knew about the Noakeses.'

Markham chuckled and the slight awkwardness passed.

'Did Doyle have a crack at any of the mourners after the memorial service?' the DI asked, his thoughts turning once more to the case.

'He managed a chat with Alice Matheson, sir.'

'Ah yes, I seem to remember your saying she was unhappy at being around Warrender.'

'According to Doyle, she *loathes* him. Called him a rapist.'

'Indeed.' Markham steepled his long pianist's fingers. 'So, Sheila Payne pointed us towards Mark Drexler and now we have Ms Matheson calling out Jon Warrender . . . And there was that incident in college where the two of them came to blows over something to do with a dining club . . . something which involved Catriona Rowlands.' He meditated on it for a few minutes.

Shooting sidelong glances at the hollows and planes of his profile, Burton reflected once again that Markham's ascetic features had nothing modern about them at all, they belonged to a bygone age. It was a face to which Caravaggio would have done justice.

'Ms Payne is Warrender's friend, which has to be borne in mind,' the DI said. 'But Alice Matheson might have her own agenda . . . perhaps she sees this as a chance to stick it to the man whom Catriona chose over her.'

Burton considered this. 'But Drexler was a boyfriend too . . . she could have hated him for the same reason.'

'Maybe the relationship with Warrender was special . . . maybe Catriona's feelings for him ran deeper, so Alice saw *him* as her rival.'

'Matheson told Doyle that Catriona's baby was Warrender's and he wanted her to have an abortion.'

'Did she indeed.' Impatiently, Markham ran a hand through his thick black hair which, slightly longer than regulation for Bromgrove CID, curled over the back of his collar in a manner that his folically challenged DCI regarded as a personal insult. 'What did the health clinic have to say?'

'No joy, sir. Catriona didn't say who the father was and they didn't ask.' Burton fidgeted as though she wished she had a notebook to hand. 'We could try DNA extraction from the foetus's bones, but that would take time and then we'd have to test Catriona's past boyfriends . . .' She frowned. 'Don't see the DCI or principal buying it to be honest.'

'"Oxford Dons in Paternity Probe",' Markham groaned. 'Not exactly the kind of publicity they'd welcome.'

Especially not with Markham being a 'Sherwin man' handpicked to save them embarrassment.

A thought struck him. 'When we first spoke to Alice Matheson, she didn't say anything about Jon Warrender being a rapist or the father of Catriona's baby . . . I wonder what made her open up to Doyle.'

'You mean, apart from his boyish charm, guv?'

'Oh, I'd never discount Doyle's ability to radiate empathy, Kate, but the timing's interesting.'

'Maybe she's afraid of Warrender . . . too scared to say anything until now.' Burton traced a pattern on the ground with her foot, thinking hard. 'Or maybe her defences were down after the service and some vino. Doyle said she knocked it back pretty quickly. Looked a bit out of it, he said.'

'Any other insights from the boy wonder?' the DI asked. 'Did he have an opportunity to speak with Perdita Cargill-Thompson? Wasn't she trying to attract Peter Hart's attention at the end of the memorial?'

'That's right, sir. Either Hart was lost in his own thoughts or he was deliberately ignoring her. She didn't stay long at the reception. Doyle said something was definitely bugging her, but she just necked a glass of white and took off.'

That was authentic Doyle, the DI thought wryly. Perdita Cargill-Thompson was far too soignée to be caught 'necking' anything.

'Cargill-Thompson's good at doing a disappearing act,' Burton said ruefully. 'Every time I tried to get hold of her at Rochford, she managed to be unavailable.'

'What about the shifty pair, 'De'Ath and Skeffington. Anything from them?'

'They were huddled in a corner most of the time.' Burton was thoughtful. 'But Doyle said he heard Skeffington muttering about some letters, that De'Ath should hand them over . . . something like that.'

'*Letters*?'

'That's what Doyle said. He couldn't be totally sure he'd heard it right because the moment De'Ath noticed him hovering he gave Skeffington a dirty look and they both shut up.'

'Well, Kate, hats off to you and Doyle.' Markham was warmly approving. 'Sounds like you mingled to some purpose.'

'It wasn't the same without Noakes there hoovering up the canapés and stuffing vol-au-vents in his pocket,' she observed mischievously.

'Lowering the tone, you mean,' the DI laughed. 'I can still see him at that wake in the Ashley Dean case . . . expressing his "deepest symphony" to one of the relatives through a mouthful of sausage roll. Hard to imagine Veronica Rowlands appreciating a similar demonstration.'

'That's a strange woman,' Burton said. 'Cold and hard.' She bit her lip with compunction, 'But then, it was an awkward occasion . . . a put-up PR job by the college. She probably couldn't wait to get away.'

The two detectives lingered on.

'It's getting colder,' Burton said eventually. 'Bet it's like a fairy tale here when it snows, all those old colleges and cloisters dripping with icicles.'

She delivered this with delighted anticipation like a child.

'You're just like Olivia,' Markham replied, oblivious to his DS's sudden stiffening at the reference to his girlfriend. 'She finds it magical watching everywhere fill up with snow like Narnia.' The DI turned his gaze fully on Burton. 'But when I think back to that business with the snowman in the New College case, I'm surprised you didn't develop an instant antipathy to the stuff!'

'I used to have nightmares about those murders,' she admitted with an air of constraint. 'Kept remembering how it ended, kept seeing the pointy carrot nose and those pebbles for the eyes and mouth. And then the white turning red . . . like some demon in the woods had cast a spell.'

She recollected herself with a shaky laugh. 'Sorry, sir, that makes it sound like *Snow White* . . . I'll be yakking about the wicked queen and poisoned apples next.'

'Not at all, Kate. There *was* a demon, but we vanquished it, remember.'

She nodded, eyes fixed on the pewter skies.

'I'd like a white Christmas in Oxford,' she said simply. 'And for us to catch whoever's doing this.' She looked full at him. 'But we don't have any leads to speak of.'

'Two colleges and two groups of suspects,' Markham mused. 'There's Sherwin: Catriona's ex-boyfriends Jon Warrender and Mark Drexler and maybe an unreported rape. Then Royston De'Ath and Andrew Skeffington with something to hide—'

'Don't forget the bursar.'

'And yes, of course, Philip Greaves,' the DI concluded grimly.

Burton took up the litany.

'At Rochford we've got Peter Hart embroiled with a disgruntled postgraduate, plus, he could've been one of Catriona's exes. Margaret Payne, his wife and loyal mainstay. Sheila Payne, her sister whizzing up and down to Oxford over the years, a friend of Warrender and the college librarian.'

The DI continued to count them off. 'Then there's the Catriona's sister, Sarah Rowlands. The under-achiever who may or may not have lost Peter Hart to Catriona.'

'And Alice Matheson who says she accepted the situation when Catriona threw her over but looks like she never got over it.'

It began to feel chilly on their bench. Markham got to his feet. 'Come on, Kate, let's walk and talk.'

Burton rounded off the roster of suspects. 'That leaves Veronica Rowlands . . . Oh, and Perdita Cargill-Thompson, who looks like she's got unfinished business with Professor Hart.'

'Ray Cunliffe's off the hook for murder, but he could be mixed up in it somewhere.' Markham adjusted his long strides to Burton's more sedate pace.

Folly Tower receded behind them as they followed the twisting paths and shrubberies of Latimer College, though it seemed the presence of that strange little mausoleum hung over the grounds like an invisible pall.

She tried to shake off the feeling of sick dread that had begun to steal over her.

'Where to now, boss?'

'Well, there's Sherwin's carol concert later, if it's a Christmassy vibe you're after,' Markham said with a mocking inflection. 'Noakesy's rendition of 'Ding Dong Merrily on High' should knock them dead.'

He found that he was glad to have had this time with Burton. 'The day is young, so let's call in at the Folly Café,' he suggested. 'It's open at weekends and they do excellent coffee.'

Burton's face had started to look pinched with cold, but she brightened up considerably at this suggestion. It felt like a small triumph to have him to herself and set the morning in a glow.

'Besides,' he said lightly, finally coming to the real reason he had asked to meet her. 'I want to discuss your future in the force. I'd expect you to sail through the inspectors' exam, so it would be pure selfishness on my part to clip your wings.'

Her heart sank like a stone, the morning's bright promise evaporating as fast as her breath in the cold air. Suddenly the day felt dull as sawdust.

Not yet. I don't want to leave you.

But a desperate smile stretched across her face and she spoke up bravely in a voice she barely recognised as her own.

'I don't know I'm ready to climb the greasy pole, sir. Mind you, Noakes says I've got all the PC bollocks off pat.'

He laughed, looking suddenly much younger, and her heart lifted in spite of the misery.

'The team hasn't lost you yet, Kate, so old misery guts won't be getting out the bunting any time soon. And whatever happens,' his voice so low it was almost inaudible, 'you'll always be family.'

With these words, he turned his face away. *Just as well*, Burton told herself. That way, he didn't see her expression at these affectionate words. By the time he looked at her again, she had mastered her treacherous emotions and schooled her features to bland friendliness.

They passed through Latimer's lodge into the High Street.

Behind them, silence fell over the college gardens once more.

11. DEATH KNELL

Oddly enough, Sherwin's carol concert did not take place in the college chapel. Instead, people were directed to third quad, having first been issued with candles and paper drip protectors.

'After the interval,' a pimply young usher told the detectives enthusiastically. 'We move into the library for selections from Handel's "Messiah". Listen out for "The Glory of the Lord" . . . that always raises the roof.'

'What's he take us for?' Noakes muttered incredulously. 'Can't he tell we're plod?'

'Must think you're a don, sarge,' Doyle grinned. 'What with you dressing the part.'

Noakes had certainly made something of an effort, the tweed jacket, maroon sweater and flannels by no means the sartorial catastrophe that might have been expected, though the look was more down-on-his-luck local poacher than visiting professor.

To Kate Burton's pleasure, a light dusting of snow had fallen, coating the quad and old stone buildings with a delicate mantle that became them very well. The evening air was strong and clear, providing a tonic for overwrought nerves, and Markham began to feel some intimations of seasonal goodwill. Even Noakes bared his teeth genially enough for the selection of rousing favourites, surpassing himself when it came to 'We Wish You A Merry Christmas'.

'Now bring us some figgy pudding,' he bellowed with an eloquence that had his two younger colleagues convulsing with suppressed laughter. DCI Sidney looked even more bilious than usual as he observed Noakes's contortions, making Markham breathe a prayer of thanks that the police conference was due to wind up the following day with their nemesis en route back to Bromgrove.

Song after song rang out and Markham, with Olivia on one side and Noakes on the other, immersed himself in the spirit of the occasion, for a short period untroubled by thoughts of murder or the ghosts of Christmases Past. After the last rousing chorus of 'God Rest Ye Merry, Gentlemen' died away and the interval was announced, he watched affectionately as Olivia twitted Noakes on the splendour of his apparel and the dexterity with which had managed to avoid setting his eyebrows alight during the more challenging numbers. As ever, the terror of CID became a tongue-tied schoolboy around her, smiling shyly at the attention and shuffling his feet as she laughingly pointed out 'the swank brigade' — including Royston De'Ath and Andrew Skeffington — who had turned up ostentatiously clutching their personal copies of the 'Messiah'.

Olivia was looking particularly lovely, Burton thought wistfully. The grey-green eyes, combined with the waterfall of red hair, gave her an otherworldly appearance that was only enhanced by the guttering candlelight. Sarah Rowlands stood near them with pupils from Forty Martyrs and the DI's eyes rested briefly on the teacher's cool blonde beauty — for Markham was not immune to feminine allure, Burton acknowledged sadly — before returning to Olivia with a look of reverential tenderness that betokened her absolute supremacy. In that moment, Burton felt ashamed of her secret hope that discord might arise between the boss and his partner and vowed anew to master feelings that had no prospect of return.

Mulled wine, savoury tartlets, mince pies and other goodies were laid out in the lobby of the library, much to Noakes's glee. But he was careful to help Olivia to the eatables before piling his own plate high in preparation for the rigours of the second half . . . no way was he facing the screechy stuff and a load of poxy arias without something substantial inside him.

The second half of the concert saw the congregation seated on the library's wrap-around rectangular balconies which rose one above the other over four floors, with the small amateur orchestra and singers in the atrium below. Markham and his companions found themselves on the second tier, this arena-style arrangement suiting him perfectly, not only for its novelty but for the fact that it allowed his eyes and thoughts to wander freely over the attendees while Handel's glorious music soared.

Immediately before the concert, Doyle had brought him some interesting information about the bursar Philip Greaves . . .

'This girl at the union put me onto someone who remembered Catriona's piece about Greaves in the *Sherwin Confidential*.' The young DC was clearly pleased with his own resourcefulness. 'Basically, Greaves had ambitions to become union treasurer, but she put paid to that by outing him. She was clever about it, never referred to him by name but described him so that everyone would know who she meant.'

'But being gay here's okay, right?' Noakes was genuinely confused. 'I mean there's *Brideshead* an' teddy bears an' all that . . . so what's the big deal?'

'Yeah, sarge, but this was twenty years ago and he was big in the Newman Society . . . that's the one for the RC god squadders — no offence, sir.'

'None taken,' was the DI's dry response.

'Well, Greaves was so far right he was practically coming out the other side. Total fascist, always pontificating on the decline of morality and how society had degenerated. Sex at the root of everything and down with sodomites, that kind of thing.'

Burton was boot-faced. 'Delightful.'

'Yeah, a right little charmer . . . banging on about family values and gay sex being an abomination while all the time he was Sherwin's very own Mister Shagnasty. The thing was, Catriona showed him up as a total fraud which didn't go down well and made him a laughing stock.'

'Presumably Greaves's lifestyle choice wasn't common knowledge,' Markham said.

'That's right, guv. Even worse was the fact that he was at it with some hunky seminarian or trainee priest attached to the Catholic Chaplaincy. It was a really colourful hatchet job. Stuff about gay saunas and drag-queens . . . all sorts.'

Noakes's eyes were so wide now they were almost outside his head, leaving Markham in no doubt that the DS's anti-Papist sentiments had just climbed to new heights.

'Hmm . . . Entertaining and scurrilous,' he said thoughtfully. 'So there was more to the hostility between Greaves and Catriona than just academic rivalry.'

'Oh yes,' Doyle continued. 'He ended up being kicked out of the Newman Society, apparently it was full of closeted gays spouting anti-gay stuff. But Greaves committed the ultimate sin of being found out.'

'I wonder where Catriona got her information,' Markham said.

Noakes's imagination was running wild. 'Hey, didn't Skeffington say he almost became a priest? Perhaps he an' Greavesie . . .' The idea of the two fellows as love's young dream was too much for the DS. '*Nah* . . . Greaves couldn't be that desperate.'

'How come Ernie never said anything about Catriona doing this exposé on Greaves?' Burton asked. 'I mean, he told us the article was just "a bit of fun" but it was obviously far more than that.'

'If he was planning to blackmail Greaves, then it would be natural for him to put us off the scent by playing the whole thing down,' Markham suggested.

'I think it was more that Ernie didn't know the full story,' Doyle said. 'Apparently Greaves threatened to sue the paper — he had the connections — but Catriona's dad whipped out his chequebook pronto and shut the whole thing down. The "in-crowd" all knew, of course, and it was kaput for him as far as the union and Newman were concerned, but otherwise it was all hushed up.'

Just like the goings-on at the Culpeper Society, thought Markham grimly.

'If Greaves was litigious, then people would be nervous of speaking out of turn,' he said. 'And Oxford's part of the Establishment, so they could wheel out the big guns to ensure everyone fell into line.'

'Even after all these years, they were definitely twitchy down at the union about me sniffing around,' Doyle agreed. 'And the bloke I spoke to carried on like he thought he was Deep Throat — it was all "off the record" and "full deniability" before he came clean about what had gone on.'

'Every valley shall be exalted and every hill laid low.'

The beautiful vocals swooped and dived as Markham contemplated Philip Greaves who was sitting at the end of a row on the opposite balcony. The warmth of the library after the chilly first half had brought out patches of hectic colour on the man's sharp cheekbones and long, pointed nose, calling to mind a clown's make up. There was nothing clown-like, however, about the set of his mouth.

Certainly the bursar wouldn't have minded Catriona Rowlands being 'laid low' after that devastating character assassination. For all that he now held sway at his old college, armoured in middle age and the dignity of his office, what happened to him as a student must have felt like a fiery brand of ignominy never to be effaced.

Greaves had made no effort to hide his antipathy towards Catriona, but whether this was honesty or some kind of diabolical double bluff eluded Markham.

Further along the row, Dr De'Ath and Andrew Skeffington sat together.

What was it Doyle had reported? Something about letters . . .

Could there be some scandal linking Greaves, De'Ath and Skeffington. Something to do with that long-ago infamy exposed by Catriona Rowlands in the *Sherwin Confidential*? Was Skeffington ever involved with Greaves? Was De'Ath's over-familiarity with female undergraduates the cover for sexual secrets of a darker kind? Had Catriona stumbled upon something that threatened the careers of all three?

Or was there another mystery lurking behind the gaunt walls of Sherwin College?

He felt almost giddy with the possibilities that teemed through his brain.

As 'The Glory of the Lord' rang out, so did Noakes's stertorous snores, eliciting disapproving stares from their fellow concert-goers.

It was bound to happen, Markham thought resignedly, what with mulled wine, mince pies and the library warm as an oven

Scanning the upper levels opposite, he caught Sheila Payne's eye. The librarian appeared to be trying hard not to laugh as Noakes sank lower and lower in his seat. Despite Sheila's vigorous nudging, Margaret Payne remained composed, a faint smile hovering about her lips the only sign that she was in on the joke. There was no sign of Peter Hart or Perdita Cargill-Thompson.

'He was cut off from the land of the living.'

'Just like George,' Olivia murmured, her eyes dancing with mischief.

At that moment, the DS came to with a noisy jerk that was mercifully covered by a loud orchestral *rallentando*. 'Hang in there, sarge,' Doyle muttered. 'Only three more movements to go . . . Ouch!' A swift kick on the shins by Burton precluded any further colloquy between the two malcontents.

Markham could only hope the DCI was somewhere aloft in the gods and oblivious to any mutiny in the ranks.

Sidney's bill of indictment against Noakes was quite long enough without Crimes Against Culture being added to it.

'The Trumpet Shall Sound' rang out and for a brief interlude he allowed himself to be transported by the rich melody and the sweet voices. It was only when the performers commenced 'Since by Man Came Death' that he allowed himself to think once more of Catriona Rowlands's remains mouldering on staircase eleven in the same quad . . . sightless sockets staring blindly through that muddy bilge while two decades of Christmases came and went.

Afterwards when they stumbled out into the night air, almost roasted from the hot atmosphere and the exhilaration of the evening, the DI called his team to order in the shadow of that same staircase where yellow police tape fluttered as a reminder of the awful discovery.

'Briefing in the incident room tomorrow at nine sharp,' he said. 'Then Noakes and I are going to interview De'Ath and Skeffington again followed by Greaves.' His gaze roamed across the lawn gleaming palely in the moonlight beneath its snowy counterpane. 'We need to get to the bottom of those letters and see if one of them will crack. Kate, I want you and Doyle to grill Warrender and Drexler about the Culpeper Society. Don't mention Sheila Payne or Alice Matheson. Just let them think we're on to the alleged rape.'

'D'you reckon the killer's someone from Sherwin then, boss?'

Doyle's voice sounded eerie and hollow as they stood in the corner of the quad, isolated and apart from the concert-goers streaming cheerfully home.

'I just don't know, Constable.' Markham felt oddly detached from the university at that moment, as though he was a wayfarer in a strange land struggling to master the language and customs of an alien tribe. The gentle pressure of Olivia's hand on his arm roused him and he said more cheerfully, 'We'll review everything tomorrow morning. Going through the full narrative will hopefully clarify our minds . . . sharpen the picture.'

''S Crimbo in five days,' Noakes mumbled drowsily. 'We don' wanna be spending it banged up here,' he gave a baleful glance round the quad, 'with all the ghosts and ghoulies.'

'I didn't have you down as the superstitious type, George,' Olivia said.

'There's something about this place,' he rumbled. 'Like there's spooks watching all the time.'

'It's the weight of history,' she laughed. 'Eight hundred years of it. I'm not surprised you can feel them in the air, all the faithful departed waiting in the wings.'

Times like this, Noakes knew why she and the guvnor were so well suited. Fluent in bloody gobbledygook the pair of them. But like a squire true to his lady's colours, he smiled agreement and shuffled his feet before heading off with Burton and Doyle to their temporary quarters.

'I suppose I could be a dirty stop out and stay the night at Sherwin,' Olivia told her boyfriend. 'But you could do without any distractions, Gil, so I'll get a taxi back to Rochford. Plus, I might as well soak up the college atmosphere and see if it inspires one last burst of purple prose.'

'I'll walk you over to the porters' lodge,' he said.

Just outside the glass-fronted office, Olivia paused, wanting to prolong the moment.

'I enjoyed tonight. Took me back to when I was little . . . Mum and Dad let me have the radio in bed as a special treat when it was coming up to Christmas. Hearing all the old favourites makes me feel happy and sad at the same time.'

'Why sad?'

'I guess because until I met you it was the one time in my life when I felt perfectly secure, cocooned in my safe place, like nothing could get me. Mum and dad downstairs keeping out the dark . . . makes me wish I could find my way back there.' Dreamily, she continued, 'Dad gave me a record player when I was thirteen . . . old school, I know, but I loved the idea of it over a tape player. It had an orange base, cream lid and a carry handle. Every night after homework and cocoa, I'd curl up in bed and listen to Gilbert and

Sullivan for hours.' She punched his arm playfully. 'Don't laugh, Gil, I was addicted to light opera! Ballet music too and Acker Bilk, I was such a square but happy in my own little fantasy world. I can't listen to any of that stuff now because it's too painful. There's no way back to the way things were.'

The wistful expression on his girlfriend's face reminded Markham of Kate Burton talking about her father and his hens.

Olivia's parents had had her late in life. An idyllic upbringing, she said. So much so, that what followed never measured up. 'Except me,' he was wont to remind her only half in jest.

Suddenly, she bit her lip, recalling Markham's far less idyllic childhood experiences and the lost brother with whom he would never share another Christmas.

He guessed what she was thinking and drew her close.

'You make up for it all, Liv.'

A stiff breeze had whipped up from nowhere making it feel colder. Stars in the inky sky above first quad glittered like pinprick jewels and little flurries of snow swirled in corners of staircases.

Markham sensed Catriona Rowlands, Ernie Braithwaite and Belinda Lycett at his shoulder like unsleeping spectres. Olivia had told Noakes that the faithful departed of history lurked nearby, but for him it was the ghosts of the murdered dead who watched and waited.

He took a deep breath. 'Come on, dearest,' he said at last. 'Let's see about getting you that taxi.'

* * *

'What the chuff's it all about?'

Noakes's throaty growl was accompanied by furious contortions of his shaggy eyebrows.

Monday 21 December found the two detectives in their incident room contemplating a folder of typed correspondence that had just been passed to them by Royston De'Ath.

De'Ath had called on them without waiting to be summoned and unfolded a peculiar story.

The letters dated back to the months before Catriona Rowlands's disappearance and, according to De'Ath, had been found when she vanished. Pressed as to how they came into his possession, he admitted that he had asked Andrew Skeffington to turn over the student's room and remove anything potentially 'hurtful and distressing to others'. He had been the chaplain in those days and Skeffington an organ scholar at Courtenay Hall.

Skeffington had apparently found a substantial cache of poison pen letters warning Catriona to stay away from Jon Warrender and abusing her in scatological detail.

Now Noakes asked, 'D'you believe all that about Skeffers being his "friend and associate", guv?' He thumped the manila folder. 'I reckon they're both pervs an' the lass had something on the pair of them . . . something to do with the piece she wrote in that college rag.'

'There may well have been something incriminating about them in Catriona's room,' the DI said quietly, 'but if so, they haven't chosen to hand it over.'

'Why did Doctor Death keep this stuff then?' Noakes demanded.

'Well, if we take what he says at face value, De'Ath was disturbed by the correspondence and felt he should keep it on file—'

'In case anyone ever fingered him for murdering the lass. A bleeding insurance policy.' Noakes sounded disgusted. 'Who's to say they're even genuine? I mean, him or his creepy mate coulda written them ready to give the police if they came sniffing around.'

'Some sort of double bluff's perfectly feasible,' Markham admitted, 'but somehow I believed De'Ath when he said the contents of those letters bothered him.'

'He had no business keeping 'em . . . shoulda handed stuff like that to our lot.'

'Perhaps he was thinking about Sherwin's reputation — his own too, if attention were to be focused on Catriona's flirtations around college or he could have been protecting someone . . . maybe even blackmailing them.'

'Like who?'

'No idea, Sergeant. But whoever the killer was, De'Ath might have secretly sympathised with them . . . maybe he even felt grateful when Catriona was no longer on the scene.'

Eyes narrowed, Noakes had another suggestion. 'Mebbe he only suspected who it was an' just hung on to the letters in case a body ever turned up.'

'Or maybe he genuinely had no idea, but some instinct made him keep them—'

Noakes's face was thunderous.

'Cos he's a sick bastard an' got his rocks off keeping them around.'

'And what about Skeffington?' he demanded. 'Are we gonna winkle him out from the organ loft or wherever he's hiding?'

'No point, Sergeant,' Markham said tonelessly. 'He'll only tell the same story.' The DI reached for his third black coffee of the morning. 'He was the one who told De'Ath to hand the letters over, remember.'

'So where does music man fit into all of this, guv?'

'Your guess is as good as mine . . . De'Ath and Skeffington are bound together in some way.'

The DS muttered various imprecations under his breath none of which were likely to bear repeating.

'But whatever the nature of their relationship, as things stand there's nothing to tie them to these murders and they know it. Handing over the letters was a shrewd move in case we did a search.'

Noakes screwed up his mastiff's features in a spasm of intense concentration. 'If them letters telling Catriona to stay away from Warrender are the real deal . . . the writer could be a bloke . . .'

'Go on.'

'A bloke who was in love with Warrender, one of the gay crowd Rowlands wrote about. Greaves or one of that lot . . .'

'Yes, I'm inclined to adopt an equal opportunities perspective on the identity of our letter writer, Noakesy,' the DI said drily. 'No reason why they shouldn't be male.'

He regarded the folder thoughtfully.

'We need to divvy the letters up between us and see if anything jumps out.'

'Can't Burton do it?'

'Equal opps remember, Noakes.'

Craftily, the DS tried a different tack. 'Yeah, but with her being a psychology graduate an' dead keen on that diagnostic handbook thingy she's always quoting—'

'*The Diagnostic and Statistical Manual of Mental Disorders*?'

'That's the fella. Well, likely *she'll* spot the medical signs quicker . . . the bits that show people might not be well, y'know, the socio-wotsit stuff.'

'Nice try but no cigar, Noakesy.' Markham's voice was firm. 'I want *your* take on our poison pen . . . any clues to their identity and so forth. If they're our killer, we can take the sociopathy as read.'

The DS gave it up as a bad job.

Markham split the correspondence into two even piles while his colleague lurched across to the Nespresso machine. After much clattering and cursing, Noakes eventually produced two coffees along with a plate of chocolate digestives thoughtfully provided by the head porter.

'How's Mr Stevenson doing?' the DI asked as he contemplated these 'elevenses'.

'Looks like the stuffing's been knocked out of him, poor ole git,' Noakes replied between slurps. 'Ernie turning up like that hit him hard. You can tell he's shitting hisself in case it turns out to be someone from Sherwin.' The DS shook his head sorrowfully. 'I think it would finish him off.'

After this, for a time there was quiet as the two men pored over the letters.

Then Noakes broke the silence. 'What's "boondocks" mean?'

'*Boondocks*?'

'Yeah. There's a bit here that calls Rowlands a brainiac bitch from the boondocks with a thing about jocks, says she's looped most of the time.' The DS scratched his chin. 'Reads like summat out of a U.S. soap. *Friends* or one of them sitcoms my Nat used to watch.'

Markham pondered for a minute. 'I think "boondocks" means somewhere out in the back of beyond — rural, the countryside — Catriona hailed from Somerset originally, didn't she?'

'So they're saying she's some sort of inbred, is that it?'

'Could be . . . or maybe it's just a dig at her for being unsophisticated.' The DI sighed. 'Or perhaps they just liked the way it sounded.'

Markham looked at his own pile.

'They've got quite a way with invective,' he said. 'High-flown in parts and then quite slangy in others.'

Noakes looked apprehensive. 'Don' tell me that means *two* people wrote them, guv . . .'

'No, I don't think so,' the DI replied. 'It seems to me like we have a single author but possibly there were moments of dissociative fugue or there could be an issue of multiple personality . . .'

'See what I mean, guv.' Noakes gave his pile of papers an emphatic thump. 'You need Burton an' her whack-job manual.'

'Well, I think Kate will certainly find this interesting. But,' he continued, with an increase of steeliness, 'I want to know *your* take on it, Sergeant.'

Noakes contemplated the chocolate biscuits as if something about the task interfered with his digestion.

'Can't work out if the writer's a bird or a bloke,' he grumbled after further scrutiny. '*Hey up*,' riffling through his pile, 'a couple of 'em accuse Rowlands of being at it with everyone, even the chaplain. De'Ath won't have liked *that*.'

'Same here . . . In fact,' the DI was skim-reading as he spoke, 'this stuff about Catriona being prodigal with her sexual favours is something of a running theme. That might explain why De'Ath wasn't falling over himself to involve the police.'

'Look here, guv.' Noakes was exasperated. 'Why did the lass keep this garbage? Why didn't she jus' chuck it down the bog? I c'n see why she might not have wanted to report it — 'specially if she were up to all sorts — but hanging on to it like this. Mind, I s'pose she coulda been waiting to let it pile up . . . so she could say she were being stalked.'

'Maybe it gave her a sense of power,' the DI said slowly. 'Maybe she liked the idea of driving someone insane with jealousy. Or maybe she had an idea who it was and planned to confront them.'

The DS made a throaty noise, like a dog who sensed something wicked prowling about.

'There's stuff in here about that weird society,' he said.

'The Culpeper?'

'Yeah . . . the one Burton says Warrender an' Drexler belonged to. A rant about how Rowlands turned good men into animals . . . *Huh*!' Noakes wasn't having that. 'Drexler were only semi-house-trained to start with.'

'Does it mention Warrender and Drexler by name?'

'No . . . but it's gotta be them two, guv.'

'Hmm. *Ah*,' Markham stiffened.

'What is it, boss?'

'This one talks about Catriona trying to trap Warrender into marriage by palming off a child on him.'

'So it was someone who knew she were up the spout . . .' Noakes scowled. 'As in half the bleeding university.'

'Yes . . . and by the sound of it, finding out about the pregnancy tipped them over the edge.'

'D'you reckon Catriona rubbed their face in it?'

'It's possible . . . Or Warrender might have vented to someone who got angry on his behalf.'

Markham rubbed his temples as though to still the pulses that were throbbing there. He had told Olivia the full picture of the college murders would be coming into focus, but currently he felt further away than ever from fathoming the truth.

Noakes took a turn about the room then wandered over to the window with its view of Plessington College's garden.

'Hey, there's a robin redbreast in their rockery wotsit,' he said gleefully. 'Meant to be lucky, that is.'

Markham smiled wearily. 'We could certainly do with some of that right now, Sergeant.'

The DS wheeled round from the window.

'Look, guv, seems to me like we should be after someone who's bats about Warrender.'

'And who might that be, then?'

'What about Sheila Payne? She's friends with him, came to that manky dinner an' all. Plus she'd hurt her foot . . . had a bandage on it.'

'So she did.'

'An' that woman from the museum thought the person with Belinda Lychee had a limp,' Noakes brought out with a flourish. He looked so pleased with himself that Markham didn't point out the correct surname.

'Dr De'Ath was using a cane the other night, Noakesy.'

'Yeah, but c'n you see him in a duffel coat an' beanie? He'd stand out a mile wherever he was. But Payne could blend in easy peasy. She's the librarian . . . handles events for Rochford too . . . prob'ly knows that place inside out.'

The DS was getting quite excited. He rolled up the sleeves of his ratty jumper as though to show that he meant business.

'We should get over to Rochford an' check her out, guv,' he said.

'I want to speak to Dr Warrender first . . . see what he has to say about this latest development.'

'You mean, tell him we think it's a bunny boiler?' the DS enquired bullishly.

'It might not be a woman, remember.'

'There's summat *girly* 'bout the way them letters go on an' on.' Noakes had done a 180-degree turn. 'Y'know the way women allus say "An' another thing" when they're having a rant. It's like that.'

'Better not let Kate hear you making these sexist assumptions.'

'Talk of the devil,' his wingman grunted as Burton and Doyle walked in.

'What's up, Kate?' the DI asked as he registered her anxious expression.

'I've just had a call from Sheila Payne, sir.'

Noakes threw Markham a significant look.

'She was supposed to have a meeting with Perdita Cargill-Thompson today — library requisitions for the Classics department — but Perdita didn't show.'

'Coulda forgot,' Noakes retorted.

'No, apparently she's a stickler for that kind of thing, it's really out of character. Sheila said Perdita seemed distracted and upset lately too . . .'

'Well, the student she's meant to be supervising had her head bashed in.' Her fellow DS was cutting Burton no slack.

Markham's face was dark with concern. 'Does she live in college? Have they tried her room?'

'Yes, but there's no sign of her, sir.'

The DI reached for his black wool overcoat and Noakes his horrible parka. 'Let's get over there. We can share intel on the way.'

As they made their way out of college, Markham thought about the letters De'Ath had surrendered. He had an uneasy feeling there was something vital he had overlooked. But for the life of him he could not grasp the elusive clue.

The clock struck the hour as they passed through the lodge.

It sounded like a death knell.

12. REVELATION

Passing through the porters' lodge, they spied the head porter and various underlings heaving a towering fir tree into position at the entrance to first quad.

''Good distraction for ole Stevenson,' Noakes muttered, then loudly, 'D'you need a hand there, mate?'

Mr Stevenson was indeed distracted but answered with his usual punctilious courtesy, 'I think we're winning the battle, Sergeant.' As if he were piloting a Spitfire, Noakes commented to Markham afterwards. 'At Sherwin we don't put decorations up till Christmas week . . . bad form to have them up too early.'

Kate Burton murmured something about the magnificence of the tree and received an approving beam before the man returned to his task.

Outside in Turl Street she unlocked her car, Noakes and Doyle getting into the back while Markham took the front passenger seat.

'Just let me get the de-icer and heater sorted, sir,' she said as her colleagues noisily blew on their fingers behind her.

In a matter of minutes, they had parked on Wellington Street and were trudging around Rochford's campus towards the main entrance. The snow crunched underfoot and there was not a soul to be seen.

'Makes you feel like Captain Scott or one of them Antarctic fellows,' Noakes commented.

'Just so long as you don't do a Captain Oates on me, Noakesy,' Markham riposted.

'That's the one who went out into the blizzard saying he was going to be some time.' When Noakes looked nonplussed, Burton explained, 'Sacrificed himself for the others cos he had frostbite or gangrene and didn't want to slow them down.'

'Oh yeah, I remember doing a project on that fella. Real hero he was . . . not like the people they let into the forces nowadays.'

Markham felt this was dangerous ground. 'What transpired with Dr Warrender, Kate?' he said hastily. 'Did you learn anything more about goings-on at the Culpeper Society?'

'I said we had information that Catriona Rowlands had been raped after things got out of hand and asked him straight out what he knew about it.' She sighed. 'But he knew I was fishing, demanded to know who gave us the story and then started blustering about his solicitor. So I had to back off.'

'Did he say anything about Mark Drexler? Anything about that fight they had during dinner?'

'Just that they'd both had too much to drink and it was something and nothing. Told me the police shouldn't listen to malicious gossip.'

'Pompous prick,' Noakes growled. 'Wonder what his missus would make of lover boy being hauled down the nick. That'd *really* give 'em summat to talk about.'

'He gave it the usual about harassment and human rights,' Burton continued. 'Seemed pretty confident. I mean, he was uncomfortable about *something* that happened involving Catriona and the Culpeper but it was obvious he didn't think we could tie him in to the murder. The call about

Cargill-Thompson going missing came in before there was a chance to get started on Drexler.'

Doyle voiced what they were all thinking. 'D'you reckon something's happened to her, boss?'

'Sheila Payne said Perdita had something on her mind,' the DI said slowly. 'Which may mean she had uncovered something . . . knew something . . .'

Something that might have sealed her fate.

They had come round to the St Giles entrance and passed through the gates into the main quad. An impressive spruce with crates of decorations waited next to the porters' lodge, suggesting that the college authorities were of Mr Stevenson's mind when it came to festive timings.

Rochford's library was spread across three floors in the central portion of the ivy-clad Queen Anne mansion, with undergraduate accommodation and tutors' rooms on adjacent wings. The more recent additions — the two Lego annexes, as Markham thought of them — overlooked Walton Street and Park Town at the outer borders of the college campus.

It was a gracious, peaceful space, thought Markham. Just what a library should be, with tall, mullioned windows flooding the long oak tables with plenty of natural light while carrels, crannies and secluded workstations afforded those less sociably inclined a degree of greater privacy. The distinctive scent of antique leather and venerable book bindings hung in the air.

He could see Kate Burton was drinking it all in with an almost reverential expression on her face. Perhaps that was what she needed, a university sabbatical — a career break that would give her another shot at higher education and make up for the disappointment she'd experienced first time round. Her dreams of university life had never been fulfilled. Instead, she'd resorted to faking it, making up stories for her mum and dad. She deserved another chance at academia. And second time around, to what heights might she not soar?

Sheila Payne was flustered. 'It's not like Peri to miss a meeting,' she said.

Peri! The DI carefully avoided Noakes's eye as he heard this diminutive.

'You said she seemed out of sorts lately,' he prompted gently. 'Not her usual self.'

'That's right. She was quite prickly when I asked if anything was the matter, so I didn't want to push it. Belinda was Peri's student, so it was only natural she should be upset. Peter —Professor Hart — said we should all give her some space, keep to business and college stuff. Said she'd come round in her own time.'

Markham nodded. 'I take it you've searched the library?'

'Yes . . . that's where you usually find Peri in holiday time.' A rueful grin. 'She'd hole up in here knowing she wouldn't be badgered.'

Markham recalled the Reynolds Museum exhibit where their latest victim had been found. 'Are there any parts of the library out of bounds during the holidays? Special collections or anywhere closed off to students?'

'Just the Daphne Parker viewing platform for the astrophysics students.'

Registering Noakes's look of bafflement, she added, 'That's a former principal of the college. She was a spook, M16. Bit of a stargazer in her spare time.'

'Oh aye. So what's with this viewing hoojah then?'

'It's nothing fancy, Sergeant. Just a little terrace with a telescope and some busts of famous astronomers — Galileo, Copernicus, Hailey, Hubble.'

The DS looked distinctly underwhelmed.

Unease stirred in the pit of Markham's stomach. 'Who has access to this area, Ms Payne?'

'Oh, the tutors' fob covers all areas, Inspector, but,' she faltered, 'Peri wouldn't have had any reason to be up there.'

Unless she arranged to meet someone, and they wanted to be assured of privacy.

'Can you show us?' he asked.

The librarian gestured to the far side of the library, where iron wrought spiral stairs led to the upper levels.

The team followed her up to the third floor and then through a door behind which was another spiral staircase.

At the top of this staircase, Sheila Payne passed her key fob over an electronic sensor that operated a heavy steel door. Passing through it, the team found themselves in an enclosed terrace with an impressive state-of-the-art telescope and counters sporting a range of scientific instruments. Rolling stacks filled the walls on two sides while a third was lined with busts of distinguished astronomers and glass-cased historical exhibits. On the fourth side nearest the Woodstock Road, a floor-to-ceiling window offered a magnificent view across the city towards the snow-covered vista of Magdalen College Deer Park.

'*Hey*, I remember *these*,' Noakes gestured to the locker-type shelves anchored to tracks on the floor with large wheels on their sides. 'From the book club investigation, remember.'

The DI wasn't at all sure that he cared to revisit that particular investigation in which retractable bookshelves had accounted for one of their most gruesome crime scenes. Judging from their queasy expressions, Burton and Doyle felt a similar repugnance.

The terrace was deserted. No sign that anyone had been up there.

And yet Markham felt his shoulder blades prickle . . .

He ran his eyes over the grey metal cladding until they fell on a discreet sliding door.

'What's through there?'

'Just the old paternoster.'

'*Eh*?' Noakes looked wary on hearing the Latin jargon.

'An old-fashioned elevator with no doors that goes round and round very slowly on a loop so that you can hop on and off. It dates back to the nineteen eighties. The college mothballed the lift when the library was being renovated. It's a creaky timber affair but part of the history of the building, so the authorities were reluctant to rip it out.'

'Can we have a look at it please.'

Something about the DI's tone and the intensity of his gaze gave Kate Burton goose bumps.

'It's just an old museum piece, Inspector . . . Only the facilities staff ever go in there.'

Markham was courteous but adamant. 'Nevertheless.'

They moved over to the doorway and Sheila Payne slid it back.

'There you go . . . *Oh my god.*'

Two wooden carriages hung crazily in the lift shaft, one slightly higher than the other.

But what made the onlookers' hearts jump into their mouths was the sight of the occupant of the right-hand compartment.

Perdita Cargill-Thompson sat doll-like on the floor, arms and legs stiff as any jointed puppet, the heavy bust warring against gravity. Her eyes were open but glazed and unseeing. A thin skein of drool dangled from the corner of her lipsticked mouth onto a navy-blue cowl-necked dress and her blonde chignon looked to be coming loose, heavy strands framing congested purplish features that were fixed in a ghastly grimace. A livid weal around the neck seemed to indicate strangulation, though there was no sign of any garotte.

Rochford's librarian made a series of inarticulate sounds.

The DI signalled to Burton.

'Take Ms Payne downstairs please, Kate, and then call this in.' He turned to the DC. 'Doyle, I want the library cleared immediately and the whole area cordoned off.'

His subordinates hastened to comply.

Noakes leaned in.

'D'you think it happened up here, guv?'

The DI looked around the terrace.

'Most likely, yes,' he said. 'Easy enough to lure Perdita up to this observatory or whatever they call it . . . maybe by sending a text or maybe *she* suggested it. Either way, the attack clearly came out of the blue, so she most likely trusted her killer.'

'Peter Hart?'

'Depends when she was killed . . . The two of them weren't at the carol service yesterday, so it could have happened then. If it was later that night, after people had theoretically turned in, then anyone from Rochford or Sherwin could've done it.'

'Only tutors from Rochford would have been able to get up here, boss,' Noakes pointed out. 'You'd need one of them fob thingies to get into the library.'

'I don't imagine it would be difficult for any of the dons at Sherwin to get hold of a pass key if they put their minds to it,' the DI replied.

'Yeah, but wouldn't it mean awkward questions if they borrowed a key from someone an' then a dead body turned up?'

'They could have lifted a staff key, Noakes. Olivia told me it's easy come, easy go at Rochford. She's got one of these passes and apparently library staff are always complaining that people leave them lying around. Or, if meeting in the observatory was Perdita's idea, then *she* could have taken them up there using her own fob.'

'That Sheila had the best chance of doing it,' the DS said. 'An' we only have her word for it about this meeting. Seems to me like it'd suit her to raise the alarm an' then come over all hysterical when we found the body.' He looked at Perdita Cargill-Thompson's ungainly corpse from which every trace of grace and refinement had been expunged. 'Poor lass,' he murmured softly. 'It's just like when we found that other kid in the mortuary at the Newman.'

The murder investigation at Bromgrove's special hospital was another case that still haunted Markham. Not least the heartrending discovery of one of their youngest victims, another pretty blonde who never saw danger coming . . .

'You're keen on Sheila Payne being our killer,' the DI said thoughtfully.

'She's sweet on Warrender, guv, so *yeah*. An' I reckon her being an outsider back then when they were all students coulda meant she were jealous of Rowlands . . . the spoiled little rich kid who got everything handed to her on a plate while Sheila was stuck there with her face pressed up against the window watching the smart set live it up.'

It was an arresting image.

'Hmm. From what I remember, Sheila's sister, Margaret, and Peter Hart weren't part of that set either.'

'Well, at least *they* were here at Oxford while *she* were slumming it in that red-brick place or whatever it was,' Noakes insisted stubbornly.

'The same is true of Sarah Rowlands, Sergeant. But neither of them seems to have a chip on their shoulder about being in the second division.'

'Payne's *on the spot*, guv . . . here on the staff at Rochford. Sarah Rowlands ain't a don or a fellow or whatnot, she's just a teacher out in the sticks. It's gotta be someone from the university. Rowlands would stand out like a sore thumb if she went wandering round the college library.'

Markham looked intently at the elevator with its grotesquely posed occupant.

'Sarah Rowlands knows Peter Hart and likely other people too . . . That could give her a reason for being here.' He shook his head. 'We can't rule it out.'

The two men moved away from the paternoster back to the window which overlooked the Woodstock Road. Outside looked picture-postcard perfect, with snowflakes coming down in downy profusion. 'It's like being in Moscow or Siberia or one of them places,' the DS said as he watched the world turn white. Meanwhile his boss was struck less by the romance of the winter landscape than by the way it seemed to highlight the loneliness of the human condition, turning individuals into mere dark stains against the landscape.

'We need Jigsaw Man,' the DS grumbled.

'And details of next of kin,' Markham added sadly.

Noakes pounded his open palm with a pudgy fist. 'Say it *is* Payne and the lass were on to her,' he said impatiently, 'why'd she agree to meet her up here? There'd been *three* murders already for chuff's sake.'

'Perhaps Perdita wasn't sure,' the DI replied. 'Or perhaps she suspected someone else and wanted to talk . . . But then she said or did something which turned her into a threat.'

'What happens now, boss?' the DS asked helplessly.

'We let the pathologist do his stuff. I'll need to see the next of kin and then I've got a conference call with the DCI.' The mere thought of the latter appointment made Markham want to smash a hole through the glass window. 'In the meantime, I want you, Burton and Doyle to go through all the statements and alibis with a fine-tooth comb. There's got to be something we've missed, Noakesy.' Again he had the nagging sense of something overlooked. 'And I want a timeline for Perdita covering her movements from the memorial service onwards.'

'Do we have another go at Drexler?' It was obvious this was a prospect Noakes viewed with some relish.

'No. Just focus on what we've got and be ready for a full case review first thing tomorrow morning.'

Noakes noticed the restless flexing of the DI's finely tapered hands.

'Bet you wish Doggie were here so you could work off some aggro before dealing with Slimy Sid.'

A harsh laugh. 'Is it that obvious?'

'Well, not to the others,' said with a hint of pride, 'but with someone who knows you like I do, guv . . .'

'Doggie' Dickerson was the DI's boxing guru back in Bromgrove — a decrepit and thoroughly disreputable character who ran a 'gym' where the town's criminal fraternity slugged it out alongside the local CID. Markham's membership was a running sore with the DCI, who emphatically disapproved of the set-up, but Markham loved the unvarnished authenticity of the premises and its dodgy proprietor.

'I wonder what Doggie would make of the dreaming spires?' he asked, gesturing round the high-tech eyrie. 'Somehow I don't reckon it would faze him at all.'

Noakes grunted. 'That's cos he'd be too busy casing the joint to notice the historical stuff.'

The DI ruefully admitted to himself that this was true. But he felt a sudden nostalgia for the sweaty, dingy club — a mad desire to burst the Oxford bubble of privilege and escape back to Bromgrove.

Instead he said, 'Tomorrow's the twenty-second. We *can't* go into Christmas with a triple homicide unsolved . . . four deaths if we count Catriona as the start of the series.'

'There's too many bleedings suspects,' the DS grumbled. 'But mebbe one of them will crack,' he added dubiously. 'Shouldn't we wheel in Greavesie an' the rest of them, twist the screws a bit?'

'You can give it out about Perdita being found dead in suspicious circumstances . . . no way are we going to be able to keep that under wraps. Throw out a few hints that we're close to making an arrest and see how they react.'

'We're not, though . . . It's a load of bollocks,' came the glum response.

'Yes, but *they* don't know that, Noakesy . . . I want to keep them on edge without going in all guns blazing.'

After this exchange, the two men resumed their contemplation of Magdalen Deer Park blanketed in snow: an ethereal winter wonderland that Perdita Cargill-Thompson would never see again.

'Afternoon, gentlemen.'

Jigsaw Man had arrived, escorted by Kate Burton and two paramedics. 'There's a service lift on the other side of the stacks,' she said, 'so the ambulance crew should be able to get the body down to the ground floor without any difficulty.'

They left the pathologist to his initial examination, waiting in awkward silence until he had finished.

'Time of death, doctor?' Markham asked when the medic re-joined them.

Something in the DI's worn expression must have struck a chord.

'I'd say around midnight last night, but don't quote me on that . . . Cause of death, strangulation. It seems she was taken by surprise, so no defensive injuries.' The man's normally colourless tone was shaded by genuine emotion. 'It was a cowardly attack from behind, and whoever did it kept squeezing long after she was dead. I'd like to see you catch this one, Inspector.'

'Me an' all,' Noakes muttered sarcastically albeit with more respect than usual in his glance.

As Perdita Cargill-Thompson's sheeted form was carried on a stretcher through the observatory, the pathologist's words echoed in Markham's head: *Squeezing long after she was dead.* Did this overkill mean their murderer was losing control of the narrative?

Heads bowed, the detectives and pathologist remained respectfully silent for some minutes.

Then, 'I better get off, Inspector.' The pathologist's expression was sympathetic. 'I'll be in touch later.'

'Thank you, Doctor . . .' The DI realised he didn't actually know the man's surname.

'The name's Merrick,' the other said, his wooden features relaxing in what might almost have been a grin. He nodded affably at Noakes. 'Though I imagine your Sergeant's come up with some other designation. People usually do.' And with that he was gone.

'Actually, think I'll stick with "Jigsaw Man".' Noakes's prejudices were generally hard to shift, but he clearly felt better disposed towards the pathologist for this glimpse of humanity.

Margaret Payne was waiting with DC Doyle on the ground floor.

'I'm going to take Sheila home, Inspector,' she said looking anxiously at her sister whose putty-coloured features were slack and almost ugly with shock. 'I think Peter's somewhere around — in his office if you need to speak to him.'

'That's alright, Ms Payne, you get off.'

To his amusement, the tutor took a scrunchie hairband from her cardigan pocket and rammed it unselfconsciously onto her head. By contrast with the dead woman, this was someone who clearly didn't give a hoot about her appearance.

Though in her early forties, she still had a freshness of youth which saved her from the vinegariness of an Oxbridge bluestocking, but he could imagine her becoming increasingly Margaret Rutherford-ish in later life. 'Come along, Sheila,' she said briskly but not unkindly, piloting her sister towards the entrance foyer.

Doyle handed a slip of paper to the DI.

'Next of kin's her mum and stepdad,' he said. 'They live out by Headington.'

'Quick work, Constable,' came the approving response. 'If you can drop me at the family's address, Kate, I'll make my own way back into town afterwards.'

'D'you need me with you, guv?' Noakes enquired magnanimously. The guvnor looked wiped out, like a bereavement visit was the last thing he needed.

'Thanks, Sergeant, but I need the three of you back at base. I'll brief you how it goes with the DCI then find my own way back to town.' Pray god Sidney was so buoyed up by post-conference euphoria (and the nearer approach of the hitherto elusive OBE) that he wouldn't demand he stage an immediate press conference with Superintendent Charleson to 'reassure the public'. Frankly, the way things stood, he wouldn't know how to pull it off.

* * *

In the event, 'back to town', meant a visit to Olivia at Rochford.

'It's not too bad,' Markham said as he surveyed the old fashioned but cosy ground-floor room with yellow-counterpaned single bed, simple pine furniture including a desk, two easy chairs and a dresser with drink-making facilities. The casement window looked out onto the front lawn of Rochford's main quad where snow drifted heavily across blue-black skies. A small electric heater supplemented the massive ancient radiators, so despite the weather the couple were warm and comfortable. Across the lawn, the lights of a Christmas tree twinkled in the principal's residence. *In the midst of death we are in life*, Markham thought sadly. At least there were no decorations in the college library, it would have seemed too cruel in the circumstances.

'How did it go with the family?' Olivia asked him.

'They were amazingly stoic . . . It'll only really hit them later,' he said. 'There are two siblings, also university lecturers — Leeds and Edinburgh — but they're coming home tomorrow.' He cradled his coffee almost as though for dear life. 'I only gave her parents the essentials . . . Couldn't bear to tell them it's most likely someone from the university killed her.'

'What about Sidney?'

'Demanding developments within twenty-four hours, needless to say. Still clinging to the idea of its being the work of "drug-crazed elements".'

'*Jesus* . . . Sorry, Gil, but he just never learns.'

Her glance fell on the thick folder next to his chair.

'Have you brought something for me to look at . . . seeing as I'm your Nancy Drew.'

He chuckled at that. 'I rate you higher than that.' A pause as he seemed to wrestle with himself, then, 'It's a file of poison pen letters. Long story short, they turned up in Catriona Rowlands's room and only came into my hands earlier today.'

Her eyebrows shot up at that.

'What kind of hate mail is it?'

'The long rambling kind . . . warning her to stay away from Jon Warrender, with lots of unpleasant personal abuse thrown in for good measure.'

Olivia digested this information then unexpectedly she smiled. 'D'you remember the Ashley Dean investigation when you brought home all those newspaper cuttings from the library and we found that photograph which blew the case wide open? Maybe history will repeat itself.'

He laughed. 'You're a mind-reader, Liv. Yes, actually, I wanted you to run your eye over the letters. You notice the way people use language . . . perhaps something will jump out at you and god knows I need a fresh perspective.'

'No worries, sweetheart, chuck them over here and I'll wade through the vitriol. In the meantime, you lean back and relax.'

Nothing loath, Markham did exactly that. Gradually, soothed by the warmth and the gentle rustling of papers, he found himself nodding off.

'The writer has to be from across the pond.'

He jerked upright.

'Say that again, Liv.'

He was suddenly wide awake, his senses alert.

'Well, they're full of Americanisms,' she said.

'That's what Noakesy said . . . they reminded him of *Friends* and soaps like that.'

'George is bang on the money.' Olivia's eyes were suddenly thoughtful, remote.

'What is it, Liv?'

'Actually, the style reminds me of something from when I was having a browse in Rochford's archives . . . looking at back numbers of *Rochfordia*.' Her gaze cleared. 'Oh yes, that was it. A piece by one of the tutors called *A Yank at Oxford*. It was quite witty, especially the way she referenced the nineteen-thirties film . . . I remember she poked fun at herself for using American jargon . . .'

'*She*?' There was a strange light in Markham's eyes.

'Margaret Payne. You know, the junior dean. The one married to the Classics prof.'

He thought back to the girl guide lookalike he had last seen shepherding her sister home.

'But she's not American,' he said haltingly. '*Is she*?'

'Her article said the family moved to the UK when she was quite young, so no American twang but she picked up some colloquialisms along the way . . . joked about them being in her DNA and getting told off for sounding like Jennifer Aniston. *Hey*, are you alright, Gil?' she asked anxiously as her boyfriend changed colour.

No twang, he thought. But he'd noticed both the sisters had an attractively un-English lilt to their voices. Now, he realised it was a transatlantic inflexion . . .

Olivia was fast catching up.

'God no,' she whispered. 'You don't think . . .'

Markham's mobile was in his hand. He needed to reach the team.

'*Noakes*.' His voice was hoarse, urgent. 'I'm on my way back to Sherwin. I think we may have a lead.'

Terse calls to Burton and Doyle followed.

Finally, he turned to Olivia.

'Catriona Rowlands wrote an article for Sherwin's college magazine which sent me in the wrong direction. But with what you've just said . . . well, maybe history *has* repeated itself . . . maybe we're still in with a chance.'

He picked up his overcoat.

'Keep your door locked and don't go out for any reason at all, do you understand.'

'"To hear is to obey."' Then, very softly, 'Be careful, Gil.'

He gave her a swift tight embrace before disappearing down the dimly lit corridor and out into the night.

13. OUT OF THE SHADOWS

Re-entering Sherwin, the DI noticed the college Christmas tree was now decked out in all its finery, topped by a silver star bearing the university logo and studded with lights winking at a variety of tempi. Touchingly, a large blue bauble bore Ernie Braithwaite's name engraved in silver. Markham suspected this was the head porter's doing; unlike the other victims, there would be few mourners for Ernie, so Mr Stevenson had secured for him a little corner of immortality.

The other members of the team were waiting in the incident room surrounded by files and piles of paper.

'I organised a takeaway for us, sir,' Kate Burton said pointing to some pizza boxes. 'Just Margheritas and garlic bread for you, me and Doyle and a Sloppy Giuseppe for sarge . . . Not very Christmassy, I'm afraid.'

'Excellent,' he said, realising to his surprise that he was suddenly very hungry. Coffee materialised at his elbow and he devoted the next few minutes to the needs of the inner man, noting with amusement Noakes's side-order of dough balls and fries. No danger of his number two fading away through lack of sustenance!

'Whassup then, guv?' the DS asked with an exuberant belch as he polished off the last of his fries. 'You said summat about having a lead.'

Without preamble, Markham updated Burton and Doyle about the cache of letters he had retrieved from Royston De'Ath. Noakes, meanwhile, looked complacent, in pleasurable anticipation of being directed to slap handcuffs on the emeritus chaplain.

Then the DI went on to tell the team what he had learned from Olivia and the conclusion he had drawn.

Noakes was incredulous.

'*Margaret Payne*? The one who looks like she's barely out of knee socks . . . no makeup . . . wears that old-fashioned Alice band thingy . . . *You gotta be kidding me*.'

Doyle too looked askance. 'But she's dead wholesome, boss,' he faltered. 'Happily married too, isn't she? Sticks to her handsome husband like superglue . . . They seemed pretty devoted from where I was standing . . .'

But Burton looked steadily at them.

'We're talking twenty years back. Things might've been very different then.'

Noakes waded into the breach. 'Lemme get this straight, guv . . . You're saying Margaret Payne had a thing about Warrender — that total waste of space — an' murdered Catriona Rowlands cos she wanted him for herself but the lass got in her road . . . then fast forward to 2020 an' she finishes off three more people to cover up what happened in the noughties . . .'

'Yes,' the DI said simply.

'I need a drink,' Noakes rumbled, 'an' I don' mean a poxy Diet Coke.'

'You can have a *Stella* from the fridge, Noakesy . . . *one beer* and that's your lot because I need you focused.'

The DS slouched across to the fridge, rooted around for his lager and returned to the fray.

'She jus' don' fit the profile,' he said stubbornly.

'*What profile*? We don't *have* a profile, Sergeant . . .' Markham gulped down more coffee. 'But I recall something Mrs Noakes said during her visit to Oxford.' The DI very nearly mentioned their outing to the Randolph Hotel, but remembered himself in time before realising that the precaution was unnecessary; Kate Burton was too engrossed by the new development to worry about any extracurricular activities.

His wingman's belligerence abated. 'What did my missus say then?' he enquired in a softer tone.

'She talked about how hard it must have been for other women who ended up being put in the shade by Catriona . . . *wallflowers* she called them.'

'I see,' Noakes temporised, clearly not seeing at all.

'And she mentioned women being the best haters too,' the DI added.

'Well, the missus is very . . .'

'Perspicacious,' Burton finished Noakes's sentence.

'*Exactly*.' The DS treated her to one of the more affable expressions in his repertoire. Being unused to this, she recoiled in surprise before warily leaning in once more.

'Margaret Payne only got together with Peter Hart in their fourth year at Sherwin,' she said. 'Plenty of time before that for her to have developed an infatuation with Warrender—'

'Lazy fat git,' Noakes interrupted rudely.

Pot calling the kettle black, Kate thought but she held on to her temper.

'Warrender was good looking when he was an undergraduate,' she pointed out. 'Women seem to like him. There's Sheila Payne mooning over him and a wife out in Woodstock. Veronica Rowlands was eyeing him at the memorial service . . . Even Alice Matheson was stirred up by him.'

'Only cos she wanted Catriona herself.'

Burton summoned up her reserves of forbearance.

'The point is, sarge, it's not impossible to imagine Margaret Payne falling for him . . . falling hard.' Burton's mind was moving at warp speed. 'From the sound of it, she was young for her age and very unworldly.'

Markham pressed home his advantage. 'You said it yourself, Noakes . . . there's something childlike and unformed about Ms Payne for all her big brain . . . maybe something unbalanced too.'

Unbalanced and stunted.

'But can you really see her strangling Rowlands an' shovelling her under a load of cement?' Noakes demanded.

'I think it may have happened along the same lines that we thrashed out at the start,' the DI said seriously. 'Margaret took advantage of post-Finals revelry to manoeuvre Catriona where she wanted her . . . perhaps got her legless — maybe even spiked her drink — and then persuaded some lad to carry her over to staircase eleven. Nobody would have thought anything of it. Just good-natured horseplay, young people letting off steam.'

Doyle tried to picture it. 'You reckon she killed Catriona on staircase eleven then, boss?'

'If Catriona was incapacitated, it would have been very easy,' the DI replied. 'And she was a slight girl, so no heavy lifting required . . . just one good shove and then fill in the hole.'

Noakes was reluctant to be convinced. 'Payne's slight too,' he objected.

'Sometimes folk get this unnatural strength when the adrenalin kicks in,' Doyle ventured. 'But then . . . what about the other three deaths? Did she really do *them* as well?'

They heard the clock tower strike the half hour, as though it tolled for those other victims.

'Ernie could have been blackmailing her,' the DI continued. 'Remember, Mr Stevenson said he gave a little jump when they were chatting in college just before Ernie disappeared, as though he had recognised somebody.'

'An' you think the *somebody* was Margaret Payne?' Noakes demanded.

'It could have been, yes. If he saw her and suddenly remembered something—'

Burton jumped on it. 'Like the fact that Margaret had once been sweet on Warrender . . . maybe even confided in him or one of the other scouts about it when she was a student. Ernie was a bit of a father figure, remember, he took the female undergrads leftovers when they were ill, that kind of thing. Maybe it all came back to him in a flash.'

'And he saw a way of making money,' Doyle concluded.

'I'm not sure it was as cold-blooded as that,' the DI said. 'He could have been fond of both girls . . . Catriona and Margaret. Thought of them both as being his *girls* rather than grown women—'

'Which blinded him to the danger.' Burton's expression was bleak.

Markham nodded. 'Again, drink played its part and Ernie was shoved into the river, having been lulled into a false sense of security by Margaret giving him money.'

'That scrap of paper in his fist . . . part of a fifty-pound note.' Noakes rumpled his hair, a sure sign of profound cogitation. 'Okay, but what about Belinda an' that Stone Age thingamajig?'

'They were academics,' Markham answered. 'Classics and Ancient History. It's the kind of rendezvous that would appeal to them both . . . and disarm Ms Lycett.'

'But why did Payne have to kill her?'

'*Think*, Noakesy.' The DI's angular features seemed more hawk-like than usual. 'Belinda was the girl we met down by the river . . .'

Burton took up the story. 'And she most likely remembered seeing Margaret hanging round Christ Church Meadow about the time of Ernie's murder.'

'Correct.' The DI nodded approval.

'Why didn't she come to *us* then, guv?' The DI could see that Noakes wanted to be persuaded but was struggling. 'She musta *known* it were dangerous.' He wheeled round on Burton. 'You said she would never have done owt daft.'

Burton remained composed. 'What if Belinda didn't suspect Margaret herself of being the killer but just thought she could trade what she'd seen in return for Margaret's influence with the research committee?'

Noakes's jaw dropped. 'You mean she tole Payne she'd make trouble for her with the police unless she put her on the PhD course?'

'From her perspective, it was a neat little *quid pro quo* . . . with the added bonus of putting one over on Hart.'

'*Jesus.*'

Seeing how his DS was properly winded, Markham let the profanity pass.

'What about the latest?' Noakes asked helplessly. 'Where did that Penelope one fit in?'

'Perdita.' Burton took a swig of Coke. 'She must have become suspicious . . . maybe saw something that made her wonder about Margaret.'

'*Why not come to us then*?' Noakes's plea was even more anguished than before. 'What made the stupid woman think she could handle it on her own?'

'Cargill-Thompson was carrying a torch for Peter Hart,' Doyle said. 'Maybe she didn't want to sneak on his missus . . . Wouldn't exactly win him over, would it?'

'Plus the three of them went way back,' Burton went on. 'Ties that bind.'

'But we're talking *murder*.' Noakes was outraged. 'Surely that justifies throwing your bestie under the bus, for god's sake.'

Burton was unruffled. 'If they all had reason to dislike and resent Catriona, that could have made it easier for Perdita to talk herself out of going to the police . . . at least not until she'd heard what Margaret had to say.'

'Perdita might have tried emotional blackmail.' This was Doyle. 'If she was interested in Peter Hart, maybe she planned to use what she knew as a way of making Margaret give him up. Make her stand aside . . .'

'Chuffing hell, this is giving me a headache,' Noakes grouched. 'Talk about fricking musical chairs.'

'Perdita might not have thought Margaret had murdered anyone,' Markham mused. 'She might even have been suspicious of *Peter* not Margaret . . . But something she said made Margaret decide to kill her.'

'Hey, perhaps Peter Hart *is* in on it.' Doyle's mind roamed the possibilities. 'A husband-and-wife team . . . *Accomplices*.'

The DI shook his head.

'I somehow don't see Hart as a murderer, and there's nothing to show he knew anything about his wife's obsession,' he said. 'I think back in the day Margaret was unhinged about Warrender, which led to her murdering Catriona. But then she married Peter Hart and compartmentalised her feelings for Warrender, put them in a box and threw away the key. Everything nice and neat and tidy . . .'

Doyle saw where this was going. 'Until Catriona's body turned up under that staircase, opening up a whole new can of worms.' Worms being the operative word here, Markham thought.

A thought struck the DC. 'D'you think De'Ath guessed who wrote the letters?' he asked.

'Who can tell what was in that creepo's mind,' Noakes muttered. 'Most likely he was gearing up for a spot of blackmail hisself . . . Warrender or Payne, take your pick.'

'Long shot but hear me out,' said Markham. 'Maybe he *knew* but held his tongue out of compassion. Then the bodies began piling up and he panicked . . . didn't know what to do.'

'*Diddums.*' Noakes was unsympathetic. 'Next you'll be telling me he planned to go an' hear Payne's confession, forgive her sins an' all that jazz.'

'Stranger things have happened, Sergeant.'

'An' Skeffers?'

'I don't imagine those two have many secrets from each other,' Markham said grimly as he began to tidy away the debris of their meal. 'I doubt we'll ever know what else they removed from Catriona Rowlands's room or what it was she'd uncovered about them. But, whatever motivated De'Ath to keep those letters in the first place, we can safely assume he and Skeffington decided they'd do best to hand them over.' Heavily, he added, 'Sherwin will keep its secrets and Oxbridge omertà makes it unlikely we'll get to the bottom of the Culpeper Society and its sleazy doings. But at least the letters gave us the first chink of light.'

'I reckon De'Ath an' Skeffington would've put the squeeze on Warrender cos of all that juicy detail an' the stuff about him getting Rowlands pregnant,' Noakes declared. 'Might even have tried it on with Payne too if they pegged her for Mrs Poison Pen.'

'You mean tried to extort money from them?' Doyle asked.

The DS scowled. 'Money, favours, kickbacks . . . all sorts . . .'

'Maybe it was the *bursar* they planned to target,' Doyle suggested. 'If those rumours about his homosexual activities were true — as in all that stuff Catriona dug up for the *Confidential* — then he'd be desperate to stop the scandal flaring up again. If De'Ath and Skeffington handed those letters over to the police along with a tip-off about Greaves's sexual history suggesting *he* was the one with the hots for Warrender, that would spell disaster for him . . . he'd go a long way to prevent it happening.'

'It's one possibility, Constable,' the DI said. 'If they guessed Margaret Payne was the author, they may even have thought about blackmailing her husband. But for some reason the letters became too hot to handle, or they feared for their own safety.' He sank back on to the chesterfield. 'Prudence dictated that they hand the letters over.'

'After three people had died,' Noakes said, disgusted.

'Yes, they'll have it on their conscience,' Markham told him.

'Don' reckon they have any,' his wingman muttered grinding his heel into the carpet as though he wished it was a tender portion of De'Ath's anatomy. Suddenly, he sat up. '*Hey*, what about the limp?'

'What limp?' Doyle was bewildered.

'Remember, the security attendant woman at the museum thought Belinda met someone with a limp. Anyone notice if Margaret Payne walked funny?'

'Foot drop,' Burton said slowly.

'*Eh*?' Noakes stared at her.

'Sheila Payne mentioned it when we went for coffee in the covered market — I've only just remembered. She had her bicycle with her . . . was joking about taking your life in your hands round Oxford. Said something about Margaret never cycling because she'd had Polio as a child and it left her with a weak ankle which played up when she was under stress . . .'

'*Under stress*,' breathed Doyle. 'She must've been pretty stressed doing what she did in that museum . . . bashing someone's head in and then strolling out like she was just another visitor.'

'Okay, so she's a hop-along,' Noakes said. 'Where's it leave us?'

'It's another piece of the jigsaw, Noakesy,' the DI said. 'As I see it, Margaret Payne is shaping up to be our prime suspect.'

'She don't look the part,' the DS cavilled. 'I mean, imagine trying to persuade a jury that someone who dresses like that's a cold-hearted killer . . . more like a trainee nun if you ask me.'

'Yeah,' Doyle chimed in. 'Payne looks like the worst thing she's ever done is hand an essay in late.'

'This whole thing started *twenty years ago*,' Burton reminded them impatiently, 'when they were all students. I'm willing to bet with some digging it'll turn out that Margaret Payne wasn't so squeaky clean after all. We'll need to try the Warneford and the other psychiatric facilities to see if she was known to them . . . adolescent mental health issues, that kind of thing.'

'Good idea, Kate. You're on that,' the DI approved as she scribbled furiously in her notebook. Noakes and Doyle in the meantime studiously averted their eyes. No way did they fancy a tour of the local mental health clinics, especially not after what happened during the Newman Hospital investigation. As Doyle put it, these days just watching series three of *The Fall* brought him out in hives, so a trip down memory lane was the last thing he needed. Burton was welcome to it.

'How about the husband?' Noakes asked. 'Assuming he twigged what she'd done, couldn't *he* have killed Ernie an' the women to protect her? Like Doyle said, they're this kissy kissy couple . . . mebbe she came clean to him an' he did the caped crusader bit . . . mebbe it were *him* down by the river . . .'

'But what about the museum, sarge?' Doyle objected. 'Peter Hart would have been too noticeable there, he'd have stood out, and he doesn't fit the security woman's description.'

Noakes rolled his eyes in exasperation. 'Perhaps it were turn an' turn about an' *she* did the museum one while *he* took care of the lass in that lift thingy.'

Burton consulted her notebook. 'They're each other's alibi for Ernie and Perdita — assuming Perdita died after the carol concert . . .'

'She did,' the DI told them. 'Dr Merrick confirmed it happened some time just after midnight.'

'Alibis for Belinda Lycett aren't corroborated,' Burton continued. 'Apparently, Hart was at work in his office while Margaret was in and out of the Bodleian. Both of them had an opportunity to get round to the museum.'

Noakes puffed his cheeks out and performed the tuneless whistle with which he was wont to accompany deep thought.

'She's jus' so *dull*,' he said at length. 'If you'd said *Sheila* Payne, then I'd buy it. You can imagine *her* seething away an' writing sexy letters but *Ugly Betty* . . .'

'Margaret Payne's not ugly,' Markham pointed out. 'Far from it. She just plays her looks down.'

'Maybe that's how Hart likes her,' Doyle agreed. 'You know, understated, demure and natural.' He shot his mentor a glance. 'Plenty of guys aren't comfortable with vampy.'

Markham smothered a grin, aware from the CID grapevine that the young DC had had his fingers burned after various romantic liaisons turned sour. Small wonder if these days he no longer cared to live dangerously.

'I'm *jus' saying*,' Noakes retorted huffily. 'With Sheila or Sarah Rowlands you could imagine 'em stalking a bloke an' going off on one . . . even the bird who loved Catriona . . . But Margaret Payne don' look like she's got it in her.'

'*Slow burn*, Noakesy,' the DI said with conviction. He turned to Kate Burton. 'When we were talking about Tudor history, you mentioned the woman who betrayed Anne Boleyn and Catherine Howard . . .'

'That's right, guv.' Burton was eager. 'Lady Rochford. The college is named after her husband's family.'

Surreptitiously, Noakes and Doyle exchanged the mother of all eye rolls.

David Starkey eat your heart out. Stroke of luck them missing Burton's seminar on the Tudors.

'You described Lady Jane as being stuck on the margin of other people's lives, weaving webs like a spider,' Markham commented.

'Yes, guv. She was kind of obscure and overlooked. That's why she lived her life vicariously through folk who were more glamorous.'

'And presumably that's what made her so dangerous,' the DI observed.

'Too right . . . In the end, she went off her head in the Tower of London before being executed.'

Well aware that the other two considered all of this thoroughly yawn worthy, Markham said, 'Your description of Lady Rochford stuck with me, Kate. I think subconsciously I must have sensed we were looking for a woman who watched Catriona Rowlands from the shadows and hated her for being everything she was not.'

'Low self-esteem which turned to psychosis . . .' Burton was re-energising on the spot.

'Something like that, yes,' the DI agreed. 'After Margaret met Peter Hart, the demons went underground and she rebuilt her life.' Markham smiled at her rapt attention. 'But they were only dormant,' he continued, 'and when Catriona's remains were dragged out from under that staircase, the old pathology stirred again . . . like that two-forked serpent in the painting on the wall of the chapel, the one you couldn't tear your eyes away from at the memorial service . . .'

'The William Blake, sir.'

Noakes cleared his throat nosily. The Tudors were bad enough, but if they got started on poetry and paintings god alone knew where it would end.

'So Margaret Payne's a psycho,' he said. 'Which means she musta done the bit with the graffiti an' flower.'

'I'd forgotten about that, Sergeant.' Wonderingly, Markham recalled the word WHORE and the broken rose petals. 'Looking back, it strikes me as something a woman would do.'

'I said them letters were *girly* too,' Noakes observed complacently.

'So you did.'

The DS looked triumphant. 'And she had roses in her study.'

It was true. Markham wondered now how he could have missed it.

The DI crossed the room and leaned against the window, resting his forehead on the frosty panes, welcoming the damp chill against his skin.

Next door, Plessington College's garden lay silent, the milky glow of floodlights illuminating the tracks of small creatures who pattered unseen and unheard around the edges of the night.

Kate Burton's voice broke into his thoughts.

'Peter Hart could be at risk,' she said.

'Unless he's in on it with her,' Doyle countered.

Slowly, Markham turned to face his team. 'I don't think he is,' the DI said. 'But in any event, we need to locate him.'

'What about Warrender?' Noakes demanded. 'It was all about *him* in the first place so what's to stop her going Tonto an' topping him too?' His eyes narrowed speculatively. 'Mebbe we c'n use lover boy to bring her in,' he said craftily. 'Set a trap with him as bait. It'd bleeding serve him right.'

The DI came to a decision.

He looked at his watch.

'Give Peter Hart a call at home will you, Kate,' he said. 'They live in one of those large Victorian terraced affairs out in Summertown. He should be there this time of night.'

'What if Margaret answers?'

'Play for time. Tell her you're checking alibis again, routine stuff . . . whatever it takes to make her think she's off the hook.'

'And if I manage to get hold of Hart, sir?' Burton suddenly looked wan and peaky as she sat hunched over her notebook. The case was clearly getting to her. Even Noakes and Doyle had shed their usual air of assumed nonchalance.

'Ask him to come in and meet us here, Kate.' The DI paused. 'Tell him to be discreet and say nothing to anyone, even his wife.'

She slipped out of the room, mobile already in her hand.

'Won't that give him a heads-up, boss?' Doyle enquired. 'If he's got any inkling, it might push him into confronting her or something.'

'I think we have to take the risk, Constable.' Their chief's face clouded. 'Somehow we need to bring Margaret Payne in.' *Before anyone else dies*. 'And perhaps we can find a way to reach her through Hart.' Now he was on his feet. 'The clock's running down,' he said. 'Kate's mental health trawl can wait till we've got her in custody . . . We have to move *now*.'

Burton slipped back into the room, her face troubled.

'No answer, sir. Of course, he could be out on faculty business or have a social appointment.'

'Not Hart,' Noakes jeered. 'He's a real Horlicks. *Newsnight*'s as good as it gets.'

Icy fear gripped Markham.

'I've got a bad feeling about this,' he said quietly. 'Let's get over there right now.'

Such was the DI's certainty, that no one demurred.

Sheepishly, Noakes reached under a cushion and produced a crushed fedora with side feather.

Christ, he's not actually going to wear that thing, is he? Doyle wondered, aghast. *Oxford's answer to Humphrey Bogart . . .*

'Present from the missus,' his mentor said gruffly, pulling the hat down over his brows.

As he contemplated George Noakes's demonstration of matrimonial devotion, Markham wondered if Peter Hart's fidelity to his wife would help or hinder them.

Either way, he sensed the climax of the college murders was close at hand.

14. FINISH LINE

Little was said as they headed to the house in Summertown, Kate Burton driving with her usual caution.

It was snowing hard, drifts clothing Oxford's ancient buildings in purest white. The beauty took Markham's breath away.

'Makes everything look different,' Noakes grunted prosaically.

'Did you ever go sledging here when you were a student, sir?' Doyle asked shyly, contemplating the smooth inviting expanse of St Giles.

'Yes, in the University Parks,' Markham said with a smile. 'That was the best place for snow-banks and for building snow-castles and caverns . . . until they collapsed from the sheer weight of it. I remember the local wildlife used to watch in astonishment as if they thought we were mad. But there's nothing like snow to bring out one's inner child.'

'I don't like the way everything looks black against it . . . like the negative of a photo,' his mentor said.

Markham smiled to himself. There was definitely a poet somewhere in George Noakes . . . perhaps wearing that gruesome trilby or fedora or whatever it was had helped tap a vein of artistic self-expression.

But the DS's mind had turned swiftly to other matters.

'Was Warrender really Mr Charisma?' There was something almost wistful about Noakes's question.

'He was what we called a "hearty", the DI said wryly. 'The sportsmen always had a certain cachet.'

'What made him so special, though?' Noakes was grappling with the conundrum. 'I mean, special enough that someone'd *kill* . . .'

'We're talking about someone with possible monomania and tunnel vision, sarge,' Burton piped up. 'Don't forget, we've come across it before,' she added. 'There was the book club case, remember. *De Clérambault Syndrome*.'

Doyle shifted restlessly. Any minute now, Burton would launch into extracts from that creepy psychology manual she was always lugging around.

But catching sight of the DC's expression in her rear-view mirror, she refrained from any catechising.

'I think Margaret Payne was in the grip of an erotic obsession which prevented her from thinking straight,' she said. 'More than likely, Warrender never spared her a second glance but she wove some kind of fantasy around him in which they were meant to be together.'

'How come she were able to go on an' have a normal life afterwards?' Noakes sounded genuinely interested.

Doyle was drawn into the debate. 'Maybe she was frightened of herself after what happened with Catriona? I dunno. Maybe that brought her to her senses . . . realising she'd committed murder.'

'She met Peter Hart the following year,' Markham pointed out. 'It seems probable she transferred the romantic intensity to *him*.'

'But you can't jus' wipe out *murder* like it never happened,' Noakes protested. 'All them threats an' letter-writing an' then throttling a lass . . . you couldn't simply blank it all out an' go on like normal . . .'

'You could if you were in a state of dissociation.' Carefully, Burton eased her way along Oakthorpe Road, aware of potholes lurking beneath the powdery snow. 'Like when you cut off from reality and pretend that bad things never happened or that you weren't even responsible . . .'

It was too much for Noakes to take in. 'How the frick does someone manage *that* for twenty years?'

'If she sealed off the past — like a watertight container — so that nothing seeped in.' Burton sought for analogies, but the baffled faces of her colleagues made her switch to simplicity. 'It's a sort of mental defence mechanism,' she said finally. 'Helps stop the personality from fracturing so people can function even after going through terrible experiences.'

'Yeah, I've heard about that.' Doyle was intrigued despite himself. 'Post-traumatic amnesia or something. They thought that Green Beret might have had it, the U.S. army surgeon who murdered his wife and kids. He got off at his first trial and then they convicted him ten years later. What was his name?'

'Jeffrey MacDonald, the ice pick killings,' Noakes replied promptly. He wasn't an *American Justice* addict for nothing, and true crime documentaries were Mrs Noakes's secret vice. 'The guy's still inside, a one-man freak show. They think he coulda whacked the family an' then buried it in his subconscious.' A prodigious sniff. 'Me, I reckon he's just a twenty-four-carat psycho.'

'Oh yes, I remember that case. There's a brilliant book about it, *Fatal Vision*,' Burton said enthusiastically. 'It argued the amnesia might've been why MacDonald was able to carry off the grieving widower pose.' Typically, Burton waited at an intersection, looking both ways even though the streets were practically deserted and there was no other traffic about. 'If Margaret Payne experienced something like that, it would explain how she was able to get her act together in the aftermath of Catriona's murder —take her degree, marry Peter Hart and generally move on with her life.'

Noakes frowned. 'Wouldn't memories come crawling out of the woodwork after a while? An' wouldn't she need to see a trick cyclist, y'know, to make sure she . . . well, didn't do it again? *Hey*,' Noakes's exclamation nearly sent Burton off the road, 'mebbe she *did* do it again . . . mebbe there's other bodies out there waiting to be found.'

'I don't think so, Sergeant.' Markham's tone was one of quiet certitude. 'Margaret Payne held down a successful academic career and marriage for the last two decades. That suggests she managed to force the genie back into the bottle.'

'Do you reckon she never gave Catriona Rowlands another thought then, guv?' Doyle sounded awe-struck at such an exercise in dissimulation.

'I don't have the psychological expertise to answer that question, Constable,' Markham told him. 'But I think there must have been a mental safety-mechanism in place . . . initially some kind of dissociative reaction followed by denial on an epic scale. Maybe she managed to persuade herself *she* was the victim and *Catriona* the aggressor. Most likely she somehow justified what had happened and then buried it.' Much as she had buried her victim's body.

'How the chuff did she cope with working in Oxford? I mean, the lass's body was round the corner from Rochford, for crying out loud. Mouldering away under that staircase the same time Payne was prancing round in a fancy gown doing her tutor bit. That's fricking *unnatural*.' Noakes rummaged under his hat, scratching viciously before jamming it firmly down again in a sure sign of agitation.

'That's the whole point, Noakesy.' The DI was gentle. 'The woman was — is still, possibly — very seriously disturbed. You or I wouldn't be capable of managing that degree of compartmentalisation and split-level thinking, but *she* was able to detach.'

'How come the obsession with Warrender didn't start up again later?' Doyle wondered. 'Surely she couldn't switch it off just like that.'

Markham considered this. 'Oh, I think the explosion of rage at Catriona might have shocked her out of it, cauterised the violent impulses, if you like. You said it before,

Constable. She would have been frightened at herself . . . And then there was the transference to Peter Hart.'

'She only started killing again when her perfect life looked like it was going to unravel,' Burton said. 'When the secret of what happened to Catriona was going to come out—'

'Unless she silenced people,' Noakes concluded.

'Essentially, yes.' Burton turned into Ewert Place. 'The discovery of Catriona's remains must have flipped a switch so that all the psychological defences she'd erected came crashing down.'

'I still can't imagine how she lived with that hanging over her all those years,' Doyle mused.

'She would have felt safe enough as time went on.' Noakes's face darkened as he recalled McMaster's shambolic site management. 'Even when they dug up the bones under staircase eleven. There were plenty of other people who hated Rowlands. She jus' had to stick with the Mother Teresa act and cling to hubby's arm.'

'But Margaret lost control of the narrative,' Markham said softly. 'She didn't count on Ernie remembering the past or Belinda Lycett manipulating the situation to her own ends. And then there was Perdita — predatory, suspicious — looking to move in on her husband . . . threatening to destroy everything she'd salvaged. No,' he added emphatically, 'the cards just didn't fall her way.'

'And finally, De'Ath handed over the letters.' Doyle punched the air. '*Back of the net!*' he exclaimed boyishly to Markham's amusement.

'It was your Olivia really cracked it, guv,' Noakes observed with proprietorial pride in his boss's sharp-eyed girlfriend, 'linking it to that stuff in Rochford's archives . . . the Yank connection an' all that.' The DS motioned towards the dreadful fedora almost as though he meant to tip his hat to Markham's partner. 'It's like ole times having her in on a case.'

Better not let the DCI get wind of it, though, Markham told himself grimly. Sidney was ever apt to weaponize Markham's 'lady friend' with whom it had been a case of mutual loathing at first sight.

At Noakes's words, Burton's hands stilled on the steering wheel, but the moment passed and then she was turning into Ferry Pool Road with its elegant terrace houses.

She drew up and cut the engine. 'It's that one diagonally opposite. Number forty-eight.'

'What happens if Payne's there?' Doyle asked anxiously. 'Do we make an arrest or what?'

'As things stand, we don't have a case against her,' the DI said. 'It's all purely circumstantial.'

'Even if De'Ath fingers her as the poison pen?' the DC pressed.

'Still not enough,' came the reply.

'An' she'd be lawyered up in a jiffy,' Noakes put in gloomily. 'The bigwigs would see to that.'

Doyle came back with another question. 'What about physical evidence?'

'What about it?' Noakes growled. 'No trace of any weapon an' she'd have worn gloves.'

'Then there's the usual issues with flawed DNA transfer, secondary touch and cross-contamination plus degradation of samples for Catriona and Ernie cos of where they were found.' Burton pursed her lips. 'I don't see us being able to make it stand up just on the forensics.'

'No, we need a confession.' Markham gazed at the Victorian house enveloped in snow like some delicate frangipane confection.

'Let's get going,' he said. 'If they're both at home, we invite them in for questioning. Make it low-key, unthreatening . . . easy as you like.' His voice sharpened. 'If it's just Hart, we find out where his wife is and put surveillance on her. In the meantime, we hole up with him at Sherwin and see where that takes us.'

Noakes gave the house a critical once-over.

'It's like Inspector Morse's gaff,' he said. 'Looks like they've done alright for themselves.'

They crunched across the snow to the front door and tried the old-fashioned bell pull.

Once, twice, three times.

Finally, the door opened.

There was an air of defeated resignation about Peter Hart. Nevertheless, the professor greeted them courteously, explaining that his sister-in-law had texted his wife asking her to come over while he put in a few hours work having left the telephone off the hook. He wasn't expecting her back till much later.

Markham had the feeling that the man already knew what they had come to tell him.

* * *

Nothing was said, however, until they were in Hart's study, a cluttered but cosy space dominated by floor-to-ceiling bookshelves and what Markham recognised as Nigerian antiques arrayed along an impressive mantlepiece.

There was something rigidly sculpted about Hart's own features, the DI reflected, once they were seated in fraying Hepplewhite armchairs and a leather two-seater that had seen better days. The professor, meanwhile, sat behind his mahogany desk facing into the room, as though glad to have this barrier between himself and the detectives. Outside the study window, snowflakes were whirling thickly in the back garden.

'You *know*, don't you?' he said, with something infinitely weary in the sound of the words.

Gently but inexorably, Markham laid out their case against Hart's wife as the man listened without uttering a word.

At the conclusion of the recital, he reached out and rested his hand on the bronze head of an Igbo warrior which stood on the desk blotter, before straightening in his chair as though he had received a transfusion of strength.

'Yes,' he said simply in the velvety tones that had struck so pleasurably on Markham's ear in their initial interview.

'When did you realise, sir?' the DI asked gently.

'Not for certain until I saw you coming up the path. But I knew there was *something*. It was at the memorial service. I caught her looking at Dr Warrender and, I don't know how it was, suddenly in that instant I had the thought that she might have harmed Catriona. But then it seemed ridiculous, so I pushed it away.'

Markham recalled the sibilant hiss Kate Burton claimed to have heard on that occasion . . . the exhalation of Margaret Payne's hatred, perhaps . . .

'Two more women *died* for crying out loud.' Noakes hadn't taken off his ridiculous trilby and the quill jiggled with each jerk of his head. 'Why didn't you tell us you thought she'd done Rowlands an' the scout?'

'I had no proof, Sergeant. And this was my *wife*.' The response was terse but dignified. 'I *love* her . . . and I didn't want it to be true.'

Christ, thought Noakes, *they're two of a bleeding kind when it comes to kidding themselves.*

'And those alibis?' Burton prompted. 'What about Ernie Braithwaite?'

'Margaret always jogged by herself in the mornings before we went out together.' He made a clicking sound in his throat. 'Hard to imagine she could do anything like that to her old scout.' Again, his hand caressed the bronze warrior and once more the contact seemed to calm him. 'When Belinda died, I honestly didn't connect what had happened with Margaret . . . there wasn't any reason to. It just seemed like one of those random crimes.'

'What about all the aggro over her not getting onto the PhD course?' Noakes rumbled. 'Didn't you think it was odd your least favourite student getting her head bashed in like that?'

The liquid eyes held nothing but sadness.

'I had nothing personal against Belinda,' Hart said. 'I was merely concerned to maintain departmental standards.'

The exquisitely moulded lips twisted. 'What happened struck me as a horrible coincidence, nothing more than that.'

'But eventually you began to have doubts about Margaret, correct?' the DI pressed.

'I had a feeling something was dreadfully wrong, but it was as if there was this vast chasm between us and I couldn't bridge it . . .'

'Very *poetic*.' Noakes's feather was once more aquiver. 'An' you *still* didn't work out she mighta done for Ernie an' the lass in the museum?'

Hart's eyes kindled with something close to anger. 'Actually, I didn't know for certain until you turned up here on my doorstep this evening, Sergeant. Then suddenly everything fell into place.'

Markham could believe it. A man like Hart — cultured, detached, immersed in academia — might continue as blind as a mole until some crystallising moment woke him to the truth.

'You felt something was wrong with Margaret,' the DI prompted. 'Had there been problems before?'

'She'd experienced neurotic episodes as a student before we got together and became engaged. I believe she saw a therapist for a time . . . CBT, that kind of thing. Naturally I didn't pry.'

If the thought crossed the detectives' minds that it might have been better for all concerned if he *had*, none of them voiced it.

'You say that at the memorial service you sensed your wife had unusual feelings for Dr Warrender,' Markham resumed.

'I wasn't sure what it was. But there was something . . . It made me uneasy.'

'What about Ms Cargill-Thompson?' Burton wanted to know what had happened with the final victim.

'Shortly before the carol concert at Sherwin, I heard Perdita and Margaret having an argument about something. I only caught the tail end of it but Mags seemed fine afterwards . . . laughed it off. Said it was something about the Hilary timetable. She was very convincing. I told myself I'd got it all wrong.'

'You and Ms Cargill-Thompson didn't attend the concert, sir,' Burton continued.

'No, I had a deadline . . . a submission for the OUP.' A swift glance at Noakes's glowering features. 'I wasn't with Peri. She was out of sorts and said she had things to do.

'Do you recall what time Margaret got home?' she asked.

'I wasn't aware of her coming to bed, but I usually take a sleeping pill after an "essay crisis".' The handsome face crumpled momentarily then, touching the bronze talisman, he recovered his composure. 'You have to believe me when I say I had no idea of her harming anyone. She went off to that concert as though she didn't have a care in the world. We had a G&T before she left . . . she was on good form.'

Markham recollected Payne's demeanour that evening, her lips curving with amusement at the sight of Noakes snoring his head off. Sharing the joke with Sheila.

Sheila.

He was struck by an unwelcome memory.

'Your sister-in-law seems close to Jon Warrender,' the DI said quietly.

'Yes, they're —what do you call it? — "having a thing", I believe.'

The atmosphere in the room was suddenly electric with tension.

'Does Margaret know about this, sir?' Burton asked urgently.

'No, she wouldn't approve at all. He's married and Mags takes a dim view of what she calls Sheila's guttersnipe lifestyle.'

Slender fingers closed convulsively on the Igbo bronze head.

'You think Sheila could be in danger,' Hart said.

The DI met his gaze squarely. 'I think if Margaret suddenly found out about her sister's liaison with Warrender, that might precipitate a crisis.'

'You mean it might tip her over the edge? A psychotic episode or something?'

'It's possible, yes.' Markham's outer calm gave no sign of his racing thoughts. 'Are you quite *sure* Margaret doesn't know about Sheila's liaison with Dr Warrender?'

Hart's eyes flickered. 'I couldn't say for certain,' he replied hesitantly. 'Sheila admitted it to me after I saw them together in Browns, but I think she knew not to tell Mags.' His voice held a pleading note. 'They're very close despite having such different personalities. Mags could never hurt her, *surely* . . .'

'Where do Sheila an' Warrender have it off? Her place? College? Somewhere else?' Noakes was never one to go round the houses, and it looked like Payne's sister could well cop it unless they got to her first.

'She told me it's never at her flat,' Hart said swiftly. With some embarrassment he added, 'They like out-of-the-way hidey holes, use Latimer College from time to time . . . Folly Tower's quite picturesque.'

The DI stared at him.

'I didn't think there was access to the public,' he said.

'Warrender and his wife contributed to maintenance work, "Friends of Folly Tower".' Hart grimaced. 'Benefactors get to have their own keys, more for the honour and glory than anything else . . . a bit of one-upmanship . . . you know, impress the relatives when they come down for a visit.'

Markham's voice sounded oddly disembodied to his own ears. 'So Warrender has a key?'

'Yes, Sheila said he got one cut for her, too. . .' Hart faltered. 'It's just now and again on a whim.' He looked incredulously at the detectives, scanning each face in turn. 'You think that's where they are . . . Margaret and Sheila . . . you think they've gone *there*?'

'I think in the aftermath of finding Perdita's body, Sheila may well have felt vulnerable,' Markham said. 'Maybe she had doubts about Warrender, wondered if he could be the murderer . . . felt the urge to confide in her sister.'

Hart looked stricken. 'Her text said she wanted to tell Mags something and it was *personal* . . . Oh my god . . .'

The DI stood up followed by his subordinates.

'We'll check Sheila's flat. If they're not there, we'll try the folly,' he said.

'Do you want backup, sir?' Burton asked, mobile in hand.

'Not yet, but I'd like you to call Dr Warrender's address.' In response to her interrogative glance, he added, 'I don't *think* she'll try to lure him to Latimer — too risky taking on him and Sheila together — but if she's decompensating, we can't know for sure.'

Burton slipped into the hall.

'I'm coming with you,' Peter Hart said, a muscle twitching violently in his cheek. 'Maybe I can get through to her.' Hoarsely, he pleaded, 'You see, I feel responsible. I didn't want to accept the truth.'

'Very well, sir.' Markham nodded to Doyle. 'Take Professor Hart to the car please, Constable.'

The DC led Margaret Payne's husband out of the room.

'What d'you reckon Payne's got planned?' Noakes grunted, his phlegmatic nonchalance belied by the keenness of his glance.

'What do *you* think, Noakesy?'

'Something that makes it look like Sheila topped herself out of guilt cos she's the killer.'

'A staged suicide?'

'Yeah . . . She don't know we've sussed her, see, so she'll try to pin the murders on Little Sis.'

Burton came back into the room.

'Dr Warrender answered, sir. I just blagged it . . . pretended I was checking something on his alibi for Perdita.'

'Excellent. So Margaret hadn't been in touch?'

'No, sir. And the neighbours were there — I could hear them in the background — so he's home for the foreseeable.'

'Thank god for that,' the DI said with feeling. 'Right, let's step on it. No blues and twos, everything under the radar.'

They stepped out into Ferry Pool Road where curtains were drawn cosily against the snowy night and Christmas tree lights twinkled like little beacons.

Beholding the tinselled fripperies of the season, Markham was struck by the hideous incongruity of their mission.

It might be the season of Santa and sugarplums, but *they* had a killer to catch.

* * *

As the DI had anticipated, there was no answer at Sheila Payne's flat in Cowley.

'Right, let's head for Latimer College,' he instructed.

There was no conversation as they drove across the city blanketed in snow.

Oxford had never looked so ethereal and remote, Markham reflected as they went through Tyburn Gates and past Latimer College's Archbishop Laud annexe which looked as though it was enveloped in a fleecy christening robe.

Some words from Olivia's favourite Shakespeare play came into his mind.

Call me but love, and I'll be new baptised.

Jon Warrender had never called Margaret Payne 'love' and because of that four people had to die.

On they went towards Folly Tower.

Parked to the left of the path leading up to Latimer's picturesque landmark was a small Fiat Punto.

'That's Margaret's car,' Peter Hart whispered.

The DI felt an exultant leap of the heart at this confirmation that his instincts had been right and the killer had chosen her sister's trysting place with Jon Warrender to enact the final scene of the drama. Then the exultation suddenly drained away as Markham wondered whether they were too late to save Sheila Payne.

To the killer's wildly skewed perception, it must seem that her sister had inflicted the ultimate betrayal in taking up with the man whose unattainability had set her on the path to multiple murder.

Would Sheila have been able to talk her sister down from that invisible ledge she had walked all these years unbeknown to everyone around her? Or had paranoia engulfed the killer in a replay of what happened two decades ago with Catriona Rowlands?

The tower came into sight, magically transformed by its icy carapace into a frosted masterpiece. The two saints on the clockface were unrecognisable in snowy cowls, but Markham's eyes barely skimmed them as he took in the octagon.

The oak door stood wide open.

It was as if the killer was beckoning them into the heart of the web.

The little group obeyed the summons . . .

On the other side of the door was a musty vestibule.

Harsh electric lighting illuminated a spiral stone staircase cut into the left-hand wall leading upwards. On the right-hand side, a set of steep steps led down into the crypt.

Guided by instinct, the DI led them down towards the crypt.

The rotunda was just as he remembered, with hook-nosed Bishop Latimer sculpted in white granite at the centre presiding over twelve Portland stone spokes that radiated outwards along the tessellated pink marble floor. Twelve for Christ and his apostles, each branch bearing three or four sarcophagi. A strange mosaic of the Protestant martyrs sent to the stake by Mary Tudor lined the chamber, the flames of the Smithfield Fires licking their way round the walls in eerie orange, purple and yellow crescents. Markham found himself looking for the wizened monkey features of Anne Askew, carried to her death in a chair because she had been so brutally racked she could not walk . . . As a student, he had wondered why the artist did not make this bride of Christ more angelic . . .

Then another set of features swam into focus with the foreshortened faces of the martyrs.

Margaret Payne stood a little to the right of the mosaic's sinewy stake piled high with faggots to which the martyrs were bound, a bat-winged Satan with red-hot eyes capering about their feet.

The woman's breath came in gasps as if she had been running. She did not acknowledge her husband.

'Inspector, thank heaven you're here. I think Sheila must have lost her mind.'

Markham waited. Something in his silence must have alerted her.

Claw hands tightened on her trench coat.

'She insisted I drive her out here then started ranting and raving about sins of the past. I thought she was going to attack me, but she just ran off.'

And still Markham didn't speak.

Beads of sweat broke out on the woman's pale forehead.

'Mags, sweetheart,' her husband said, from behind Markham. 'It's over . . . *We know*.'

A shocking transformation came over the schoolgirl features as they contorted into a mask so full of malevolence as to rival Satan's sly leer. The pleasant dry tones sank to a hiss. 'You know *nothing*.'

Noakes shambled forward, removing his hat. 'Best take this off, hadn't I,' he said conversationally to Margaret Payne, 'seeing as we're practically in church.'

The sheer ordinariness of it took her by surprise. The mad light went out of her eyes and she looked bewildered.

'My missus were in love with a fella once,' Noakes continued as though they were the only two people in the place. 'Came close to ruining her life for him . . . And she mighta done if things had fallen out differently.' He rubbed the nap of his hat and became more confidential still. 'I don't mind telling you, the whole thing ripped me guts out . . . turned me into someone else for a while. Proper nasty . . . till I got help.'

The DI hardly dared breathe. Tears pricked his eyes. It was the nearest Noakes would ever come to revealing the painful backstory of the Bluebell case. And all for the sake of the tormented woman in front of them and a life that hung in the balance.

Noakes's small shrewd eyes held a wealth of understanding. 'You cared too much about someone an' that sent you down the wrong path when you were only a kid. Coulda happened to anyone.' Steadily, the DS advanced nearer to her. 'An' then later on . . . We know you didn't really want to kill folk. You jus' panicked. But look here, lass, you've still got something to live for, that's why your fella's here.'

Something rippled across Margaret Payne's features as she looked at the tall figure of her husband and her face seemed to clear. Doyle said later that it was almost as though she'd been exorcised or something.

Then her gaze returned to Noakes. She didn't speak but gestured upwards so it looked like she was praying, mirroring the upraised hands of the martyrs on the mosaic behind her.

'The belfry?' Markham prompted gently. 'Is that where Sheila is?'

An infinitesimal nod.

'Noakes, with me,' he rapped. 'The rest of you stay here.'

He nodded to Kate Burton who began reciting the words of the caution.

Replacing his hat with a sweeping gesture that was almost courtly, Noakes promptly followed the DI.

* * *

The stone steps leading to the upper floor were of polished masonry. They felt regular and solid underfoot, but there were no bannisters and only the light from downstairs to guide them. The DI kept close to the wall while Noakes advanced slowly as a snail, finally getting down on his hands and knees and feeling before him inch by cautious inch.

Markham had never been up to the clocktower, having previously only visited the rotunda. It felt like climbing up an exposed scaffold and for a moment he wondered if Margaret

Payne had sent them on a wild goose chase, intending them to break their necks trying to a rescue a woman who was already dead. The mere thought of it brought the sweat out on his body and turned his joints to water. With angry courage, he forced the fear down.

At last they reached their goal, the vertiginous ascent leaving them panting and giddy.

But there was no sign of Sheila on the narrow landing at the top of the dim shaft. Just a low doorway, a battered cupboard flush against the stone wall and bare floorboards spattered with bird droppings.

'Bound to be bats an' chuff knows what up here,' Noakes muttered, squinting about him and gingerly testing the planks on which they stood.

He looked up through an open trapdoor above them.

'Well, Sis ain't in that attic thingy,' he concluded through chattering teeth. 'D'you think that poor cow down there,' with a jerk of the thumb, 'is having us on?' He revolved slowly in the cramped space. 'I'll jus' check this broom cupboard wotsit over here. Nope, only a statue,' he announced with some puzzlement. 'With a sort of hook jobbie on the back.'

Markham felt a premonitory tingling in his palms as the cupboard disclosed St Eanswythe's long painted curls.

The dark-haired saint who resembled Sheila Payne.

'What is it, guv?'

Markham was remembering their arrival at the folly.

There had been *two* statues covered with snow standing either side of the clock in front of their arches. They had seemed to him like Trappist monks in their long white cowls . . .

Ignoring Noakes's alarmed cries, he plunged through the doorway onto the clockface's narrow stone balustrade.

'Give me a hand, Sergeant . . . *Quickly*!'

'*What the . . . ?*'

It looked to Noakes at first as though his boss was embracing the right-hand statue in some sort of religious delirium. Then the snow-shrouded form moaned, and he understood.

'There's a belt holding her up,' Markham muttered. 'It's fastened to that hook behind on the wall.'

Heaving and tugging with numb fingers, they finally succeeded in freeing Sheila Payne and half-dragged half-carried her between them through the doorway to the top of the shaft.

'Ring for backup and an ambulance, Noakes.'

With much cursing and blowing on his fingers, the DS managed it at the third attempt.

'Is she alive?' he asked Markham who was frantically brushing heaped snow from the shrouded figure and chafing its frozen hands.

'Yes, but I think she's in shock and likely suffering from hyperthermia. Let's put our coats over her.'

It seemed an eternity before they heard the sirens below and voices calling up to them.

As paramedics winched the casualty down to ground level, the DI placed a hand on Noakes's arm.

'You did well back there, Sergeant,' he said simply.

'I tole the lass she had summat to live for, guv, but it were a lie. A big fat lie.' Despite the bitter cold, the DS now looked too warm, fanning himself furiously with the trusty trilby. A downcast expression stole across the lived-in features. 'She'll be in the funny farm for god knows how long,' he muttered. 'Prob'ly be a hundred by the time they reckon she's safe to be let out.'

'Love is never wasted, Sergeant,' Markham said softly. 'However long it is, I think Peter Hart will wait for her.'

Noakes gave a shaky guffaw.

'An' they say romance is dead.'

Looking at his deputy, the DI felt bound to conclude that the spirit of chivalry found champions in the most unlikely places.

* * *

The late afternoon of Monday 28 December found Markham's 'gang' ensconced in their favourite pub, the Grapes in Bromgrove, its brassy proprietor Denise having made the back parlour over to them so that they could relax in peace.

It was an unfashionable hostelry whose charm resided precisely in its refusal to move with the times. The front lounge resembled a ship's cabin, its motley collection of nautical instruments and bric-a-brac clashing violently with the Prince of Wales patterned carpet. But Denise — darling of the seafaring community and a passionate fan of the royal family — was unconcerned. 'I know what I like and I like what I know' was her motto, so it looked as though the Grapes would remain for ever becalmed amidst the changing tides of fashion.

Noakes was relieved to be out of the public eye where no one could see the bobbled reindeer jumper that Natalie had insisted he wear.

'C'mon, Dad, *lighten up*. Ugly sweaters are *cool*,' she said with a certain sly malice. 'And you're always saying you admire that Olivia Mullen's *original* dress sense.'

To Muriel and Natalie, firmly of one mind on this particular subject, Markham's partner would always be 'that Olivia Mullen'.

Olivia herself had kept a straight face when complimenting him on his festive attire. 'It's adorable, George. You look just like Colin Firth in *Bridget Jones's Diary*,' she said gleefully.

Colin Firth, eh? He'd take that any day.

'How's Judas Iscariot doing?' Olivia went on, for such was her nickname for DCI Sidney. 'No, don't tell me, crowing like a demented rooster about "his" success in cracking the college murders.' She took a hefty gulp of gin and tonic. 'And to think he blocked you every step of the way. If it had been down to old slimy boots, you'd still be rounding up druggies and local misfits.'

Markham grinned.

'Sidney's certainly done a good job spinning it as a psychological profiling triumph . . . his people showing Thames Valley how it's done.'

'The fact the killer's a nutcase helped too.' Doyle was flushed and happy, having found romance at Christmas with a comely sergeant in digital forensics. 'I mean, it's not like one of the university top brass was an evil psycho or anything . . . She's *ill* . . . couldn't help it.'

'Well, the jury's still out on evil psychos,' Markham retorted.

'*Yeah*,' Noakes spluttered. 'De'Ath, Skeffington an' Greaves for starters.'

Kate Burton had been quietly sipping her buck's fizz. She seemed somehow more settled and assured since the Oxford investigation, and Markham had been delighted by her announcement that she wanted to take the long-deferred inspectors' exam.

'Your *Trumpton* analogy wasn't so farfetched after all,' he had told her after the events at Folly Tower. 'Up there in the belfry, I remembered what you said about those clockwork figures coming out to strike the time. Then when I saw that statue in the cupboard, I knew Margaret Payne had substituted her sister for St Eanswythe.' Burton had been pleased at that and still more gratified when the DI said, 'Our killer had a great deal in common with Lady Jane Rochford. After you told me about her, I was more ready to believe we might be looking for a woman.'

Now she said, 'Is there anything De'Ath and Skeffington could be charged with, boss?'

'How about perverting the course of justice?' Noakes growled. 'Or do them public school toffs at Sherwin jus' wanna bury the mess six feet deep an' play cricket on top?'

Markham's lips quirked.

'I'd say that's an accurate assessment, Noakesy,' he said. Then more soberly, 'I doubt we'll ever know the truth about Catriona's dealings with those two.'

'Maybe *she* was a blackmailer,' Doyle put in. 'Certainly sounded like she had *something* on them.'

'An' that Philip Greaves were a wrong 'un,' Noakes insisted.

'I imagine there were lots of undercurrents swirling about Sherwin,' Markham said. 'And somehow they went right over my head,' he added ruefully. He contemplated his Châteauneuf-du-Pape thoughtfully. 'I daresay Ray Cunliffe could tell a tale or two. I never liked the man. But that particular chapter's closed for the time being. Sir Philip Mirfleet and co have enough clout to protect their own. And now we've got our killer . . .' He shrugged helplessly.

'Why'd we allus get the nut jobs?' Noakes demanded suddenly. 'Why not the straightforward whack-a-mole crimes . . . *bish bash bosh*.' He brought down his pint so heavily that it slopped all over the pine table.

'That's because we're,' Markham adopted Sidney's nasal honk, 'an *elite* unit, Sergeant . . . every case an intellectual challenge!'

'Sod that,' the DS grumbled. 'Seems like the ones we chase have allus got some bleeding *condition*.'

'Well, that poor woman certainly does,' Olivia chided. 'In the Warneford with — what is it, Gil — traumatic psychosis?'

'Correct,' he answered quietly, reluctant to expand on his visit to the Oxford psychiatric facility and the harrowing spectacle of Margaret Payne's deterioration.

'At least her husband's staying loyal,' Burton pointed out.

Markham resisted the temptation to close his eyes at the recollection of Peter Hart's despair.

Sensing his discomfort, Burton returned to the issue of loose ends.

'Do you think there ever *was* anything between Margaret and Dr Warrender?' she asked. 'I couldn't help wondering if he ever led her on.'

'With whatever might have happened in that creepy club of his, he's lucky we never charged him with rape.' Noakes's face showed purple with outrage above Dasher and Blitzen.

'Again, I fear we'll never get to the bottom of what happened between Catriona, Warrender and Drexler,' Markham sighed.

'Nor the truth about who fathered Catriona's child,' Burton added sadly, thinking of the little foetus retrieved from under staircase eleven.

'Leave it to Karma,' Olivia said softly.

Denise bustled in with menus, and the little group was soon squabbling amicably over starters and sharing platters.

Typically, however, their thoughts wandered back to Oxford and the college murders.

'I wonder why Payne and Peter Hart never had kids?' Doyle speculated idly over his onion rings.

Markham noticed Olivia's knuckles turn white as she gripped her cutlery tighter. Only he knew about the secret abortion that weighed so heavily on her conscience. But her voice was light as she said, 'Perhaps they were enough for each other.' She smiled across the table at Markham. '"For love, all love of other sights controls, And makes one little room an everywhere",' she murmured.

Noakes feared an outbreak of arty-fartiness.

'Thank chuff they didn't have sprogs,' he said spearing three roast potatoes at once. 'No knowing how *that*'d turn out.'

'Do you reckon Payne was doolally about Warrender again at the end and that's why she attacked her sister, cos Sheila told her she was seeing him?' Doyle enquired.

'The team at the Warneford are still piecing it together,' Markham replied. 'But yes, it looks like her obsession with him had revived with a vengeance under the strain of the murders.'

'Did Sheila not suspect Margaret at all?' Olivia asked curiously.

'She had latent misgivings but like Peter Hart, she pushed them away as being unthinkable,' Markham said. 'It wasn't until Margaret came round that night that the truth began to dawn on her.'

'Did Sheila confront her?' Olivia tried to picture the scene.

'Sheila's still in the John Radcliffe,' Markham explained, 'so it'll be a while before we get the whole story, but it appears she asked Margaret outright if she knew anything about the murders.'

'And then Margaret wigged out?' Doyle asked eagerly.

His boss deliberated for a moment. 'Essentially, yes. The combined impact of learning about Sheila's affair with Warrender plus being cross-examined like that tipped her over the edge. She forced Sheila into her car at knifepoint and then, well, you know the rest.'

'Did Perdita tax her with being the killer too?' Olivia asked.

'I think we have to assume so.' Markham spoke gravely. 'Perdita thought *she* was the one in the driving seat but had no idea what she was dealing with.' He looked around the table at his colleagues. 'When we get the whole history from the Warneford, I believe it will all be pretty much as we imagined it.'

Noakes felt things were getting altogether too gloomy for the festive season.

'Remind me what subject *you* studied at Oxford, boss?' he asked, sawing away at the roast turkey for dear life.

'PPE, Noakesy. Philosophy, Politics and Economics.'

'Not English or Classics, George,' Olivia teased. 'Despite his tiresome habit of firing quotations at you all the time.'

'Oh, Noakes is used to it by now,' Markham laughed. 'Comes back at me with a few of his own.'

The DS beamed.

Like the missus said, the University of Life was what counted.

* * *

Afterwards, walking home hand in hand through the frosty streets of Bromgrove, Olivia was meditative.

'How awful for Margaret Payne, feeling different from everyone,' she mused. 'It must have been like going through life encased in a thick glass bubble.'

'She's begun to smash her way out of it, Liv.'

'Sounds like George helped her.'

'Yes, the last thing I expected was that he would bring up the Bluebell case like that. But that's the thing about Noakes. Just when you think there's nothing left to learn, he surprises you.'

'What next, now you've solved the Oxford murders, Gil?'

'I'll just have to see if we can't nab one of those exciting whack-a-mole assignments.'

His lover's laughter pealed out in the crisp night air.

Whatever the New Year had in store, she was looking forward to it.

THE END

ALSO BY CATHERINE MOLONEY

THE DI GILBERT MARKHAM SERIES

Book 1: CRIME IN THE CHOIR
Book 2: CRIME IN THE SCHOOL
Book 3: CRIME IN THE CONVENT
Book 4: CRIME IN THE HOSPITAL
Book 5: CRIME IN THE BALLET
Book 6: CRIME IN THE GALLERY
Book 7: CRIME IN THE HEAT
Book 8: CRIME AT HOME
Book 9: CRIME IN THE BALLROOM
Book 10: CRIME IN THE BOOK CLUB
Book 11: CRIME IN THE COLLEGE

Thank you for reading this book.

If you enjoyed it please leave feedback on Amazon or Goodreads, and if there is anything we missed or you have a question about, then please get in touch. The author and publishing team appreciate your feedback and time reading this book.

We're very grateful to eagle-eyed readers who take the time to contact us. Please send any errors you find to corrections@joffebooks.com. We'll get them fixed ASAP.

Printed in Great Britain
by Amazon